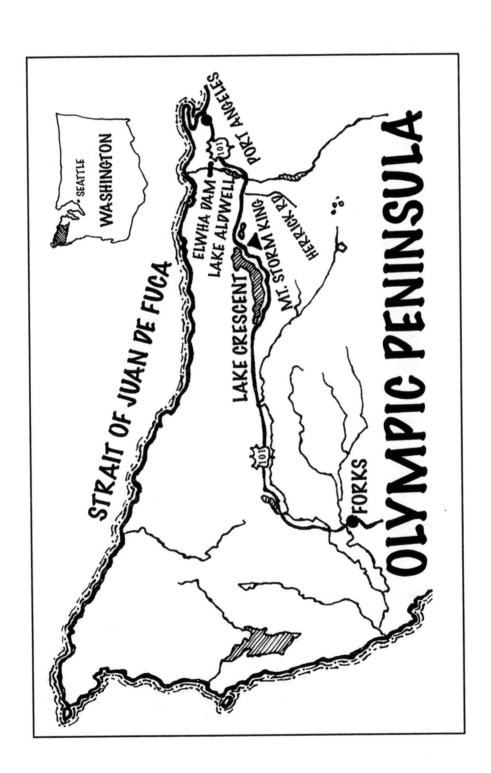

STORM KING'S
GRAVEYARD

STORM KING'S GRAVEYARD

ROB SORENSEN

Halo Publishing International
7550 WIH-10 #800, PMB 2069,
San Antonio, TX 78229

First Edition, July 2023
ISBN: 978-1-63765-397-5
Library of Congress Control Number: 2023906745

Halo Publishing International is a self-publishing company that publishes adult fiction and non-fiction, children's literature, self-help, spiritual, and faith-based books. We continually strive to help authors reach their publishing goals and provide many different services that help them do so. We do not publish books that are deemed to be politically, religiously, or socially disrespectful, or books that are sexually provocative, including erotica. Halo reserves the right to refuse publication of any manuscript if it is deemed not to be in line with our principles. Do you have a book idea you would like us to consider publishing? Please visit www.halopublishing.com for more information.

DISCLAIMER

Storm King's Graveyard is a work of fiction inspired by one of the Pacific Northwest's most famous historical crimes. The settings on the Olympic Peninsula, in the state of Washington, are real, and facts in the "Lady of the Lake" section have long since been public record. That said, throughout the book, I have not hesitated to adapt characters and events to enhance the fictional narrative.

Any resemblance to other characters, living or dead, are completely coincidental.

For those readers interested in the true history of the "Lady of the Lake" section, there are many excellent reference books. For THE most authentic information, visit the Clallam County Historical Society and their staff for exact details.

For Alexis,
My light in every darkness.

ACKNOWLEDGMENTS

Without the inspiration and support of many, this book would not have been possible. My sincere thanks to those who contributed time, expertise, and empathy. More specifically, Dr. Travis Sorensen, who served as editor, critic, and dedicated supporter. Glenna Campbell, Dr. Robert Bond, Bob Lovell, Bobbie Jean Krieder, Dr. Staci Sorensen, and Dr. Josh Herbeck.

A very special thank you to dust-jacket designer, mapmaker, and joy to work with, Kelsey Redlin.

These people provided suggestions and encouragement, and I cannot thank them enough for their contributions.

The most important person in the publication process of *Storm King's Graveyard*, however, is my wife, Alexis, who spent countless hours reading, correcting, typing, making suggestions, and cheerleading. Without her patience and belief, there would have been no book.

CONTENTS

THE LADY OF THE LAKE

1937-1942

DISCOVERY

The mist lifted slowly, as if it were a massive curtain being raised by a delicate hand. The two fishermen sat in their truck, watching in silence as the lake began to reveal its true colors, the sullen gray water turning to azure blue in the awakening morning as the sun lit the lake's surface.

It was early on a long Fourth of July weekend in 1940, and the two men had arrived in darkness at the public boat-launch area on the highway side of Lake Crescent in the state of Washington, fifteen miles west of the city of Port Angeles. They were in no hurry, talking quietly and smoking cigarettes while waiting for the half-mist, half-fog on the surface of the lake to finish rising, as it did almost every day of almost every summer, almost every year. They left the truck and stood at the lakeside, savoring the moment in silence. When the lake was almost unveiled, they finished their smokes and eased a battered fishing boat into the waters of the lake.

The older man's name was Albert Jackson, a retired logger who lived with his wife on a farm on Eden Valley Road, ten miles from Lake Crescent. Friends called him Jack, and he was an avid outdoorsman who had fished the lake for years. Jack was famous for catching the landlocked Beardslee trout that grew to enormous sizes in the deep waters of the lake.

His partner, Jeremy Reed, was an equally rabid fisherman, and this morning they had chosen to use the younger man's boat, hunting for trophy-sized fish.

The anglers were soon afloat, spooling out fishing lines and looking forward to reaching the small stream closest to the boat launch. The rivulet, called Barnes Creek, tumbled off Mount Storm King and into the lake, depositing a conveyer belt of drowned insects and other fish-food tidbits into the deep waters. The mouth of the creek was a favorite spot for fishermen, and the two men were eager to be the first to work the area in the soft morning light.

They trolled past the honey hole without tempting a fish. Jeremy, seated beside the outboard motor and steering the boat, felt the tense muscles in his back relax and said to his partner, "Well, I guess the big ones are sleeping in this morning."

Jackson grunted and answered, "Be patient, boy. The mouth of the creek has some fish, but it's too shallow for the big ones. We ain't lookin' for no minnows. I think we should troll across the lake so's we can focus on the deep water in front of the Devil's Punch Bowl. We'll leave the pan-sized fish here for the other guys."

The Devil's Punch Bowl was on the other side of the lake, almost two miles away. They could fish their way across the water, but at trolling speed, it would take some time. Both fishermen settled in for the crossing. The morning sun was warming the air and coloring the surface of the lake a striking dark blue.

Jeremy yawned. As the boat purred along, the gentle pace and soft thrumming of the outboard motor did little to lessen his drowsiness. When they were close enough to the other shoreline to make out the rugged cliffsides of their destination, he started to pay closer attention.

Rolling his head on his neck, the young man scanned the water in front of the boat, enjoying the approach to the spectacular expanse of rain forest and craggy rock-line ledges of the steep cliffs. The shoreline was squeezed between the lake and a massive display of trees packed like a dark-green carpet above and behind the craggy face of rock.

He switched his focus back to fishing, watching the water ahead of the boat, and was surprised to spot something floating on the surface of the lake. Jack was sitting in the front, his eyes locked on the tip of his own fishing rod.

"Hey, Jack, looks like somethin' floatin' up ahead of us… Maybe there's a big one hidin' underneath it."

Jackson turned his head to look and grunted, "Huh. If there is, it'll be hidin' about two hunnert feet below it." Pausing, he mused, "Don't usually see stuff floatin' around this time of the year. Must be a log or somethin'. Just make sure we don't tangle our lines on it."

"No problem. I got this."

There was a slight breeze on the water, and steering around the log, they were pushed closer to the floating object than Jeremy had planned. Both men watched the flotsam to break the monotony of the vast surface of the lake.

As the boat slid past, Jeremy said, "What the hell is that? It don't look like a log to me."

"I dunno," said Jack, pulling at the brim of his black cowboy hat to shade his eyes for a better view.

"Let's check it out. This might be a good time to wake up the big boys for breakfast anyways."

Jeremy shut off the motor, and they began retrieving the yards of fishing line that both men had been trolling. When they finished reeling in, they set down their fishing poles and noticed that during the delay they had floated away from the object on the surface of the lake. Jeremy restarted the motor, throttling the boat to a crawl, and as they grew closer, both fishermen studied the bundle of what was beginning to look like a stretched-out pile of waterlogged rags or trash. Almost to the debris floating on the water, they exchanged glances.

Jackson shrugged. "This is kinda weird. It ain't no log," he said.

Whatever it was, it appeared to be wrapped in a tarp or blankets and trussed up in coils of rope. It was oddly horizontal, floating low and looking as if it had been in the water for a long time.

Drawing closer to the bundle, Jeremy slipped the outboard motor into Neutral, and Jack picked up an emergency paddle from the floor of the boat. As the boat coasted up beside the bundle, he gave the waterlogged cluster a tentative poke, exposing a quick peek of white.

Frowning, Jackson said, "Damn. If I didn't know better, I'd say this thing almost looks like a human body."

"Nah, I don't think so. Everybody knows this weird-ass lake don't have floaters. It must be a deer or somethin'."

"It's not no deer, Jeremy." Scratching his chin, Jack said, "It looks like it might be one of them body-form thingies they use in Montgomery Ward to show off clothes for broads."

As the men studied the object in silence, a cool morning breeze ruffled the water, and the open end of the object rolled a quarter turn in the wind. A long mane of dark hair rose gently from the end of the bundle and floated on the surface. Like a clump of brown sea kelp, it undulated in the water.

Jack jerked back and almost fell overboard before landing hard on the front seat of the boat. "Jesus H. Christ! This ain't no dress form. This here's got human hair. It's a goddamn body!"

Jeremy answered, "A body! No way. It can't be."

The old man was shaking. "Well, it is. This is crazy!"

Jeremy said, "What should we do? Load it into the boat?"

"No, no. Don't touch it! Jesus H. Christ. I do not believe this is happening. We gotta get over to the ranger station by the lodge and let the park rangers know what we found! They'll get people here quicklike. Goddamn. This is crazy."

Jack's distress convinced his friend the object was indeed a body. He cranked the small outboard motor as high as it would go; the engine shrieked, shattering the morning calm and rousting a trio of cruising mallards squawking in noisy protest.

The discovery of a body actually floating on the surface of the lake was so rare, and the body's unveiling so startling, that neither fisherman could talk. They were shocked they'd found a body…and just as surprised that a body had found them. The dark, deep waters of the beautiful lake never floated things to the surface.

They just disappeared.

MOUNT STORM KING

Throughout the centuries, Lake Crescent has been one of nature's most puzzling enigmas. The lake, with its size, depth, and icy-cold water, coupled with the winds and waves from furious storms, could always—and still can—change from a breathtaking photo op to a raging death trap in a matter of minutes. Locals have long known about the dangers and are careful to monitor the weather. This potential for natural disasters is not uncommon. Many northwestern lakes of this size have histories of boating accidents and drownings.

Lake Crescent's history is much darker. Bodies of its victims sink rapidly, and they never float up to the surface of the lake. The vanishing acts of drowning victims have foiled every attempt of scientific research or technical explanation. The body the two fishermen found was an anomaly. Even though the incident was as unusual as an Olympic Peninsula heatstroke, it would be the condition of the corpse—wrapped in blankets and hog-tied from throat to ankles—that would create a national uproar.

* * *

According to the Klallam Indians' tribal history, Lake Crescent was sacred grounds for Storm King, the god of the Elwha River Valley. Since the beginning of time, Mount Storm King has ruled the lake and all of its surrounding peaks, forests, and creatures. The tribe's storytellers say that, ten thousand years ago, the native Klallams and a neighboring tribe fought a bloody three-day battle on the shores of the river at the foot of Storm King, the god. Tired of the fighting, he tore rock from the mountainside and threw massive boulders into the Elwha River to separate the combatants. The carnage from his tirade was so formidable that it killed all the warriors of both tribes and dammed the river, creating the lake.

To ensure the tribes did not forget his rage, Storm King cast a curse over the newly created wilderness lake. The body of anyone who died in his lake would never be recovered.

As the years passed, the Klallams came to believe the lake's bottomless abyss was filled with evil spirits who would seize—and hide—the bodies of drowning victims. So effective was the punishment, tribal members refused to visit the lake.

To this day, the mountain god has enforced his curse with astounding tenacity. Most of the bodies of those who die in the lake, regardless of ethnicity, are seldom recovered, and the families of the victims are unable to say goodbye to loved ones in their family tradition.

Amazingly, the tribe's time line for the invocation of the curse has been documented by geologists who have confirmed that a massive earthquake or landslide created the lake somewhere around eight to ten thousand years ago, which is spot-on with the Klallam Tribe's legendary time frame. The disappearance of drowning victims remains an enigma, and the lake's depth, cold temperatures, and deepwater currents continue to swallow the dead.

Following Storm King's creation, the mountain's empire was soon as beautiful as ever, a wonder of bright-blue water nestled in virgin forests surrounded by the snowcapped Olympic Mountains. Storm King—so named for its gathering of the first storm clouds blown inland from the Pacific Coast— defines the character of the entire Olympic Peninsula. The mountain and the lake create a vista so spectacular they were eventually established as the eastern gateway to the Olympic National Park. That staggering beauty and the macabre history of the lake created a unique natural treasure…and a centuries-old, haunted underwater burial ground. It is a watery crypt without coffins, tombstones or white crosses to mark the resting places of the dead.

On that quiet day in July 1940, the two fishermen who discovered the floating body knew they had found a human corpse. What they did not know was the bundled body would soon stun the world. And in a most unlikely twist of fate would connect a working-class family of Nova Scotia immigrants to the legend for the next eighty-five years.

SOAP

On the day the body was found, Harlan McNutt was at home with his family at their ranch east of the city of Port Angeles. Having just finished his freshman year at George Washington Medical School in Washington, DC, he was on break for the summer. The phone rang in the family's living room, and Harlan took the call.

A raspy voice said, "Harlan, is that you?"

"Yes, it is. What can I—"

Before he could finish, the voice interrupted, "Thought so. This is Charlie Kemp with the county sheriff's department. Your dad told me you'd be home for the summer. Glad I caught ya. I got a little problem here, and I need some help. Our coroner is out of town for the Fourth of July holiday."

Harlan waited. When the sheriff didn't continue, he said, "And…"

"Whaddaya mean, and? Like I said, I need a coroner. Both of the regular docs are out of town for the holiday… or hiding. We've got a murder-victim's body at the funeral home. I need a doctor."

In those years, the population of Port Angeles was less than ten thousand people, and most everyone knew everyone else. Charlie Kemp needed a doctor, and when he could not find anyone else, medical student Harlan McNutt was close enough.

"Charlie, I can't do an autopsy. I'm a first-year med student. We are not that far along."

"I don't need no auto-topsy. I need a doc to take a look and give me some idea of what the fuck is going on. You're my boy. How soon can you get here?"

Harlan was the first male McNutt to go to college, let alone grad school. During his first year at George Washington Medical School, he had worked on a grand total of two human cadavers, which was standard procedure for every medical student pursuing a degree.

Sheriff Kemp did not care. Harlan was the only health person available, and Kemp was too excited to wait for the official county coroner to get back to town.

Even before leaving the peninsula for the East Coast, Harlan had been a favorite son for the small, blue-collar town of Port Angeles. A child phenom with a photographic memory and unlimited curiosity, his pioneer family connections had exposed him to local city officials and a good portion of the population. In those days, folks were close, and one did not say no to a neighbor who needed a favor.

* * *

The body found in Lake Crescent had been taken to a funeral home in town and placed in a shed beside the mortuary while authorities waited for the undertaker to be located and summoned. It was in this outbuilding where Harlan met the sheriff and two of his deputies. The deputies had jury-rigged a temporary table out of sawhorses and a sheet of plywood, and the tattered bundle was lying on it in the center of the room.

The wiry Kemp was pacing the grimy floor of the shed, and Harlan could smell the strong odor of the man's chewing tobacco he repeatedly spit on the worn, rough-planked floor.

Short in stature, Charlie wore a policeman's cap with a plastic bill and the pie-shaped top that one would expect to see on the head of a captain of a naval vessel, or a high-end hotel doorman in Washington, DC. Although the two deputies who completed the sheriff department were in uniform, Charlie Kemp was wearing a plaid sport shirt and a pair of work dungarees. Behind his back, underlings of the Clallam County Sheriff Department referred to the sheriff as the Little General and attributed his behavior to a serious case of Napoleon complex due to his lack of height.

Tugging Harlan by the elbow, Charlie led him toward the body resting on the makeshift table. "What do you think, Doc? Have you ever seen anything like this?"

Harlan stared at the bundle. The only human corpses he had worked with in the past year had been clean and sterile, provided by the school as refrigerated laboratory specimens. Every first-year student in the program was assigned their own cadaver each semester to study during anatomy class and dissection sessions.

McNutt shook his head and leaned over the trussed-up package. It was late afternoon, and the bright summer sun shone through dust-caked windows, providing a measure of light.

Harlan's first impression was that the decomposition had hopelessly damaged the exposed skin at each end of the bundle of the rotted blankets and rope. The face, hands, and parts of the feet were stripped to the bone. But even with the grotesque disfigurement, it was obvious the corpse was a woman.

Although the face was without a nose, eyes, or lips, a full head of long, reddish-brown hair remained, and from neck to ankles, the rest of the corpse appeared to be intact. It was wrapped in a tarp and tattered blankets held close to the body by coils of industrial rope. The blankets were shredded at the edges and faded to a shade of cold gray. He could see some patches of clothing beneath the blankets, and although the clothes she wore were beginning to decompose, the dark-green dress she wore was surprisingly well-preserved.

"May I take a closer look?" he said to the sheriff.

"Well, hell yes. That's what you're here for."

Harlan nodded. Loosening the rope and peeling the blanket gently off the shoulders, he began to look closer at the body. The other men watched as his eyebrows knitted behind his horn-rimmed glasses as he focused on the body. He did not speak, and as the exam lengthened, Charlie Kemp squirmed and cleared his throat, unable to restrain his impatience.

Harlan whispered to himself and took a step back, still studying the corpse. His mind scrolled through his memory of past textbooks and lectures, reviewing the information presented during his studies and from his own vast reading background. He took a tongue depressor from his pocket and used it to test the consistency of the skin and underlying tissue. His eyes opened wide as he poked and prodded.

Finally, he stepped away and peered in disbelief at the strange corpse he had been examining. "My God," he said. "This is incredible."

"What!" said the sheriff. "What the hell are you talking about?"

Looking at Kemp, Harlan said, "Something has taken place here that I've never heard of before. I cannot believe what I am seeing. The skin and body tissue of this cadaver seem to have changed into some type of congealed preservative!"

Kemp's mouth dropped open as he stared at Harlan. "Whaddaya mean, congealed?"

"I'm not sure what I mean. I have never even read about something like this. But what I do know is we need someone who does to examine this body. I cannot imagine what's taken place here."

Kemp said, "Harlan, I have no idea what the hell you're saying, but I do know none of that bullshit is going to keep me from checking out a murder victim."

Harlan tried again, "Look at what's happened to her flesh, Sheriff. Her body is as white as snow and perfectly preserved. I can see bruises and scratches on the white skin. When I touched them, I knew something wasn't normal. There is even no post-mortal smell!" Shaking his head, he said, "I realize it does not sound possible, but it looks and feels like her body tissue has turned to some kind of gelatinous material...like putty or wax. Maybe even soap."

"Soap?! No fuckin' way."

"Yes, I know. But look at this. I can actually scrape pieces off if I want to. Listen, I'm no expert, Charlie. I do not know what

33

this means. But I do know we need to be really careful here, and we need to get an experienced doctor…and probably some scientific specialists here who can do a full autopsy. This is unbelievable. And inexplicable. Not to mention the most incredibly fascinating thing that I've ever seen!"

"Yeah, maybe. But this here lady has obviously been kilt. We need an ID. Let's get the rest of the rope and rags all the way off and see if we can find anything."

Harlan pleaded, "If we do that, Charlie, you should get someone to take post-mortem pictures as we go. And the tissue is fragile. All of us need to handle this body as carefully as possible."

Charlie said, "I don't care if her body turned into cookie dough. I got a job to do here, son. And we're gonna do it." He didn't wait for Harlan's approval and began to loosen more coils of rope.

Once the rope and blankets had been clumsily removed by the deputies, Harlan said, "Charlie, this is crazy. This cadaver has the potential to have significant scientific value. We have got to handle it with the utmost delicacy. I think it is way too fragile to work on here."

Charlie grunted.

Harlan tried to slow the sheriff down. Staring at the strange torso, he shook his head. "Maybe we can check her mouth to see if the teeth are intact."

"Whatever. Just do somethin'."

Harlan took a fresh tongue depressor, from the kit he had cobbled together after the sheriff's call, and spent a good ten minutes working carefully around what was left of the face. The teeth were exposed but tightly clenched.

As Harlan worked, Sheriff Kemp stalked about the shed, spitting tobacco juice, his face growing redder and redder with every passing minute.

When Harlan looked at Kemp and shrugged his shoulders, the sheriff grunted again and said, "I'll get her goddamn mouth open."

Stomping over to the corner of the shed where there was a pile of stacked kindling, the sheriff grabbed a sturdy piece of cedar and walked back to the body. Ignoring Harlan, he shoved the makeshift pry bar into the rigid mouth.

Harlan said, "Charlie, you need to be care—"

Before he could finish, the sheriff leaned his weight on the piece of wood. Everyone watched in horror as the jawbone detached from the skull and tumbled to the floor, scattering the transformed body material as it exploded from the bone. The waxy, soft flesh separated into fragments the size and color of store-bought cottage cheese.

Harlan stared at the mess, too shocked to speak. Everyone's eyes were locked on the surreal splatter of bone and particles of what was once human tissue. Nobody moved.

Finally, Harlan whispered, "Oh my God."

But as the shock of the careless handling ebbed, his eyes focused on the disaster, and he saw something besides human debris. In the middle of the pile lay an odd-shaped piece of man-made substance. He dropped to his knees and picked it up, cradling it in one hand.

Fumbling in his bag with his free hand, he found a small brush and began dusting the gelatinous material from the object. When he finished, he held it up to show the sheriff. It was an upper-dental plate with a multi-tooth bridge. Six teeth aligned in a row. They were almost the same color as the cadaver's aforementioned body tissue.

The same shade of a bar of commercial bath soap.

LADY OF THE LAKE

When Harlan left the mortuary and returned to the Mc-Nutt ranch, he was on fire to understand the strange phenomenon he had just discovered. He hurried to his family's home library, which had been assembled by his parents in an effort to keep pace with Harlan's ever-present desire to learn. Passing his mother, who was reading a novel in the living room, he stopped and said, "Mother, you will not believe where I have been and what I have been doing!"

Closing her book, she asked, "Whatever do you mean? You look flushed. Are you all right?"

"I'm absolutely all right. I have just had the most exciting experience of my life. There was a body discovered floating on Lake Crescent this morning. All of Charlie Kemp's regular medical people are out of town, and he asked me to examine the corpse!"

"Oh my. I'm sorry."

"Oh no! Don't be sorry. I did my first partial autopsy. And I'm almost certain that the woman's body is an anatomical aberration. It's…I don't know…it's almost like the body has been purposely preserved. It is unbelievable. She was obviously murdered and sunk in the lake, but the body decomposition is not like anything I have ever heard of. That cadaver has turned into something besides human flesh.

More like wax or dough. It was soft, but pliable. Intact, but fragile. Almost like putty. Or soap."

His mother frowned in disgust, then rolled her eyes at her son. "Harlan, don't be ridiculous. You know we do not believe in witchcraft or fairy tales."

"I know it sounds improbable," he said, "but I can assure you this is real. I scraped flesh off that body with a tongue depressor and then watched as Charlie knocked her jawbone off her face and onto the floor. It is absolutely real, Mother, and I can't wait to find out how. Or why. I've been thinking about it all the way home, and I've got some ideas. I'll be in the library doing some research."

His mother followed him into the room, hurrying to keep up with her son, who never stopped talking.

"This is not a normal post-death body reaction. I have never seen anything like it. I have never read about anything like it. It has got to be some kind of chemical process. Like the Egyptians with their mummies, or something like that."

Two days later, Dr. Irving Kaveney, the official Clallam County Coroner, returned from vacation and examined the dead-woman's body at the funeral home. He confirmed the state of the dead-woman's body was not in a natural state.

When word of the body's conversion to a soap-like statue broke, the news swept across the Northwest's newspaper network like a west-to-east thunderstorm. From a small town in the country's last frontier came a spectacular story of a body preservation akin to the discovery of fossilized dinosaur skeletons in Southern California's La Brea Tar Pits in the early nineteen hundreds. Newspapers down the coast and as far east as the Rockies quickly titled the murder victim the Lady of the Lake.

As news of the strange body began to spread, front-page headlines throughout the Pacific Northwest reveled in the sensational nature of the discovery. Headlines all featured some version of the same message: "MURDER VICTIM'S BODY TURNED TO SOAP." Pressure on the Clallam County Sheriff Department increased with every passing day.

Harlan McNutt may have been the only person involved who was obsessed by the scientific rarity of the body's condition. For the young med student, this was not just a murder victim. It was the discovery of a corpse that defied forensic history.

When the body was discovered in 1940, times were very different. The remoteness of the peninsula, coupled with the small population of the town, slowed the process of gathering scientists or archeologists capable of unraveling the mystery of the floating-body's condition. Which left the curious first-year med-school student determined to find the answer to what could cause such a baffling occurrence. Like his role in the autopsy, this research was highly unusual. Even in the early 1940s, a young student was seldom, if ever, called upon to perform a crime-scene autopsy or serve as a forensic scientist.

But Harlan McNutt was not your standard schoolboy. Harlan was born in Port Angeles in 1914. He showed signs of genius from an early age—reading at three years old, fascinated by mechanical apparati when he was five, and solving college-level mathematics problems before graduating from junior high school. He was small-boned and soft-bodied. His health as a youngster was delicate, and he had escaped the coming-of-age rituals of most boys growing up in logging country—setting chokers, limbing downed trees, or doing the things other loggers didn't want to do. Instead, he was recognized as an academic prodigy, and the local populace had no doubts about his ability to contribute to the crime's resolution.

When the local doctors were unable to solve the mystery, Harlan talked Sheriff Kemp into allowing him to transport a sample of the mysterious body tissue to the University of Washington Science Department. Staff members, using chemical analysis, determined the most likely explanation was a reaction triggered by a process called *saponification*— a chemical change that converts fat into fatty acid and is commonly used to produce commercial soap. The process is almost unheard of in the human body; it requires a perfect-storm mixture of waterborne chemicals and near-freezing temperatures to trigger a physical reaction in order to develop soap. It was the literal creation of a soap mummy.

Later, the body was examined by a team of elite doctors and scientists who confirmed the University of Washington's theory. The resultant outcome of the preservation of the torso was so complete that strangulation bruises were still visible on the neck, and the dark marks Harlan had noticed on her chest stood out like blotches of black ink. The woman had suffered a violent beating, been strangled, wrapped in blankets, and hog-tied by coils of rope.

Meanwhile, the story continued to be featured in newspapers as far away as the *Los Angeles Times*, the *Chicago*

Tribune, and even the *New York Times.* The strange killing and the stranger state of the recovered body mesmerized readers with its haunting mystique. The discovery of this human-soap sculpture was eventually acknowledged as the first full-body cadaver of its type in modern criminal history.

THE BARMAID AND THE BEER MAN

As the media and its eager followers focused on the sensational news of a soap-statue murder victim, no one had a clue as to who had suffered the Edgar Allan Poe-like deed. It would be a year later before the background story would unfold, and by then, the locals had long since connected the mystery to the legend of the Klallam Indian Tribe's history of Mount Storm King's dreaded curse.

Although it started on the other side of the country, almost four decades before the fishermen's discovery of the strange body floating on the lake, the victim's past was as dark as the mountain's.

In the late 1930s, the country was battered and bruised, just beginning to move forward after the Great Depression. Thousands of Americans had lost their life's savings and homes. Many of these poor souls had relocated from the cities and farms they had created, in desperate search of new beginnings.

America's historical method of coping with hard times was moving to the West and starting over. But the West did not go on forever, and in the mid-1930s, only the Pacific Northwest remained as the continental United States' alleged Last Frontier.

It was the opportunity to start over and the quest for a better life that brought a pretty, young barmaid from South Dakota and a local beer-truck driver together in the most remote corner of the country.

* * *

Hallie Latham was born in Kentucky, the fifth child of what would become a family of thirteen children. The first daughter to join the family, she learned at an early age how to survive. In a family with four older brothers, she understood from the day she started to walk that she would have to fight for every inch and morsel. Hallie's childhood was not a struggle…it was a battle. Survival of the fittest. Do or die. Prey or predator.

Hallie's parents were poor tobacco farmers struggling to make a living. She was a skinny, sunburned kid always covered in dust, wearing patched and faded dresses and smelling like the farm. Her parents made her quit school at age thirteen to help with the flood of brothers and sisters. She served as nanny, helped her mother in the house, and worked in the fields when needed.

She was a young girl when the Lathams moved to the Dakotas, hoping to homestead a farm capable of supporting the family. Times were difficult, and very soon she longed to escape the poverty and hardship.

By the time she was eighteen years old, she had blossomed into a beauty and, in that year, married a traveling salesman named Floyd Spraker. It was a step up for Hallie, and the couple soon produced a daughter whom they named Doris Marie. Hallie's husband sold for a national housewares company, and she and her daughter were often alone while her husband was on the road. As time passed, the domestic bliss and frequent absences of her husband wore thin. She longed for a better future. She was still young, pretty, and ambitious. Her obsession for improving her life was uncontrollable.

On Halle's twenty-ninth birthday, Mr. Spraker was on the road, and his schedule kept him away from home. The following day, she packed her bags, took her daughter to her husband's family, and filed for a divorce. She was out of town before Mr. Spraker returned from his trip.

She took a waitressing job in a small town in South Dakota, and six months later met a young man who worked in the kitchen of the same restaurant. The two fell in love and married.

Hallie's second marriage was shrouded in mystery from the beginning. She was seven years older than her new husband, Don Strickland, but on the marriage certificate, she falsely registered her age as five years younger than she was. She also lied about her previous marriage, recording her current status as widow. The newlyweds remained in South Dakota and scraped by working in the restaurant business.

Less than a year later, the marriage collapsed. Similar to those who tried to beat hard times by starting over, Hallie decided to go as far west as she could go. She chose the country's last wilderness on the rugged and remote Olympic Peninsula in the state of Washington. Sparsely populated, blanketed by virgin timber, and surrounded by water, it was the perfect place to start a new life.

When Hallie Spraker-Strickland arrived on the Olympic Peninsula, she was still a very attractive woman. She was tall and shapely—buxom, even—with perfect skin, wide-spaced dark eyes, and arched eyebrows. Her mouth was wide for the face, with lips often stretched in an unsmiling straight line. She had a stunning mane of reddish-brown hair, the dark-auburn shade of a well-waxed rosewood tabletop. When introduced to any new acquaintances, the women she met never failed to envy her hair. Thick and shiny, it was so stunning it was impossible for other women not to envy. The men she met paid little attention to the perfect head of hair, but seldom failed to notice her Mae West-like voluptuous figure. It was a body that stirred envies of a different kind.

Hallie found a job working as a barmaid in a lakeside resort west of the city of Port Angeles. The Lake Crescent Tavern was a popular nightspot for locals and tourists. It was where she met Montgomery J. Illingworth.

Monty drove a delivery truck for a local beer distributor and was also a regular customer at the lake tavern's bar. He was six years younger than Hallie and was enjoying a lifestyle of womanizing and drinking during the post-depression, post-prohibition years of newfound freedom. He had moved from Southern California to the peninsula in search of adventure and good times. He was divorced and, by all accounts, had chosen the Olympic Peninsula as the most remote location possible for a man trying to avoid paying child support to his ex-wife. Despite the shaky background, Monty was considered to be a nice guy, fun loving, and affable. A perfect fit for the small town's thriving beer business. He was tall and fit, had thick black hair, was cleanshaven, but had a beard so heavy there was a constant five-o'clock shadow on his cheeks and chin. His eyes were almost as black as the heavy eyebrows that framed them.

The two newcomers met at the resort during a delivery in the late fall of 1935. It was the third stop on Monty's regular route. Only the bartender and new-hire Hallie were there prepping for the lunchtime opening.

When the bartender introduced the two, Monty embraced Hallie, then held her at arm's length and said to the barman, "Holy shit, Merle, where did you find this beautiful piece of work?"

Hallie laughed and said, "Aren't you the shy guy."

Monty looked into her eyes and said, "No. Can I buy you a beer? Or a Bloody Mary?"

"I'm working." She looked over at Merle. "Maybe later tonight though."

Monty laughed, turned her away from the arm's-length staredown and, as she walked away, slapped her playfully on the bottom. "I'll be back way before quitting time, honey," he said. And that was how it all began.

* * *

One warm summer day in May, Hallie had a weekend off. She and Monty were dating on a regular basis and were visiting one of Monty's resort accounts on the nearby shores of Lake Sutherland. The neighboring lake, with its warmer water for swimming and good fishing, was popular with natives and visitors alike. It was a Saturday afternoon, and most of the customers at the Maple Grove Bar were tourists sharing drinks with a few of the locals.

When the couple walked in, Hallie watched as Monty introduced himself to the room and called to the bartender, "Pete, get these folks a round on me."

The customers, all seated at the bar, were mostly men, but there were two middle-aged women sitting near the bar sink in the center of the group. All of them responded by hoisting their glasses in a mock toast and a chorus of polite thanks.

A dark-haired woman, wearing a floppy-brimmed straw hat said, "Thank you, handsome, I'll return the favor for you when I finish my drink."

Monty smiled and gave her a wink, then joined Hallie at a small table near the windows overlooking the lake.

Hallie sat with her boyfriend, answering his questions distractedly, her back straight and her eyes locked on the woman in the hat.

When the waitress returned to the couple's table as they finished their drinks, she delivered a single glass of beer and set it in front of Monty.

The woman at the bar turned and looked at them, smiling at Monty. Raising her glass, she took a small sip then turned back to visit with her friend.

Hallie's eyes narrowed, and she muttered, "That bitch." She shoved her chair back and, getting to her feet, walked to the bar and tapped the shoulder of the lady with the hat. When the hat turned around, exposing the lady's face, Hallie struck a hard slap to the lady's cheek. The skin-to-skin blow echoed like a gunshot throughout the room and rocked backward the woman on her barstool, knocking the hat to the floor.

"Keep away from my man, you little bitch. He's taken!"

Before the shocked bar patrons could react, the woman jumped off her seat and launched a windmill of furious, mostly harmless punches.

Hallie, bigger and stronger than her attacker, responded with clenched fists, landing punches on the top of her assailant's head.

Two of the bar rats jumped into the fray. Monty, grabbing Hallie from behind, locked her arms to her body and, apologizing to the bartender and the woman, dragged his struggling date out the door.

Standing in the parking lot, he shouted, "Are you crazy? You are gonna get me fired doing that kind of shit. What the hell is wrong with you?"

Hallie, breathing hard, stared at him. Then looked back toward the entryway of the bar. "I should have knocked her goddamn teeth out."

* * *

One month later, in June of 1936, Monty and Hallie were married. After the wedding, the Illingworths kept up their connection to the local nightlife. They spent most of their money and time drinking every night and partying hard on weekends. When Hallie was working, Monty hung out in other bars on his delivery route. Weekends together, they drank hard, talked rough, and quarreled constantly.

Just weeks after the wedding, Hallie began to show up at work with bruises on her face or a puffy eye or lip. It was not unusual for the couple to have loud arguments on the tavern's porch during Hallie's smoke breaks or at closing time when they would bicker all the way to the parking lot.

Monty's inability to resist other women, or reject their advances, fueled the couple's strange sexual attraction to one another. Hallie's jealousy, and subsequent need for reinforcement of her own desirability, triggered the Neanderthal baseness of the couple's attraction. The result was frightening, and Hallie's friends and family urged her to leave the relationship that was spiraling so obviously out of control.

Hallie refused. At some level, the caveman with the club, dragging his woman to the fire by her hair, was exciting—and irresistible—to both of them.

As their second Christmas together approached, along with its glut of seasonal parties, the rocky marriage was held together only by a shared desire for psychological abuse and physical destruction.

* * *

It was the twenty-first of December 1937, and Hallie and Monty Illingworth had each received invitations to two different Christmas parties scheduled for that night. They quarreled about which party they were going to attend. Hallie wanted to stay near their apartment in Port Angeles, and Monty wanted to attend a beer party, in the city of Port Townsend, hosted by his beer-distributorship employer. Neither would relent, and the two ended up at parties in the two different towns.

Closing time in the bars in those days was 2:00 a.m. Monty's beer bash was fifty miles away, and the weather was threatening snow. Monty was not home when Hallie got back to their apartment.

The past few months, Monty had come home late with growing regularity, a situation that was troubling for his insecure wife. Her husband worked in a unique social industry, and the barmaid understood the nature of the job. Taverns and restaurants were his livelihood and required a fair amount of social interaction. But recently, he was away longer and later.

When Monty wasn't home that night, she decided to fix herself a nightcap to cope with her concern and frustration while she waited. She turned out all the lights, leaving only one bulb burning on the pole lamp in the corner of the room, and sat in her husband's favorite chair, drinking the whiskey, smoking cigarette after cigarette, and watching the clock on the wall ticktock the time away.

It was 3:35 a.m. when the front door finally opened. The storm was still raging, and a burst of cold air crossed the room. When the door clicked shut, a shiver ran down Hallie's spine. She licked her lips, hating the tension and the hint of perverse excitement that had run down her back. Hallie waited, staring at her disheveled husband. She stubbed her cigarette out in the ashtray beside the chair and, still holding her glass of whiskey, rose unsteadily to her feet.

"Where the hell have you been?" she asked in a husky voice. "Are you drunk?"

Monty had capped off his night of drinking with friends and customers by putting a six-pack of beer on the seat of his truck—his own misguided way to keep himself alert—and driving home in the storm.

"Shut your mouth, Hallie. I'm too tired to deal with you now."

"I don't care if you're tired or not, you bastard! I'm sick of you playing around with other women and coming home at dawn. I've had it with your bullshit tomcatting around!"

Moving toward her husband, she stopped just close enough to stay out of his reach. "Damn you," she shouted, slashing the whiskey and ice cubes onto the rug between them and throwing the empty glass at her husband.

Monty tried to duck, but the glass bounced off the back of his shoulder and exploded against the wall behind him. His bleary eyes opened wide, and his face darkened with rage. He yelled, "You crazy bitch!" and rushed at his wife.

When the two collided, he grabbed her by the shoulders and shook her like a rag doll. She fought back, kicking and screaming, punching and scratching his exposed face. She tried to bite his hands and forearms to loosen his grip.

Monty shouted, "Goddamn you, Hallie, don't you bite me!"

Hallie clamped her teeth onto the forearm of her husband's right arm.

Trying to escape the biting, Monty threw a vicious jab to the side of Hallie's head, then rained body punches to her upper torso as she tried to protect her face. They stumbled across the room. The two knocked Monty's easy chair over and sent the room's pole lamp crashing to the floor.

Hallie was crying and begging, "Monty, stop! Please stop!"

The air stank of cigarette smoke and beer, and the room was dark after the pole lamp fell, but that did little to put an end to the fight. They had battled on many occasions during their short time together. But Hallie knew this time was different.

Monty finally got his hands to Hallie's throat, a tactic he had used before when using breath-control play during passion. When Hallie felt the strong fingers tightening around her neck, she managed to say in a hoarse whisper, "Please, Monty, not again."

And then...everything went black.

DETECTIVE HOLLIS B. FULTZ

Three and a half years later, the body of an unidentified woman floated to the surface of Lake Crescent. The discovery of an apparent murder victim preserved by a bizarre freak of nature rocked the city, and the stunning news went public. Identification of the victim was difficult, and continuing pressure to solve the case overwhelmed the small town's local law enforcement.

Sheriff Charlie Kemp and local county officials requested homicide assistance from the state, and the Washington State Attorney General's Office sent its top criminologist, Hollis B. Fultz, to Port Angeles to assist the Clallam County Sheriff Department with the case.

Detective Fultz arrived in the city, on a damp and dreary late-summer day, wearing a rumpled tan raincoat and carrying a black umbrella. He was a man who did not fit the image of pulp-fiction, hard-nosed detectives. Middle-aged, dark hair beginning to gray, round glasses protecting a pair of eyes the color of black coffee, puffy bags of skin below them, and heavy, salt-and-pepper-colored eyebrows above.

Despite the bland first impression, Hollis Fultz had a statewide reputation as a successful criminal investigator. His assignment to the Lady of the Lake case was special, and his arrival created a buzz with both city officials and well-read local residents.

The sheriff and the detective met in the basement jail of the county courthouse. Fultz opened the meeting by saying, "Okay, Sheriff, tell me what you've got here."

Kemp grunted, "Well, Mr. Fultz, we've gotta doozy for you. As you know, the victim has been sunk for quite a while. I don't know about you, but around here we've never seen anything like this kind of killin'. Excuse my French, but this is the strangest fucking thing that I've ever been around. We got us a body turned into a soap statue, hog-tied, and sunk into Lake Crescent. And we can't investigate normal-like because the body ain't got no face on it, the fingers are stripped to the bones, and there's no way we can get prints. All we know is it's a woman…and somebody kilt her. That's pretty much what we got here."

Fultz let the man talk and listened without comment. He had read the newspapers and the attorney general's report on the crime and was aware of the city's frustrations.

"So not much to go on, huh?"

"Nope. Nothin'."

The attorney general's office in Olympia had warned Fultz that the sheriff was not a homicide detective and was skeptical about the value of the recovered dental bridge as evidence. In fact, Kemp considered its owner to be impossible to track down using such an unusual clue.

"You know, Charlie, these days forensic evaluation of a victim's dental records has become a fairly common alternative for ID confirmations. In this case, it seems like it's the only thing we got. Why don't we just take a look and see if it might be a start?"

Kemp snorted then said, "A needle in a haystack, Mr. Fultz. It looks like everyone's fake teeth to me, and it coulda come from anywhere."

"I'm sure you're right, Sheriff, but what else have we got?"

When Kemp didn't answer, Fultz said, "Is the dental bridge here in the office?"

Kemp nodded.

"Good. Why don't we take a look at it and figure out whether or not it might help?"

Charlie shrugged. "Yeah, fine. We can look."

After examining the dental piece, Fultz said, "Charlie, here's what I think we should do. I know it's a long shot, but I think we should take some pictures of this bridge and get us a local dentist to write a detailed description of the work. I can have my people put together a list of dentists from across the country, and we can mail the pictures and comments throughout the dental industry. Who knows? Maybe we'll get lucky."

Kemp grumbled, "Probably a waste of time. There must be thousands of them things out there. But what the hell? At least we can tell the newspapers we're doin' something."

Once Fultz convinced the sheriff that it was the only clue they had, Kemp surprised him by organizing the survey in a cooperative and professional manner. At the sheriff's request, Fultz had his team in Olympia put together a contact list, and they mailed the information to several thousand dentists across the country. Kemp posted ads with the industry's national trade association members. To provide incentive for the dental industry, Kemp offered a reward of one hundred dollars to any dentist who could identify the patient who received the bridge.

Then they sat back to wait. And wait.

* * *

One year later, the long-shot mailing paid off. Sheriff Kemp received a letter from a dentist named Albert McDowell in South Dakota. The doctor was positive he had done the work on the unique six-tooth bridge. Dr. McDowell insisted that there could be no doubt about the identity of the dental work or that of his patient. He had custom-built the plate nine years earlier, and it had been a labor-intensive project. He remembered the procedure and the attractive young woman for whom he'd built the bridge. The dental patient's name was Hallie Latham-Spraker.

Once Fultz had a probable identification for the victim, he began his search for the dead-woman's killer. He started with the files of the Port Angeles Police Department and the Clallam County Sheriff Department. Those records would include a history of missing persons, and if Hallie Latham-Spraker was on the list, it would provide a solid starting point for an investigation.

It took the detective less than a half hour with the missing-persons files to discover the body of the Lady of the Lake matched an unresolved missing-persons victim. The woman had disappeared three and a half years earlier. Married to her third husband at the time she vanished, she was then known as Hallie Illingworth. With the match made, Fultz met with Charlie Kemp to learn more about Hallie Illingworth's background and personal relationships.

Sheriff Kemp was amazed at the news. "Well, I'll be goddamned. Are you sure, Hollis?"

"I'm sure. Now we have a possible connection. I need you to fill me in on everything you've got on the missing-persons case. What can you tell me about this woman and her husband Charlie?"

Rubbing his temples with both hands, the sheriff looked at the detective. "Umm. It's a bit of a story, Hollis…and you ain't gonna like it."

Hollis said, "Charlie, I've been doing this for a long time. Nothing surprises me. The missing-persons report says she was married and she worked in a bar. That's it. Just relax, and tell me what you've got."

Shrugging his shoulders, Kemp sighed and started to talk, "Okay. Like you said, Hallie worked as a barmaid at the Lake Crescent Tavern. I guess she didn't show up for work three days before Christmas. 'Bout three years ago, I think. After the holidays, her family east of the mountains reported her as missing.

"We went to question her husband Monty. Great guy, drives a beer truck…or did then. He swore he hadn't seen his old lady since Christmastime, when he and her had a quarrel over a personal issue. He said he didn't report nothin' about her disappearance to us because she was cheating on him and had run off with a lover. He was positive about it. Said it was a sailor who was shipping out to Alaska.

"Based on the reputation them two had—Hallie being a loose cannon and Monty a womanizer—it seemed to be pretty reasonable. I mean, we'd answered a handful of domestic violence and noise complaints called in by their neighbors. It was common knowledge them two never got along." He stopped, shot Fultz a defensive glare.

Hollis was quiet, his face impassive. Finally, he shrugged and said, "And then?"

Kemp sighed again. "We followed up on the Alaska thing and didn't get nowhere. No records, no sightings, nothin'. We all thought she had pulled off a disappearing act and wasn't no way to track her down. Over Hallie's family's objections, we finally put the case in the inactive file."

Fultz said, "That's perfect, Charlie. Obviously, we need to start with the husband. Always start with the victim's closest family member. Let's bring this guy in for a little visit."

Chewing on his lower lip, the sheriff cleared his throat and said, "I wish we could. Like I said, all of my people and everyone else in town thought that Hallie had run away with another man. Monty was granted a divorce from Hallie a few months later. Shortly after that, he and his girlfriend moved to Los Angeles."

Fultz's jaw dropped, and he stared at the sheriff.

Kemp bristled. "What!? The whole fucking town knew that was what happened!"

"Relax, Charlie. I'm not being critical. I'm just…confused."

"Well, don't be. Who wouldn't run away if they were getting the shit kicked out of them every other day?"

"You're right, Charlie. Who wouldn't? But I think it might be a good idea to put together a time line on this stuff. It seems pretty clear to me the husband was the one who wanted to leave town as soon as possible."

He smiled at the touchy sheriff. "I know how hard you guys work these days. How about if I do some legwork, and you and your crew mind the store? I will keep you posted every day so we're all on the same page. Deal?"

Sheriff Kemp sniffed and grumbled, "Deal."

A SUSPECT

After his meeting with the sheriff, Fultz did some research and confirmed that Monty Illingworth and his lover, Elinore Pearson, had begun living together less than a week after Hallie's disappearance, and to his great surprise, he found out that Illingworth had indeed been able to secure a divorce only five months after his wife's disappearance. Monty and Elinore had moved to Los Angeles after the divorce was finalized.

The two lawmen set up a meeting with Clallam County Prosecutor Max Church to assemble a strategy for a full investigation of Monty Illingworth. The men contacted the LAPD and requested that Monty Illingworth, who was then living in Long Beach, California, be detained and held as a person of interest in the state of Washington's Lady of the Lake murder case.

Two days later, Fultz and Prosecutor Church flew to California to interview the suspect. Max Church had set-up a meeting with the suspect in an LAPD interview room.

While they were waiting for the prisoner, they decided that Fultz would do the talking. The detective began the interview with a polite request, "Mr. Illingworth, can I ask you a few questions?"

Monty nodded, and before Fultz could respond, he followed the nod with his own question, "Yes, sir. About Hallie, I hope. Have you guys found the killer yet?"

"Not yet. But we need you to fill in some blanks for us. Tell me, did you ever think that her vanishing act might involve foul play?"

"No, Hallie was a tough cookie. I never thought she would have been killed."

"Really? Her departure seems a little odd to us. No note? No contact? No communication with her family or friends after she left you? Seems a little unusual."

"Hallie was about as unusual as it gets. She was a pretty girl, but a pain in the ass as a wife. Drank too much. Had a short fuse and a foul mouth. I never should've trusted her."

Fultz was quiet for a few seconds then said, "Well, Mr. Illingworth, it seems that the discovery of her body rules out her alleged run-off with a boyfriend. Can you think of anyone who might have a reason to kill her?"

Illingworth sat with his arms folded across his chest. His face was pale, and Fultz could see that he needed a shave. "Yeah," he said "About half the people who knew her."

"Really? How so?"

"Like I said, Hallie had a quick temper and could be out of control when she got mad…which she did a lot. Plus, she was jealous as hell and not afraid to knock other women around. Ask anyone who knew her. She wasn't easy to get along with."

Fultz was quiet again, watching Monty closely. Finally, he said, "Folks tell me that you and your wife fought like cats and dogs. That Hallie showed up at work more than once with bruises on her face…maybe even a black eye every so often. In fact, some of the folks I've talked to say there was an extremely violent side to your marriage."

"Mr. Fultz, Hallie was a big girl. She could take care of herself. Sure, we had some fights, but I can tell you she wasn't afraid to hit back."

Fultz could see that Monty was a good-sized man. Tall and wide shouldered, with big hands and feet. Loading and unloading beer kegs all day when he was in Port Angeles had made him strong and hard. And he still appeared to be in good shape.

The detective was also aware that Hallie herself was tall and sturdy and had a reputation for being feisty. It would take a powerful man to overcome, hog-tie, and transport her to the lake. Monty looked like a powerful man.

"Mr. Illingworth," he said, "we want you to know that you are a prime suspect in our investigation."

Monty's face faded to an even whiter shade of pale than it had been when the interrogation first began. "I didn't do it.

Lots of people had reasons to hate her. I'm telling you I did not do it."

Fultz nodded. "We'll see. Now that we know for sure that Hallie is dead, it changes everything."

* * *

The following Monday, the Long Beach police—the closest major law enforcement to Monty's home residence—agreed to Illingworth's extradition. Fultz, Kemp, and Max Church met in Sheriff Kemp's office the day after the accused man arrived.

"Gentlemen," Fultz said, "this is crazy. We know this guy's the killer. Moved to California? With a new girlfriend only a month after his wife's disappearance? Come on. The new love affair screams motive...and the quick exit out of town confirms it."

Church grimaced. "I agree. But to cinch the deal, we need something to connect him to the body."

"You're right. But I'm not done yet. We're going to get him."

* * *

It was January of 1942, the country still reeling from Pearl Harbor, when Fultz finally got a break. Working the area around Lake Crescent, he retraced Monty's delivery route from the city to the resorts and bars closest to the lake.

Nearest to the Lake Crescent Tavern, at Sunnybrook Resort, he spoke with the proprietor, Harry Brooks, "Mr. Brooks, I'm sure you've heard about the progress in the Lady of the Lake case. Monty Illingworth is in custody here now, and we are asking locals for any information they might have about Hallie Illingworth's disappearance. We know he delivered beer to you on a regular basis. Is there anything you can tell us that might help us retrace Mr. Illingworth's stops or visits or comments that might be helpful? We know he was making deliveries shortly after Hallie vanished."

Brooks pulled on a bushy black mustache and said, "I saw that you fellows brought Monty up here for questioning. It actually reminded me of something weird that happened back in those days. This was before anyone knew she had disappeared."

Fultz said, "Really? What was that?"

"Monty stopped by a day or two before the holiday and said he had some trouble with his truck up the road a piece and asked if I had any sturdy rope he could borrow to drag his rig out of a muddy pull-off he'd gotten stuck in. Said he had a buddy up here with a car, but they needed some rope.

"I didn't think anything about it. I loaned him about fifty feet of rope from a spool of industrial grade I had in my shed, and he was gonna return it later. He never did get it back to me. It was no big deal.

"I never thought about it again until they found the body in the lake. But it just didn't seem like anything that might be helpful, so I pretty much just forgot all about it. Everyone around here thought Monty's story about her running off was absolutely true. Even me. And no lawmen ever contacted me about anything. I forgot all about it."

Fultz's jaw tightened as he struggled to suppress any sign of interest. "No big deal, we're just trying to tie up a few loose ends. Any chance you might have some of that rope still around?"

"I do. You want to take a look at it?"

"Yeah, I might as well."

The two men walked out the back, and Brooks unlocked a padlock on the door of a weathered shed with four inches of rain-forest moss on the roof.

When Fultz saw the spool of heavy rope coiled in a back corner of the storage area, he scratched his head and faked stifling a yawn. He had seen a very similar-looking rope in the Lady of the Lake's evidence locker at the Clallam County Sheriff Department.

Brooks said, "I don't think I've touched this rope since the day Monty borrowed enough to drag his truck out of the ditch."

Fultz nodded. Clearing his throat, he said, "Would you mind if I took twenty or thirty feet of this stuff just in case Sheriff Kemp wants to check it out?"

"Hell no. Do you think it might be part of the murder?"

Fultz shook his head. "I doubt it. We are just being careful. You never know."

But Detective Fultz knew.

THE TRIAL BEGINS

It was raining in town on the late February morning the trial began. Not quite cold enough to snow, but gray and damp, the misery factor was exacerbated by the heavy moisture content of the coastal air. A hoard of bundled-up spectators gathered hours before the scheduled courthouse opening, filling the wide entry steps to the building's front doors and overflowing onto Lincoln Street, the main arterial running north and south in front of the courthouse. The trial's venue was a classic brick structure complete with a domed tower featuring four separate clockfaces, each pointed outward like the four directions of the compass. In an area of the country where timber and wood products were the lifeblood of the community, the stately, all-brick structure bordered on sacrilege for the town of loggers and mill workers. But for the next eleven days, it would be the most famous building in the Pacific Northwest.

Courtroom staff expected a large gallery, and when the doors opened, the crowd elbowed its way up the stairs to the second-floor courtroom where seating filled rapidly as locals and visitors battled for open spaces. A dozen newspaper men bickered over the best seats in the press section. The room was packed to capacity in a matter of minutes. Courtroom staff scrambled to find alternative seating for the overflow crowd, and folding chairs filled every possible space. The unfortunate latecomers were sent home to try again on another day.

When the lucky ones in the crowd were seated, four of Hallie Illingworth's siblings were escorted to their reserved-seating area. Minutes later, the bailiffs brought the accused man's mother and live-in girlfriend to their front-row seats. Spectators strained for the best views, twisting and half-standing from their seats. An excited buzz of conversation escorted the families from the entry doors all the way to the front of the courtroom.

Finally, Montgomery Illingworth and his attorney strode into the courtroom beside an attending bailiff.

"All rise," intoned a bailiff as Judge Ralph Smythe entered the courtroom and approached the bench.

The crowded room rose in unison with noisy scraping, throat-clearing and subtle stretching.

Judge Smythe was a tall man with a cadaverous body so thin that his robe draped on his frame as if it were a wet towel hung on a bathroom hook. His brown hair, turning to gray, and bony body gave him the look of a man much older than his late middle age.

Smythe scanned the room as if trying to comprehend the trial's huge drawing power. He looked at the jury. Eleven men and one woman. All the males dressed in an assortment of dark suits and every man sporting a unique version of how NOT to tie a necktie. Smythe's gaze turned to the tables of the prosecution and the defense, and he nodded to the attorneys for both sides. Finally, he faced the unfamiliar press corps, a group of rumpled strangers holding notebooks and tablets, ready for the event to begin. The judge delivered a slight dip of his chin to the newsmen.

"Well," he said, "be seated, please. Welcome to all of you. It appears we will be dealing with a unique trial today."

Judge Smythe's first impression of frailty—suggested by his skeletal physique and the soft voice of his welcoming remarks—vanished when he changed to his business voice. Strong and precise, the rich baritone quickly neutralized the slight body, and the crowd leaned forward in its seats.

"Before we begin, we need to review a little courtroom etiquette here. You will all be expected to remain silent throughout the trial's proceedings. Respect the seriousness of a murder trial, and do not express emotions of any kind. Violations of this etiquette, from public or press, will result in your expulsion from this hearing. Despite appearances, this is not a circus. It is a court of law. Make sure you treat it that way."

He gave the gallery, then the prosecution and the defense, a hard scan. Taking his seat behind the bench, he said, "Mr. Prosecutor, your opening statement, please."

Clallam County Prosecuting Attorney Max Church rose from his chair. Church had been elected to his position twice and had the reputation of being both a skilled lawyer and an honorable man. He was completely bald and had a deep scar running from the middle of the naked head to just above his right ear, a vivid reminder of a farm-machinery accident suffered when he was a teen. It was the kind of scar you noticed once and then looked past it to the man whose character overshadowed the disfigurement.

Church adjusted his black-framed glasses, while walking to a position facing both judge and jury, then said, "If the court pleases, Your Honor, we will prove—quickly and emphatically—that Mr. Montgomery J. Illingworth did intentionally beat, strangle, and kill his wife, Hallie Illingworth. And following that heinous act, attempted to conceal the body of his murdered wife in a particularly unseemly manner."

He stopped, letting the packed room think about his words. When the pause began to grow uncomfortable, he turned toward the bench and made eye contact with the judge.

"That's it, Mr. Church?"

"That's it, Your Honor. That's all it needs to be."

"Well, I'm not used to such a brief opening from you, Counselor, but I'm sure you will make up for it as we move along."

The judge looked toward the defense table, where attorney Joseph Johnston sat beside his client, Monty Illingworth, and said, "And you, Mr. Johnston, are you ready for your opening statement?"

Rising slowly, Johnston said, "I am, Your Honor. I want to thank Mr. Church for his brevity. Perhaps I can put a little more meat on the bone for the members of the jury.

"My client has been unjustly accused of a crime that he did not commit. We intend to prove to the jury that there is no valid reason for Mr. Illingworth being accused, that details of the murder have been poorly handled by law enforcement personnel involved, and that there are definite questions about the actual identity of the victim.

"Mr. Illingworth has been unceremoniously extradited from California where he has been a respected citizen of the city of Long Beach for several years, and is now holding a job that will contribute to the cause of America's new war as a bus driver transporting workers to factories where they are desperately needed to help produce wartime necessities.

"We need to resolve this injustice quickly and get Mr. Illingworth back to where he can continue to contribute to the war effort." Looking intently at the jury, he continued, "You folks can help make that happen. These are difficult times, and we need all of our patriots, like Mr. Illingworth, to do their part for our country."

Johnston was a handsome man with a full head of thick white hair. He was wearing reading glasses, and his blue eyes shone behind the lenses in the square wire frames. He wore a navy-blue suit and a solid gray necktie perfectly knotted. In contrast to Judge Smythe, his voice had the rasp of a heavy smoker. Even so, he was equally eloquent, and fellow lawyers considered him to be a gifted orator.

The first witness to take the stand was Harlan McNutt. Now in his fourth year of medical school, Harlan looked nothing like the country-boy med student who had first examined Hallie Illingworth's body. The small-town image had been erased by his years in cosmopolitan Washington, DC. He wore a brown herringbone suit and vest, accented by an olive-and-tan necktie; the vest was completed with a pocket watch and matching gold chain. He sported a trimmed mustache, aging him nicely and highlighting his wavy brown hair and brown eyes. Even the tortoiseshell glasses he wore picked up the colors of his features and apparel.

After Harlan was sworn in, Prosecutor Church began questioning him about his examination of the deceased-victim's body. "Dr. McNutt," he said, "can y—"

"Objection, Your Honor. This witness is not yet, and was not at the time of his examination, a doctor," said Defense Attorney Johnston.

"Sustained," replied the judge.

Church said, "Of course, Your Honor. My mistake."

Johnston snorted from the defense table.

The prosecutor began again, "What was the condition of the body?"

Harlan said, "The body was, I believe, one of the most incredible cadavers anyone has ever seen."

"And why was the body so extraordinary?"

"Because the body tissue had not decomposed in a natural manner. There was no smell. There was no bloating. It was an almost perfectly preserved, waxy statue."

Church let the answer hang in the air. "Really? Do you know what caused this phenomenon?"

"I do now. With Charlie Kemp's approval, I met with a group of scientists and doctors from the University of Washington to solve the puzzle. Through an amazing process under perfect conditions—a chemical reaction between near-freezing water, rare waterborne minerals, and the body fat of the victim—the body tissue of the corpse was astonishingly well preserved. By a freak scientific conversion, the woman's wrapped and unexposed body fat had turned into a puttylike consistency of crude soap. The process is called *saponification*, and it is quite an unusual natural phenomenon."

"Did you say crude soap?"

"Yes indeed. The body tissue had gone through a metamorphic conversion to change the human tissue into the texture and color of a rough bar of Ivory soap."

The courtroom stirred at the statement. Everyone in the room was aware of the strange condition of the body, but few knew the scientific explanation of the strange phenomenon. Nor had they heard before the visceral oral description of the body.

Church remained silent, giving the jury a chance to imagine the horrific visual, then asked, "Could you tell us a little more about the condition of this soap-like cadaver?"

"Yes. The unusual state of the body preserved the markings of a premortal beating. There was a significant amount of bruising. The neck was highly discolored and had hand- and finger-shaped marks clearly imprinted. The woman was strangled as obviously as if someone had painted the hand outlines on the neck."

"Were there any other indications of foul play, Mr. McNutt?"

"Yes. The shoulders and chest were covered with bruises the same color as the finger marks around the neck. The woman had obviously been severely beaten."

"I see. And the ropes that were removed prior to your examination, Mr. McNutt? Can you tell us what you remember about the ropes?"

"I can. The rope was coiled around the body, securing the blankets she was wrapped in. The coils were spaced maybe two to three inches apart. They were dirty and old looking, but still intact."

Church said, "So this was a methodically executed work of bondage?"

McNutt said, "I don't know. I believe she was dead at the time she was bound. She wasn't going anywhere."

Church was quiet. After a pause, he looked at the jury and said, "No further questions, Your Honor."

The judge nodded toward the defense table. "Mr. Johnston, do you have any questions?"

"I do, Your Honor."

Walking slowly toward the bench and the seated witness, he stopped in front of Harlan, cocking his head and rubbing his chin. "Mr. McNutt," he said, "how long had you been in medical school when you were asked to view the body?"

"One year."

"And during that one year, did you have extensive experience with autopsy?"

"No, only during the anatomy sessions in the lab. Everyone had their own cadaver kept in refrigerated storage."

"One cadaver? And that qualified you to examine a body unlike any other in the history of crime?"

"No, sir, it did not. I was aware of my inexperience and explained that a skilled coroner was essential. That said, I believe any person in this courtroom would have recognized the damage and obvious violence inflicted on the body. Handprints crossing the larynx are not too challenging."

"A simple yes or no would suffice, Mr. McNutt. Again, were you professionally qualified to examine the body?"

"No."

"Thank you." Johnston paused then said, "Remind me again. How many years did you say you had been in medical school?"

"One. One year of med school at that time."

"No further questions, Your Honor."

EARLY TESTIMONY

The trial moved forward at a steady pace. Max Church presented a stream of witnesses, including South Dakota dentist Albert McDowell, whose astute recognition of Hallie's dental bridge confirmed that the Lady of the Lake was indeed Hallie Illingworth.

Coworkers, family, and friends all testified as to the palpable tension of the Illingworths' relationship. Hallie's nuclear family confirmed that the corpse recovered was their family member—there was no doubt the mane of dark hair and the familiar bone-battered waitress feet, and even the clothing on the body, belonged to their sister Hallie Illingworth.

As for the defense, Joe Johnston grilled dentist Albert McDowell at length, trying to negate the credibility of the doctor's conclusion. Dr. McDowell was steadfast that the uniqueness of the custom bridgework left no doubt of the patient's identity.

Johnston continued to dispute the validity of the body's identification and called witnesses who claimed that they had friends in Alaska who had seen Hallie there after her disappearance. He called several reputable Port Angeles citizens to provide glowing character references for the defendant. Resort bar owners and downtown night-spot managers testified that Monty Illingworth was popular with local workers and customers, especially with the female members of kitchens and waitstaff.

* * *

As the second week of the trial began, the excitement of attendees and the public interest of followers of the case continued to build. Monday was the day the sparring would end, and the main event would begin. Key witnesses—a Lake Crescent Resort owner, Detective Hollis Fultz, and the defendant himself—were on the week's docket.

The morning started when Max Church called Harry Brooks, the owner of the Sunnybrook Resort on the shores of Lake Crescent, to the stand and quizzed him about the rope Detective Fultz had obtained from the resort owner's storage shed. Brooks explained his tardiness for making the connection between his rope and the crime. Like all his neighbors, Brooks had believed that Monty's story was true. It was not until the body was found and identified—three and a half years after Hallie's disappearance—and Monty was arrested that he considered a connection. In fact, not until Fultz asked about the rope did it cross his mind.

Johnston's cross was awkward, and he was forced to focus on Brooks's poor memory rather than the content of the man's testimony.

Judge Smythe called for an hour-long lunch break following the defense's cross.

* * *

Detective Hollis Fultz was sworn in right after the lunchtime recess. Most of the spectators were expecting a replica of the

1940s heroic literary detectives like Raymond Chandler's Philip Marlowe or Dashiell Hammett's Sam Spade—ruggedly handsome, chain-smoking, and hard-drinking tough guys who punched and pistol-whipped their way to justice. Hollis Fultz did not fit the stereotype. The fifty-four-year-old was nothing like those famous fictional characters. His look was more intellectual than rugged.

Despite his appearance, Fultz himself was not only a famous detective, but also a successful true-crime author. Had trial attendees read any of his books and bothered to look at the author's photo on the back cover of the dust jacket, they would have seen a man who looked nothing like a tough private eye. But there was a presence about him; it was as if his talents were obvious. As he took his seat in the witness chair, he showed no sign of nerves and ignored the anxious crowd and the cluster of eager newspaper reporters.

Prosecutor Church began his questioning of Hollis B. Fultz with a request for an explanation as to how Fultz was connected to the Hallie Illingworth murder case.

Fultz nodded. "We were contacted by Sheriff Charlie Kemp to assist with the investigation following the discovery of a victim's body in Lake Crescent. Since that contact, I have been consulting…at Sheriff Kemp's request…on the case. I have some experience with these types of crimes and was happy to assist."

Church said, "Indeed. I'm sure the county appreciates your help. Can you tell us, sir, what your team has discovered? Give the jury your professional summary of the investigation."

"Of course. In this particular case, the background research indicated the Illingworths were involved in a contentious marriage from the beginning. There was witness feedback pointing to the violent nature of the couple's relationship. During the marriage, Hallie had shown up at work with bruises and black eyes. Neighbors had twice alerted the police, reporting frightening domestic disputes with the pair fighting and screaming threats and streams of crude profanity.

"The very night before the victim disappeared, fellow members of the tavern staff where Hallie Illingworth worked reported the couple had a heated shouting match on the front porch of the bar."

Church asked, "And what happened next?"

Fultz answered, "Three and a half years later, Mother Nature gave us a huge break when the body floated to the surface of the lake. Apparently, bodies don't usually surface in this water, but to insure this one would never be found, the killer anchored it with weights tied to ropes. The body turned to soap, which is lighter than water, so when the ropes rotted, the body floated up. And that changed everything. Once we were able to ID the body, we were able to connect the dots with forensic research…the information that has been shared throughout this trial."

"And one more time, please. What was the victim's name, Mr. Fultz?"

"At the time of her death, it was Hallie Illingworth."

Church let Mr. Fultz's words hang in the air for a while. He looked at the jury…then at the judge. "No further questions, Your Honor."

The judge recessed for a break before the cross.

* * *

When the break was over, the gallery's seat holders hurried back to their places.

"Are you ready to cross-examine the witness, Mr. Johnston?" said the judge.

"Yes, Your Honor. We are." Johnston took his time getting to the bench and appeared to be deep in thought. "Mr. Fultz, during your investigation regarding this case, did you at any time attempt to follow up on the reports referencing sightings of Hallie Illingworth in Alaska?"

"No, sir, not personally. However, both Mr. Church and Sheriff Kemp contacted law enforcement entities up north and got no confirmations to support those rumors."

Johnston asked, "But those rumors had to start somewhere. Would you agree that their very existence creates a gray area in your investigation?"

"No. Every case I've been involved with throughout my career has dealt with similar issues. In this particular situation, no witnesses whatsoever were found that could substantiate the possible sighting."

"Oh, but we have witnesses who say they heard Hallie was seen in different places after 1937. It's very possible the victim could have been there at one time, is it not?"

"Anything is possible, Mr. Johnston. But, despite the alleged sightings, no official entity was able to confirm Hallie's presence in Alaska. That fact supports the theory she was never there. Especially when we have a body that was underwater for three and a half years."

Johnston quickly responded, "You have *a* body. We think there is some doubt about whose body you have. My question was, isn't it possible Hallie might have been seen in Alaska? Yes or no?"

Fultz sighed and answered with an it's-not-possible inflection, "Yes. It's possible."

"Thank you. And isn't it also possible that Dr. McDowell's identification of the dental piece that was used to identify the body could be erroneous?"

"No."

"No? Why not?"

"Because a victim's dental work is as unique as a person's fingerprints. Unlike vague gossip or rumors."

Johnston ignored the answer. "And the rope, sir? I find it difficult to believe that is *the* rope found on the body. All the rope in the world and that piece is identical to the rope that bound the body? Even if it is truly a match, isn't it possible that there is room for error there as well? I'm sure there are other local citizens—maybe even someone seated in this courtroom today—who might have purchased the same product from the same store."

"No."

"No?"

"No. The rope has been confirmed by experts to be the same as the rope securing the body. It was borrowed the day after Hallie Illingworth disappeared. There is no doubt about the crime lab's forensic evidence."

Johnston turned toward the jury. "I don't understand, Mr. Fultz. If, as you have admitted, rumors can be in error, is it not possible that other evidence can be in error as well? As you said, anything is possible." Shaking his head, as if he had been seriously wronged, the defense attorney said, "No further questions, Your Honor."

AN UNHAPPY JUDGE

The next day, the weather was clear and cold, a clash of seasons, with spring hopeful and winter determined to stay. Courtroom spectators came early; they arrived blowing on cold fingers, but smiling with anticipation. Rumors that key witnesses might take the stand had swirled around the city.

The courtroom was filled an hour before start time. Judge Smythe had agreed to allow an unusual standing room only, and a small group of latecomers squeezed tightly against the back wall. After the room was full, family members of the victim and the accused were in their assigned seats at the front of the gallery. Two of Hallie's sisters sat together with their spouses. Monty's support consisted of his mother, Flossie Illingworth, and his live-in girlfriend, Elinore Pearson. The two women came in arm in arm. Their show of solidarity was unexpected, and as they walked down the aisle, the gallery's buzz rolled behind them like a rogue wave on a local beach.

Elinore was ten years younger than the deceased Hallie Illingworth and five years younger than Monty himself. In many people's opinion, she was even more beautiful than Hallie had been. She had tawny-blonde hair and Scandinavian blue eyes. Her skin was fair and her facial features more delicate than Hallie's. She was shorter than her rival and slender in comparison, with fewer curves, but had a well-proportioned figure. The women in the gallery searched for flaws, but had to settle for calling her "pale" or "too skinny."

Elinore Pearson's connection to the story was almost as bizarre as the murder itself. Monty and Elinore met when Elinore was sharing a rented Port Angeles apartment with Hallie's own younger sister. Hallie had brought her husband to meet her sister, and by chance, both the sister and her roommate were home when the couple arrived. Elinore was beautiful.

Monty was smitten. A short time after the introduction, whisperings began that Monty and Elinore were secretly seeing one another. And then Elinore moved in with Monty just days after Hallie's alleged departure.

Trial spectators were eager to hear details of the suspected love triangle. The effect of the arrival of Monty's mother and his girlfriend in tandem was electric. The tension in the hot, crowded courtroom was palpable. The crowd smelled blood.

When Monty Illingworth entered the courtroom, his eyes went directly to the pair. The two women were seated side by side. Both dressed for a formal party, including stylish fedora-style hats with feathers tucked into colorful hat bands, a current fashion rage in the early forties. They sat touching shoulders, their arms intertwined and holding one another's hand.

Monty flashed the two a smile before taking his regular seat beside Joe Johnston at the defense table. Illingworth did not look like a truck driver this morning. Wearing a dark suit and a red-patterned necktie, the outfit included a gleaming white handkerchief folded neatly in the suit's front breast pocket. His dark hair was slicked back, and his usual five-o'clock shadow shaved as smooth as a piece of typing paper. Despite the roguish attire, a closer look revealed a less confident impression. His movements were jerky, and there was a hint of dampness at the edge of his low widow's-peak hairline. He licked his lips repeatedly and seemed uncomfortable with the necktie and suit jacket in the warm, overcrowded courtroom.

Following a nod from the judge, Mr. Johnston said, "The defense calls Montgomery Illingworth to the stand."

Monty was sworn in, accepting the oath with a confident "I do!"

* * *

Judge Smythe said, "Your witness, Mr. Church."

Prosecutor Church stayed seated, shuffling papers and not looking at the man seated beside the bench. Courtroom spectators squirmed, scooting closer to the front of their seats as Church continued to stall. When Judge Smythe cleared his throat, the prosecutor finally stood up.

Walking slowly toward the bench, Church stopped in front of the defendant, looked into his eyes, and said, "Mr. Illingworth, did you kill your wife?"

The crowd exploded with a gasp, and Monty jumped to his feet as if he had been shocked with a cattle prod. His eyes opened wide, and saliva crawled from the corner of his mouth as his mouth gaped open. Looking at the gallery, he shouted, "I did not kill anyone!" His face was red, and he gulped in air as he tried to gain control.

The crowd continued its raucous disruption, and the judge, as shocked as the defendant, began banging his gavel as hard as he dared, trying to quiet the courtroom and shouting at Monty, "Sit down, Mr. Illingworth! Please be seated!"

Defense attorney Joe Johnston was standing and shouting over the din, "Objection! Objection!"

Smythe stood up behind the bench and boomed, "Order in the court! Order in the court!"

While bailiffs scurried to restore order, the ruckus began dying down.

The judge said, "That's enough from all of you!" Turning his attention to Monty, he lowered his voice and addressed the upset witness, "Mr. Illingworth, please be seated."

Still breathing hard, Monty sat down, his face a burning red and his eyes filled with hate.

The judge glared at Church, struggling to control his own ire, and spit out, "That was a totally unacceptable question, Mr. Prosecutor...and you know it! If you want to interview this man to support your case, you will do so in a civilized manner. And I am warning you. If you try another stunt like that, you will be dismissed from this case." Still struggling to control his rage, he added, "Which I should do anyway. Do you understand me?"

"I do, Your Honor. I apologize. It won't happen again," Church said in his most contrite voice.

"Thank you. It better not. Courtroom etiquette, as you well know, does not allow badgering or harassment. We all know your opening question was reprehensible. Even a hint of that kind of behavior again and I will have you jailed for contempt. We are talking about a man's life here, not vaude-ville theater!"

Turning to the court reporter, the judge said, "Norma, strike the prosecutor's comment from the record." Then to the jury, "Members of the jury, you will ignore that question and disregard it in any discussion regarding a verdict."

Judge Smythe took another deep breath and turned his attention back to the upset witness. "Mr. Illingworth, I apologize for the prosecutor's rudeness. You can have as long as you need to compose yourself, and let me know when you are ready to start over."

Monty nodded curtly and, with a feigned show of bravado, said to the judge, "I'm good, Your Honor. Let's go."

Smythe said, "Are you sure? Do you want a recess? We can take a break here."

Illingworth, still flushed and fighting to control his shaking body, nodded. "I'm okay."

The judge looked at Monty's attorney. "Mr. Johnston, is your client ready to testify? Do you want a break to regroup?"

Staring at Church, Johnston said, "Let my client decide, Your Honor. He is an innocent man, and Mr. Church's cheap tricks have only served to reveal the prosecution's desperation to the court and the jury. I'm ready if my client is ready."

Smythe looked again at Monty, who had managed to collect himself. "Mr. Illingworth? Are you certain you are comfortable continuing the questioning?"

Illingworth nodded.

"All right," said the judge. "Mr. Church," he growled, "Why don't you try again."

Church said to Monty, "My apologies, sir. That was my mistake. I'm truly sorry. Let me start over, if you will."

Eyes flashing, Monty nodded again and tried to appear indifferent.

Church spoke quietly and said, "How long had you and Hallie been married when Hallie disappeared?"

"I don't know. A couple years maybe."

"Actually, the records indicate closer to eighteen months."

Monty shrugged. "Close enough."

"During that time, did you and she fight often?"

"Hallie fought with everybody, not just me."

"A simple yes or no will suffice, sir."

Illingworth shrugged again. "Yeah, I guess."

"Were these fights ever violent?"

"Yes. But it was a two-way street. She could hold her own."

"She could hold her own?" Looking at the jury, Church raised his arms in silent disbelief. "Tell me, Mr. Illingworth, did *you* ever show up at work with bruises or a black eye on *your* face?"

Monty's neck and cheeks began to fill again with red rage. He swallowed and cleared his throat, then snarled at the prosecutor, "Maybe. I don't remember."

"You don't remember? Okay. See if you can remember an answer to this question. Did you see other women when you were married to Hallie?"

Monty shifted his position in the witness chair and said, "I worked in the beer business. I saw other women and men every day I delivered."

"Based on earlier testimony, I'll take that as a yes. Were you intimate with other women while you were married?"

Monty was silent for a few seconds. "No."

"No? So earlier testimony from your coworkers, Hallie's coworkers, and various bar patrons was untrue?"

"Everyone can have an opinion. My answer is no."

"I see. They tell me another woman moved in with you just days after your wife disappeared. Is that true?"

"Maybe. I don't remember how long it was. Hallie had run off with another man. I wasn't going to take her back. I got a life too."

Church's soft approach disappeared. "I think your marriage behavior has been adequately established by earlier testimony. Let's change the subject here. Perhaps your memory will be better discussing something that would have taken place in a more sober environment.

"On December 22, 1937, did you borrow a length of rope from Sunnybrook Resort on Lake Crescent?"

Monty hesitated then said, "I did."

"And can you explain how that rope was traced back to you? The same kind of rope that bound Hallie's body at the bottom of Lake Crescent?"

"It wasn't me. Somehow, someway, that rope came from somebody else. Maybe someone stole it out of my truck after I got the truck out of the ditch."

Church stared at his witness for a long time. He turned and looked at the jury. Over his shoulder, he said to the judge, "No further questions, Your Honor."

It was almost one o'clock when Church ended his session with Monty. The judge called a halt to the day's proceedings, "We will begin the redirect tomorrow, Mr. Johnston. We will all be fresher and more alert. We are growing closer to the conclusion of the trial, and after Mr. Church's antics, I don't want anyone too upset to be able to think straight. Including me." Looking around the packed courtroom, his gaze swept over the tables of the defense and the prosecution. "We will begin proceedings at 10:00 a.m." Then Judge Smythe paused, took a deep breath, and said, "One more thing. I want to meet with both attorneys in the judge's chamber as soon as we clear this room."

Slamming his gavel on the desk, he growled, "Court is adjourned."

* * *

In a small town like Port Angeles, lawyers were seldom enemies. They spent too much time together as friends and at meetings or service clubs or kids' sports activities. They played golf and drank together. Superior court judges were elected by the public, and most candidates came from the pool of local-bar associates. Arguments and hard feelings were limited to the courtroom. The resultant judge-attorney relationships were usually cordial and politely professional.

The meeting in the judge's chamber after the day's early dismissal took less than forty-five seconds. With the two attorneys standing in front of his desk, Smythe said in a soft but cold voice, "Church, if you ever try that again, I will throw your ass in jail for contempt of court. Do you understand me?"

"I do, Your Honor. It won't happen again."

"That's good, Max. Now, get the fuck out of here."

THE VERDICT

The next day, Monty took the stand to be questioned by his own attorney. Both men knew the prosecution had presented a compelling case, and Joe Johnston knew convincing the jury his client was telling the truth, and everyone else was lying, would be difficult.

But from the very beginning of his testimony, Monty looked to be at ease, showing flashes of the charm that he was said to possess. Johnston led him through a litany of questions, each trying to counter incriminating earlier testimony.

Monty dismissed each as untrue or an incident he was unable to recall. Several times he used a version of "I'm a beer-truck driver. I've been known to knock back a few brewskis myself. Sometimes I don't remember details."

There was little drama to the redirect, no raucous interruptions. Only two good old boys visiting in a relaxed and down-to-earth manner. It was all Mr. Johnston could do, and Monty's good looks and outgoing personality made it difficult to imagine him as a ruthless killer.

* * *

The following day was March 5, 1942, a typical early-spring Pacific Northwest day with dark skies and cold rain. The weather and the daily news about Japan's recent attack on Pearl Harbor did little to lighten the tension. This was the last day of a murder trial. The mood was somber; both sides were quiet, their faces drawn and serious. Both lawyers would present their closing statements.

Judge Smythe, addressing both tables, said, "Gentlemen, now that we have returned to normalcy, are you ready to deliver closes this morning?"

The two attorneys nodded.

"Very well. Mr. Church, please proceed."

Church walked to the front of the bench and turned to face the jury. "Members of the jury, this is the time when you will conclude your civic duty. You have heard every word from every witness called in this case. You have processed a great deal of information. Your decision will determine how justice will be served.

"Mr. Illingworth has told us that his wife was not afraid to fight back. I expect that is true. Hallie had been fighting back her entire life. One of thirteen children in a poor-as-dirt family. A victim of the Great Depression, broken marriages, and migratory moves, always searching for a better life. Who among us would not fight back? But, despite her fighting spirit, Hallie was no match for a strong man. And even if she had been, she did not deserve to die at his hands."

He stopped, lost in thought. Then said, "Let me share with you what the prosecution believes happened on the night Hallie Illingworth died. It is critical that you understand the details of this dastardly crime.

"Both husband and wife had been out on the town, by themselves. Both were drinking, and both were drunk when they connected at their apartment in the early morning of that fateful day.

"They had a terrible fight. Mr. Illingworth was bigger, stronger, and younger. In his rage, he slapped, punched, and finally strangled Hallie to death. After he sobered up, he wrapped her body in blankets and loaded it into his truck.

"In the morning, he drove to the lake, borrowed some rope from one of his customers, then used that rope to secure the body. Then he tied some type of heavy anchors onto the body with the rope and borrowed, or stole, a lakeside row-boat and dropped his wife's body into the deep waters of Lake Crescent. He wanted to make certain the body would remain underwater."

Church let his words hang in the air. When he spoke again, his voice had softened. "After Mr. Illingworth sank the body, he created a web of lies about Hallie's unfaithful departure, wrangled a quick divorce and, only days later, left town with another woman and moved to California.

"Unfortunately for the accused, the elements of nature played a trick on him. Three years later, the anchor ropes rotted through, and a once-in-a-lifetime chemical reaction of cold water and mineral acids delivered a body that had turned into soap."

He paused then added, "The irony of Mr. Illingworth's actions is, if he had just thrown the body in the lake, nature and the lake's curse would have, most likely, done the job for him.

"Once forensic science was able to identify the victim, and despite the accused man's assorted lies and denials, every piece of evidence points to Mr. Illingworth as the killer. A man who took his wife's life, tried to conceal her body, cohabited with another woman, and fled the peninsula.

"There is only one possible killer, and as jurors, you must react accordingly. You must assure that justice be served. You must do the right thing. You must find Monty Illingworth guilty of murder."

After Church returned to his seat, Joseph Johnston moved to the railing of the jury box. Looking into the eyes of every person on the jury, he tried to transfer the compassion he felt with the intensity of his eye contact and the serious expression on his face.

Finally, he said, "The prosecution would have you believe that my client's marriage was violent and abusive. That his wife was a fragile and tormented woman and that Monty himself was a skirt chaser and an unfaithful husband. That Mr. Illingworth was a monster.

"As you could see from yesterday's testimony, nothing could be further from the truth. This man is still highly thought of in our community and, while he was living here, was hired by a company that requires great people skills and goodwill.

"The prosecution would have us believe that Hallie Illingworth was defenseless and vulnerable. Testimony, however, revealed a different story. Hallie was definitely *not* a fragile woman. She was a tough woman with an explosive temper. As her husband testified, there were many people—men and women—with more reasons to harm her than his own."

Gathering his thoughts, he took a deep breath. "Were there times when the couple fought over domestic differences? Of course. Every marriage has some spats. Was Monty active in the city's watering holes? Of course. It was his job. A hard-working, hard-playing citizen, not unlike the rest of us.

"As jury members, the task that you have been chosen for will not be easy to complete. I urge you to approach your duty with an open mind.

"The prosecution has presented a case with many questionable theories. And little rock-solid evidence. The most critical evidence—the identification of the body by a general dentist from South Dakota, from a procedure performed over twelve years ago. The rumors that the deceased was seen in other areas of the country were not adequately researched or pursued by local law enforcement. The rope that supposedly ties my client to the body can be purchased right here in town by any one of us.

"All of these issues, and more, are subject to doubt. And doubt, ladies and gentlemen, can make or break a man's life.

"The judge will give you instructions prior to your meeting in the jury room. A decision must be agreed on based upon the principle of something having been proven beyond a reasonable doubt. We believe justice will be delivered based on the intent of that principle."

He let the words hang in silence and then said, "Thank you all for your time and dedication. God bless."

* * *

Four hours later, the jury returned to the courtroom. When Judge Smythe asked the jury foreman if they had reached a verdict, the man answered, "We have, Your Honor. We, the jury, find Montgomery J. Illingworth guilty of second-degree murder."

The killing, in the jury's opinion, was a crime of passion and not a preplanned death. Thus, the accused had avoided the first-degree charge and a sentence of death by hanging.

The judge's punishment was announced shortly after the verdict was revealed. Monty was sentenced to life in prison.

* * *

After the trial was over, the McNutt family embraced legacy of the mystery and shared the excitement of a family member's role in the saga. The Lady of the Lake became another chapter in Klallam Nation tribal history of the Storm King's curse.

The irony of the chapter is, if Monty Illingworth had just deposited Hallie's body in Lake Crescent without the rope tethers to hold her down, odds are the body would never have been found, and the freak of nature that shocked the world would never have occurred.

Someone challenged the mountain god's hex. And lost.

As always, in the deep waters and dark shadows of Storm King's front yard, drowning victims—by accident or choice—continue to vanish. The lake and the legend remain...and have changed not at all.

STORM KING'S WRATH

1947-2012

PRELUDE

There is an old story—untrue but fitting—about the naming of the city of Port Angeles. As the tale goes, in 1774, a Spanish explorer named Captain Juan de Fuca, sailed out of the Pacific Ocean and into a large seaway leading inland to unexplored territory. The weather turned, and a terrible storm hammered the small ship and terrified the crew.

On the verge of disaster, they spotted a long hook of land extending into the water and wrapping around a protected bay. With shredded sails and battered hull, the sailors managed to reach calmer waters in the safety of the natural harbor, where they spent several days repairing ship and sails.

The shaken captain recovered quickly and throughout the following days had time to consider his good fortune and the jaw-dropping beauty of the landscape that bordered the bay—snowcapped mountains stretching from sea to sky and dense forests of evergreen trees as far as the eye could see, all teeming with a variety of coastal wildlife. To express his gratitude for God's blessings, he christened the area, and the harbor itself, Port *Angilia*, which in English translates to Port of Angels.

Three hundred years later, local residents still think of the town as heaven and the surrounding untamed Olympic Peninsula as their own private treasure.

Despite their passion, history has shown that few nirvanas have avoided their own darker side. Where there is beauty, there is peril. The highest mountains, the fastest rivers, the deepest lakes draw the most attention…and provide the greatest risk. The splendor of Mother Nature's artwork, and the mankind within it, comes with challenges and a hunt-or-be-hunted existence. The peninsula is a wilderness paradise, and where there are predators, there will be prey.

THE NEXT GENERATION

Two days before the fifth anniversary of Monty Illingworth's life sentence for murder, the McNutt clan welcomed another member to the family. Harlan's cousin, Mary Ann McNutt, had married a pilot who had been shot down and captured in Germany early in the war. Roy Webster was a hometown hero, and Mary Ann was very proud of him. She thought her new husband had only one flaw—he was not Scottish. To ensure their son never forgot he was part of her own heritage, Mary Ann named him Duncan Magnus Webster. It was 1947, and Duncan Magnus's birth was welcomed by the family, but unnoticed by others due to the massive influx of postwar babies soon to be christened Baby Boomers.

The world war eclipsed all interest in domestic issues; the Lady of the Lake and all other nonwar news was ignored by the general public. But when the war ended in 1945, the country was eager to resume, and improve on, every aspect of prewar lifestyle

Dr. Harlan McNutt returned from service in the US Army Medical Corps in Northern California. As with all veterans exposed to the horrors of the war, the experience would eventually change his life.

Meanwhile, the Lady of the Lake had not been forgotten. Harlan assumed the role of unofficial caretaker of the legend and reveled in sharing the tale with any interested listener.

By the time Duncan was eight years old, he himself had listened to the story at every family gathering, and as he grew older, he never tired of its telling, be it on a summer camping trip with family seated around a beach fire or in one of a handful of farmhouses of relatives and in-laws sprinkled around the county. As a young boy, Duncan had heard his uncle tell the tale so many times and knew it so well it had become a part of his own memories…as if he himself had been present when the tale unfolded.

THE GYPSY

Duncan was an early grower, and his physical head start accelerated nature's normal time lines, which played a huge role in his own formative years. Everything seemed to happen to him before the same changes took place for his friends. Early maturity can have some advantages, but being a young boy in a man's body was not one of them. When puberty kicked in for Duncan as a sixth grader, he was determined to avoid anything that might be different from his friends and classmates. As a result, he was sensitive about his early start and had an aversion to any kind of teasing—thus earning him the reputation of being a shy boy with a short fuse.

In those days, there were six elementary schools and one private Catholic school in the city, and when boomers from each school entered grade seven, all of them merged at Roosevelt Junior High. The school district, not having time to handle the explosion of postwar students, had only one junior high school. All the seventh graders in the city joined all of the eighth and ninth graders already sharing classes at Roosevelt.

Suddenly, for Duncan and his friends, there were girls everywhere. For an early-grower's hormonal development, this abundance of the opposite sex created conflicts of interest. Duncan was tall, had dark hair, and was shaving every morning before school; he was desperate to hide the dark whiskers starting to grow on his cheeks and chin. Even worse was gym class—it was hard not to stand out in a shower room full of prepubescent classmates.

By the eighth grade, Duncan's brain was catching up to his body. His friends were maturing by then, and he was not the only boy whose body and mind were changing. The awkwardness of being ahead of the usual growth curve was waning, and he was very interested in the opposite sex. Athletics had boosted his confidence, and his social skills had improved dramatically. He could talk and joke with girls and was beginning to recognize when someone was actually flirting with him.

It would be toward the end of that summer, just before going back to school as a ninth grader, when Duncan's life would change. And he would have little to do with the transition.

* * *

Duncan's first real boy-girl party of his junior high school years was organized by his classmate and neighbor Jimmy Locker. Jimmy and a pack of his male classmates had spent a week in August sweating like pigs at preseason, two-a-day football practices, a poorly disguised torture program preceding the opening of the area's junior high fall football season. Jimmy was celebrating the end of the practices and the last weeks of summer vacation.

The partygoers gathering in the Lockers' basement family room that evening were excited and nervous. The boys had taken care to clean dirty fingernails, Butch Wax their football crew cuts, and find clean shirts and pairs of khaki or corduroy pants. The girls were all in dresses or skirts and sweaters, their short hairstyles perfect and faces glowing.

Most of the guests had already arrived when Duncan got there, and as he came down the stairs of the Lockers' basement, he did a quick scan of the room. He could see the girls were grouped on one side of the cleared-out mock dance floor, and the boys were gathered around the food on the opposite wall. The room was decorated with the school's colors; there were maroon and white ceiling streamers and clusters of white balloons at the ends of a table full of snacks and sandwiches. The room was warm, the lights bright, and Roy Orbison was playing on the hi-fi at conversation level. Two impatient young ladies were already in the center of the floor, swaying to the music, talking, laughing, and waiting for the actual dance music to get things going.

Jimmy was meeting kids at the bottom of the stairs. He said to Duncan, "Hey, Web, welcome to where it's happenin'."

"Yeah. Looks good, Jimbo."

Jimmy leaned closer. "You see those two girls on the dance floor?"

"I see Ginger. Who's the other one?"

"That is our newest classmate. Just moved in a few weeks ago. Her dad is the new pastor at our church, and my mom insisted I invite her. Not bad, huh?"

"I guess."

"You guess? What are you…blind? She's a fox!" He lowered his voice and said, "She's built like a brick shithouse!"

Duncan looked again at the girls on the dance floor. He knew what Jimmy meant, but he could see very little resemblance between a sturdy outhouse and the newcomer swaying to the music.

Jimmy said, "Her name is Gee-tan, or something weird like that...just in case you're interested."

"Not me, man, we've got football to think about."

Shaking his head, Jimmy said, "Yeah? Well, tonight we got something else to think about. If we're lucky."

Jimmy knew Duncan liked girls. He also knew Duncan was not a dancer. At junior high social functions with dancing involved, Duncan made a point of being semi-invisible. Most of his buddies had older sisters or were less self-conscious. Duncan's own dancing background was limited to sneaking a quick peek at the *Mickey Mouse Club* to check out Annette Funicello, or awestruck viewings of Dick Clark's *American Bandstand* on his family's black-and-white TV.

Duncan watched the two girls on the floor. They were enjoying the music and seemed to be comfortable being the only ones out there. Duncan was studying the girl dancing with Ginger and was startled to see her staring back at him. He looked away and pretended he hadn't seen her.

Jimmy was working both sides of the room now, shooing the other girls across the floor to mix with the guys at the food table. In seconds, the guests were gathered in small groups around the food, the boys chattering despite mouths stuffed with chips or cookies and the girls sipping on paper cups of fruit punch. The two dancers joined the group. Roy Orbison sang on, unnoticed, in the background.

When the feeding frenzy died down, Jimmy decided to kick-start his party. He grabbed his buddy Scooter Bennett and asked the football-team's hyper quarterback to get the party guests' attention.

Scooter obliged, letting loose a shrieking thumb-and-finger whistle that stopped all conversations in mid-sentence.

Standing beside the stereo, Jimmy shouted, "Are you guys ready to rock and roll?"

The group—both boys and girls—responded with a rousing "Yay!"

Jimmy dropped a vinyl record onto the turntable. There was a brief humming before the needle connected, and then Chuck Berry's electric guitar blasted the opening riff of "Johnny B. Goode."

The room erupted in cheers, and most of Duncan's friends chose partners as if they knew what they were doing, laughing and flexing and screwing around with one another on their way to the dance floor. In a matter of seconds, the dancers were locked on to the music.

Duncan watched, cursing his lack of dancing skills. He knew he was not a dancer, but he wasn't deaf—it was Chuck Berry, for crying out loud. It didn't get any better than that. None of the guys were touching their partners, but they all seemed comfortable working on their own dance moves and trying to find the courage to hold his partner's hand or begin a conversation with the girl.

As the evening moved on, Duncan sat in a circle with other nondancers, talking sports and the prospect of being the top dogs in the school during their final year at Roosevelt Junior High. The loud music and excited kids made it difficult for the nondancers to communicate. All of them in the circle were having trouble hearing, and Duncan was leaning forward in order to follow the trash talk and jokes.

Just then, Jimmy stopped the stereo and, while changing the record on the turntable, announced to the room, "Let's slow things down a bit and try a ladies' choice."

"Harbor Lights" by the Platters began to play, and everything changed. Jimmy turned off the ceiling light in the corner of the room, and the dance floor grew darker and softer. The music was sultry, a welcome contrast to the hard-rock beginning of the party, and the slow music created an aura of teenage expectations.

Duncan rose to head for the bathroom to avoid anyone looking for a partner. With his back to the dance floor, he was telling the guys he'd be back shortly when he felt an impatient tapping on the back of his shoulder. Turning to check out the shoulder tapper, he stared straight into the stunning lavender-blue eyes of the pretty girl he'd been sneaking peeks at on the dance floor throughout the evening.

"Hey, handsome. It's your lucky day. I choose you," she said.

Duncan stuttered out a terrified, "I…uh…I beg your pardon?"

"I…choose…you."

"Okay. For what?"

"For this dance, dummy. For this night. Who knows? Maybe for something else."

Duncan couldn't breathe, let alone move. He mumbled, "I don't know how to dance."

"You don't have to. We'll just stand very close together and sway to the music a bit. I'll stand on your feet if you want me to. It's okay. I don't bite."

Dragging him onto the floor, she smiled sweetly and placed his arm around her lower back. Holding on to his other hand, she pulled him close. She didn't stand on his feet, but started to move her own in a tight circle just inches at a time. She smiled again and said, "Just relax. You're doing fine."

Duncan had no idea what he was doing, but he knew she felt too damn good to let go. After a few slow revolutions, his muscles began to relax, and the girl, moving her hand to the back of his neck, used her fingers to caress the stubbly hairs of his new haircut. The soft fingers sent a shiver down his back, and he pulled her closer to his body.

She was wearing a dark-green dress, snug on the top and fuller on the bottom. The only girl at the party with longer hair, the mass of amber-colored curls was secured with a green scarf tied like a headband across her forehead. He could smell the fragrance of her hair, feel the softness of her body, and was over whelmed with a stupor of joy throughout the last twenty seconds of the song. Neither of the dancers said a word.

When the music stopped—way too soon for Duncan—she towed him off the dance floor. When she let go, she slid two folding chairs into a quiet corner and sat down, patted the seat of the other chair, and said, "Let's talk," then waited for him to say something.

"Okay. Is your name really Gee-tan?"

She laughed. "It's pronounced Ja-tawn. It's French. I like it."

"Oh...I like it too."

She could have said her name was Lizzie Borden, the axe murderer, and if she said she liked it, he would have told her he liked it too.

"And you?" She said, "What's your name?"

"Duncan."

"First name or last?"

"First."

"Okay, Mr. Chatterbox. Tell me about yourself."

As the night went on, Duncan started to loosen up and even let Gitane drag him onto the dance floor for most of the rock songs. He had no idea what to do, but he could tell none of his buddies did either. He just listened to the music and shuffled to the beat. The truth was, his goal for staying on the dance floor was to be close enough to Gitane to make sure no one else had a chance to be her partner during the next slow song. He got lucky two more times.

At 11:00 p.m., Jimmy's parents came down the stairs and nodded to their son.

Walking over to the stereo, Jimmy thumbed through the stack of records, and as the current song on the turntable faded to its conclusion, he called out, "Okay, everybody, last dance. We'll make it a belly rubber," and put the record on the turntable.

The sultry voice of Brenda Lee singing "I'm Sorry" drew every couple onto the floor. Duncan scanned the room and saw a group of odd couples—short boys snuggling their faces close to off-limits territory, taller guys slouched awkwardly low to be able to rest their chins and lips on top of the heads of shorter girls. Only one dim light had not been turned off by thrill seekers, and the darkness was inhaled by the dancers. Everyone was drugged by the unfamiliar closeness and using the sensuous tempo of the song to draw out the body contact as long as possible.

At that moment, Duncan thought his night out could not get any better. As it turned out, he was wrong.

When the lights came on, the mood vanished, and the partygoers headed outside, where parents of most of the girls waited in cars for their daughters.

Gitane Harper took Duncan's elbow and dragged him over to Jimmy's parents. "Don't worry about me getting home, Mr. Locker. Duncan's going to walk me the four blocks."

Jimmy and Duncan had been next-door neighbors since first grade, and the boys had spent countless hours in each other's homes. Jimmy's dad had teased Duncan about his reserved behavior for years. He winked at Duncan and said, "Duncan, I'll leave her in your hands. Just behave yourself."

Duncan's face turned red. "I will, Mr. Locker, honest."

Jimmy's mom and dad both laughed.

Minutes out the door, as they walked slowly down the sidewalk, Gitane asked, "Do you have a smoke?"

"A smoke? I don't smoke."

"Too bad. It's kinda fun."

Duncan didn't answer, numbed by the pleasure of walking down the quiet street, hand in hand with his new neighbor. When they got close to Gitane's house, they stopped under the droopy cedar tree on the corner beside the sidewalk.

Taking both of his hands in hers and looking into his eyes, she said, "Kiss me." Duncan knew he must have looked scared to death when she whispered, "Don't worry. I'll show you how." And she did.

After Gitane went inside her house, Duncan floated home in a daze. He was certain this night had been the best night of his life. First dance. First kiss. First touch. He would never forget the thrill of every new sensation.

GITANE, THE DEVIL, AND THE PURPLE COW

G itane Harper was a revelation.

Five foot four inches tall with blonde shoulder-length hair and amazing blue-violet eyes, she was nothing like any girl Duncan had ever been around. He got the impression that, like him, she had been ahead of the normal-growth curve. Unlike him, her hormonal instincts kicked in at the same rate as her body. He was pretty sure she had chosen him because he looked older than the rest of the guys at the party.

Over the next few weeks, Duncan slowly pieced Gitane Harper's story together. Her parents met at a church in Saint-Lô, France, just after the American invasion at Normandy. Her American father was a military chaplain, and her French mother a member of the Saint-Lô congregation's choir. They connected briefly and then began to exchange letters, and the friendship soon turned into a romance.

When the war ended, the two were married. They stayed in France for a year, then moved to Seattle, where Gitane was born in 1947. According to Gitane's mother, it was a difficult birth, and the baby survived after a life-or-death stay at the hospital. The child's toughness touched her parents' hearts, and her mother named her daughter Gitane, which is the French word for gypsy, in honor of her baby's tenacity and survival instincts. Never was a chosen name more appropriate.

The new girl in town and Duncan Webster began an opposites-attract relationship. School did not start until mid-September that year, and the last weeks of that magical summer were the best times of Duncan's life. September was always the nicest time of the year on the peninsula, and during that year's record good weather, almost every day was sunny and warm. The couple rode bikes to local parks and had picnics at which they spread out a blanket and lay in the sun, listening to rock music. When the sun went down, they went to movies and took walks on the beaches close to town. They spent hours swimming with friends at Maple Grove on Lake Sutherland, hitchhiking rides with anyone willing to drive them out there.

The weekend before school started, Duncan talked Jimmy Locker's older brother, Jeff, into giving the couple a ride to the lakes. There were three lakes west of town, and Duncan choose to bypass the usual Lake Sutherland hangout and take Gitane to Lake Crescent, guessing that Gitane would be blown away by the grandeur of the clear blue water, the primal setting of the Olympic National Park, and one of its most spectacular attractions.

Duncan was excited to share the lake's history and his own family ties to the spectacular lake. As soon as they were dropped off at the head of the Spruce Railroad Trail, he started to talk, "Most everyone around here knows the story of the Lady of the Lake and its connection to local history. It's a pretty cool legend, and I'm pretty sure someone will mention it to you if they see us together. You should know what they'll be talking about."

He took a deep breath and said, "It's kinda gruesome, but kinda cool too." He waited, watching for a reaction.

"So?"

Duncan said, "I've got an uncle who played a role in the whole thing—it was a murder from the 1930s, so bizarre it's still known as the legend of the Lady of the Lake…because the female victim had been in the lake for three years, and when her body finally floated up, it had turned to soap."

"Whaaat? That must be bullshit."

"It is not. I have a ton of books I'll share with you if you want. It's a long story. But *everyone* who lives around here knows about it. My uncle has told the story a hundred times, and I've known and loved it for my entire life. It's an awesome story."

He paused and said, "But that's not the only reason I want you to see the lake. This trail will take us to the Devil's Punch Bowl, where the body was found floating on the water. It's a great place to swim and has some scary cliff-jumping areas. I've got a hunch you might like it."

"Devil's Punch Bowl, huh? I like it already. Are we going to skinny-dip?"

"No. It's cold as ice, even if you're wearing a wet suit… let alone being naked. It's deeper and colder than what we're used to in Lake Sutherland, and way more remote. Besides, there may be people there."

Gitane sniffed. "Well, we can come back some other time."

Duncan continued his story, "My grandfather worked on the logging train that carried timber from the West End to the mills in Port Angeles in the early nineteen hundreds. Grampa Doug said the railroad guys actually started the name Devil's Punch Bowl because it was the most dangerous place on the route. Narrow tunnels that had been hacked through the cliffs, rockslides, and tracks right beside the water were really dangerous."

When they reached the Devil's Punch Bowl, Gitane's eyes sparkled as if they were suns bouncing off the surface of the lake. The craggy cliffs along the shore, the flat edges that marched like the steps of a ladder to jumping spots, launching pads that required the skills of a rock climber and the balls of an elephant, the green trees, and the sapphire-blue water—it was an adrenaline junky's dream come true. Gitane Harper loved it.

They spent the rest of the day jumping off the face of the craggy cliffs, into the cold water, shivering themselves warm in the sun, and then jumping again. Gitane was thrilled, going higher and higher with every jump.

Duncan made it to the second shelf level once, then announced, "Discretion is the better part of valor."

Gitane wanted to come back when they could skinny-dip.

* * *

As school started for their freshmen year, they were inseparable. Gitane waited for football practice to end. Duncan then showered, and they would walk hand in hand to her house and fool around until her parents got home from work. He would hustle home in time to eat with his parents.

As the school year moved on, they experienced a few bumps and crises. Their opposites-attract connection worked for Duncan, but Gitane began to grow restless.

"Shall we smoke? Can you get us something to drink? Do you think you could sneak your dad's car out so we can drive out to the spit to make out?"

Duncan's answer was always the same. "No. No. And no."

Eventually, while Duncan was at football practice after classes, Gitane began walking from the school to the Purple Cow. The Cow, as it was called, was a convenient hamburger joint just two blocks from the field and a hangout for the outlaws of the school and their girlfriends. Every day after school, the place was packed.

The guys all had greasy hair combed into an Elvis-style ducktails at the back of their heads; they wore blue jeans, white bucks, and packs of cigarettes rolled in their tee-shirt sleeves. The girls were all in long skirts and pullover sweaters, some wearing a guy's ring on a chain around their neck to let everyone know they were unavailable. All of them had bouffant hairstyles, black or brunette, plastered in place with too much hair spray. They wore bright-red lipstick that left smears of attitude on their Pall Mall cigarettes. For Gitane, there was no problem getting a smoke. There was always a jukebox blaring and an undertow of teenage rebellion.

The guys in lettermen's jackets called the Purple Cow Hoodsville. Duncan's girlfriend called it interesting. She loved the jukebox, the swearing, and the shock value her preacher's-kid, unexpected presence on-site created.

Despite her new interests, Duncan and Gitane remained a couple based on a puppy-love version of staying true to one another. Duncan continued to focus on sports, but his social skills were growing by the day as his girlfriend pushed him past his comfort level. The physical attraction remained strong, and a coming-of-age curiosity grew bolder as time passed. The kissing and touching got more intense, and only fear of a junior high school pregnancy kept them from letting things go too far.

In the springtime, Duncan was working out on the school's track after classes. Gitane continued to kill time at the Purple Cow until her boyfriend's conditioning sessions were over. On a misty-aired April day, Gitane left the Cow early and surprised him, waiting outside the boys' locker room.

"Hey there," she said.

Since he was usually the one waiting, he answered, "Hey. What's up?"

Standing with her hands behind her back, she said, "Nothing much. I have a surprise for you."

"Yeah? What is it?"

Gitane brought her hands from behind her back and said, "A Roosevelt Teddy." Handing him a foot-high, stuffed teddy bear, she smiled and said, "It's not just a toy. He's brought you something special."

Duncan looked at the bear, turning it around to check it out. It was brown in color and wearing a pair of round Theodore Roosevelt spectacles and the cowboy hat with the side turned up and pinned to the crown. Tied around the bear's neck with a maroon ribbon was a round tin locket about the size of a fifty-cent piece. It was deeper than the coin, and he could see there was a push latch to open the lid. He glanced at Gitane, imagining illegal or sexual items that might fit into a round piece of jewelry this size.

Gitane laughed. "It's nothing bad, silly. It's one of your favorite things."

Duncan wasn't so sure. He popped the lid and used two fingers to extract its contents. When the locket opened fully, he sighed in relief. It really was one of Duncan's favorite things—a lock of Gitane's honey-colored blonde hair.

He suspected the surprise she gave him might be a peace offering to let him know that, despite their differences, they would be okay. Or a gesture to suggest she was going to change her wild-child image. Whatever it meant, he thought it was sweet of her to give him something connected to his beloved teams and classmates.

The next morning, hurrying down the hallway to algebra class, Gitane was not waiting for him at her locker. No big deal. The two always met again at lunchtime and shared a quiet corner table in the cafeteria.

When Duncan got there, he was surprised to see a strange girl sitting in Gitane's usual chair. As he sat down in his seat across from the newcomer, she looked up at him and smiled with bright-red lips.

"Surprised?" she said.

It *was* Gitane. The long blonde curls were gone. And the short-cropped haircut she wore was dyed as black as a one-eyed man's eye patch. Duncan was baffled by Gitane's change, but he knew he shouldn't be—only Gitane would come up with such an unusual way to say goodbye. She was moving on.

When summer began, they were officially high schoolers, and by the time school started in the fall, Gitane had discovered upperclassmen with driver's licenses and date money. And they had discovered her.

It had been a life-changing young love destined to fail from the start. But for Gitane Harper and Duncan Webster, it was their first love. And everyone only gets one of those.

* * *

Through the next three years at Port Angeles Senior High School, the two of them went their separate ways. Gitane reveled in the abundance of guys driving muscle cars like GTOs and Chevy Malibus. Car guys with swagger. Even as her classmates began to drive, she preferred the upperclassmen. Older. Bolder. Edgier.

Duncan's social life was the exact opposite. All through his high school years, he dated only three different girls, all of them on a boyfriend-girlfriend basis. He was a one-girl guy and always most comfortable being part of a couple.

Despite their contrasting personas, Gitane and Duncan maintained a cordial relationship with one another throughout high school. They had some classes together, cheered each other on in school activities, and shared the occasional dance at proms and pep dances. The relationship was platonic but sweet, the bond unspoken but permanent.

Different degrees of new loves come and go. One day you might meet the true love of your life. But even then, the heart seems to reserve a special place for the one person who shared your first love.

GRADUATION

When Duncan and Gitane graduated in June of 1965, it was the largest graduating class in Port Angeles High School's history, and the giddy seniors were ready to celebrate. The party was restricted to class members.

Duncan was between girlfriends at the time and was soloing at the party. Gitane, denied the company of her older circle of outlaws, was also unescorted. Consequently, since they had walked together for the graduation ceremony, they decided to partner up at the all-night party to share the occasion with old friends and reminisce about the glory days of growing up as boomers.

To no one's surprise, Gitane snuck in a fifth of Jack Daniel's Whiskey, which was fine by Duncan, a nondrinker who decided graduating from high school might be worth the experience of losing his alcohol virginity. The night was the end of a major passing in their lives, and other grads would have no problem sharing the bottle, undaunted by the no-alcohol-allowed party rule.

Gitane, always aware of her ex-boyfriend's caution, urged him on, "Come on, Duncan, it's graduation. You don't need to be a tight-ass tonight!"

The town's Elks Club ballroom was decked out in the green and white of all Roughrider sports teams. The music system pumped out sixties favorites by the Rolling Stones, the Beatles, and the Beach Boys. Grads wearing Class of '65 tee shirts blanketed the dance floor, which was surrounded by a ring of Monopoly-money gambling tables of Black Jack and poker. It was a night of camaraderie and unleashed freedom.

As the hour approached midnight, a few couples began to drift away, headed for illegal keg parties or small private gatherings. Others chose to remain to take advantage of the all-night faux-gambling and festivities. Gitane's bottle was long empty, and Duncan expected her to split for a place to smoke and joke.

But she surprised him by saying, "Hey, let's go to Seattle."

"Seattle? What for?"

"I've got another pint of Jack in my car. You can drive. We'll work on the whiskey, and I might smoke a joint. Come on. Let's do something exciting. We can head for the Seattle Center tomorrow and do the rides and stuff."

The whiskey, the adrenaline rush of the party, and the exaltation of newly acquired freedom won out. "Okay, let's do it!"

They snuck out a side door without notifying the chaperones and walked hand in hand into the night. When they got to the 1959 Ford Fairlane that Gitane's parents had given her in a failed attempt to gain some control over their wild child, Gitane kicked off her shoes and took a pre-rolled joint out of her purse.

"Join me?" she said.

"No thanks, Git. Not my thing."

"Too bad. I thought Mr. Straight Arrow might be coming around a bit."

He laughed. "Maybe. But this is not a good time. We're tired. And driving. You go right ahead. I might take another sip or two of the whiskey when we get there."

They drove east toward Bainbridge Island, where the ferry connected to Seattle. Gitane smoked the doobie and fell asleep before they crossed the county line. Duncan woke her up when they got to the ferry landing around 2:00 a.m. Not a single car was in the holding area's parking lot.

"Looks like the boat's shut down for the night. There won't be a ferry now until the morning. I'm gonna find a place to park, and we can get some sleep for a few hours."

"Good idea. I'm sliding down the wall."

Rolling his eyes at her, he said, "No shit, you haven't moved a muscle for an hour now."

Gitane raised a middle finger and scratched her nose.

Duncan laughed, then drove back up the hill to Bainbridge High School and pulled the car onto the baseball field behind the school. The Roughriders had played the Spartans team there three weeks earlier, so he knew where they were going. The night was moonless and the abandoned field was dark and quiet. Duncan parked beside the third-base dugout and turned off the car.

"Here we are. I will take a couple of sips of your booze, just to be polite. Maybe it will help me get some sleep."

They sat in the front seat, letting their eyes adjust to the dark, looking for any visible stars, and talking quietly about the party. After a few minutes, the talking stopped, and they sat quietly, resting their eyes.

Gitane broke the silence. Leaning her head on Duncan's shoulder, she said, "Aren't you going to kiss me good night?"

He teased her, "Do I have to?"

She was quiet again. Then, looking straight into his eyes, she pulled the sweater she was wearing over her head. "Yeah," she said, reaching behind her back and unhooking her bra. "I think you do."

Duncan had seen Gitane naked when they were dating, and although they had done most everything else during their time together, both of them had feared a possible pregnancy, so they had managed to settle for safer alternatives. During those days, they had been in junior high, and birth control pills were not available for young girls.

It might have been the freedom of graduation. It might have been curiosity about what they had missed out on when they were together. Most of all, it might have been the Jack Daniel's and the marijuana.

Gitane whispered, "Let's get in the back seat."

"Good idea," he said in a husky voice.

Before he could close the door on the driver's side of the Ford, Gitane had shed her remaining clothes, except for her panties. Before they could get comfortable, she had unbuttoned his shirt and loosened the belt that held up his corduroy pants.

"Gitane, I don't have a condom."

She whispered, "You don't need one."

Duncan didn't believe her. But he didn't care.

There were no soft kisses or tender caresses. No whispered sweet talk and nothing close to foreplay. Only a frantic coupling driven by lust and memories. The urgency was desperate, and it was over for both of them in minutes. The long day, the late night, and the Jack Daniel's put them quickly to sleep, Gitane's head resting on Duncan's shoulder, still in the back seat of the car.

When the sun came up in the morning, they skipped the ferry ride and drove quietly back home.

* * *

Three months later, Jimmy Locker and Duncan were driving out to a beach party at the mouth of the Elwha River just west of town. It was late August; the sun was glowing in a cloudless sky, one of those sucker-punch teasers trying to fool you into thinking summer would last forever. The skies were blue, and the temperature was a dozen degrees warmer than usual.

Turning off the highway, Duncan started down the Place Road toward the beach. The road was famous for the quarter-mile, straight stretch where the gearheads gathered at midnight on weekend nights to drag race their muscle cars. The faded blacktop was crisscrossed with burned-rubber tire tracks.

The guys smiled at the memories. Even non-racers loved the excitement, noise, and edgy threat of a possible bust by a cruising sheriff. Duncan and Jimmy were talking about those nights and hoping they would continue as they grew older when Duncan spotted a motorcycle coming toward them from the end of the stretch of the drag-strip road. As the bike came closer, they could see that there were two riders; based on the bike's weaving approach, the front rider must have been getting a how-to lesson on riding a motorcycle.

"What the hell do we have here," Jimmy said.

As the cycle drew closer, they looked at each other and shrugged. They could see that the front rider was a girl. Riding behind her was a long-haired guy wearing a tank top and a pair of dark sunglasses.

Duncan pulled over to the side of the road to stay out of the way. As the riders went past the car, the boys were shocked to see that the girl was their neighbor Gitane Harper. Like her passenger, her long hair was flying in the wind. She was laughing and shrieking, her arms locked on the handlebars, struggling to control the bike. Her passenger had his arms wrapped tightly around her chest. Like Gitane, he was holding on for dear life, each hand cupping one of her breasts as he leaned against her back and shouted sweet nothings in her ear.

BETTER LUCKY THAN GOOD

Later that summer, when President Lyndon Johnson reactivated the military draft, the trouble in Vietnam became the most unpopular war in the nation's history. Twenty-seven million American soldiers fought during the ten years of that confrontation. Twenty-two million of them were drafted. That war was lost. It's difficult to win a war when the great majority of your soldiers don't want to be there.

Fifty years after that unpopular war ended, the scars still remained. Many military veterans and their families would deal with issues traced directly to the war in Vietnam. The frustration, casualties, and postwar psychological damage were epidemic and life-changing.

Just before Duncan's nineteenth birthday, he received a letter from the local draft board and its dreaded director, Ms. Ruby Linton. The war in Vietnam was escalating. Duncan and all of his classmates were prime candidates for military service.

Duncan called Jimmy Locker to share the news. "Hey, Jimbo, I just got a letter from Uncle Sam. Guess who gets a trip to Seattle for a predraft physical?"

"I know. I got one too, and I heard a bunch of the guys got Ruby's little invitation. All you guys will probably be in 'Nam in six months."

"What do you mean, 'you guys'? We're all in the same boat here…literally."

"No way, man, I got a bum knee."

"Jimmy, you're six four and weigh 245 pounds. You're an All-League tackle on the football team. And you didn't miss a single game. I'm pretty sure you can pass a physical."

* * *

The local draft board provided a special bus to Seattle for potential draftees, in order to conduct physical exams for suitable candidates. Duncan's group of Port Angeles classmates included a handful of football players. Jimmy and Duncan sat together on the way over and, like all the guys on the bus, tried to act as if the trip were no big deal.

As the bus got closer to the exam center, the group's false bravado faded. Jokes ceased, and conversations were terse. When one of Duncan's friends, seated two rows behind them, tried to lighten the tension by throwing a skinny joke at him, Duncan's temper flashed.

Jimmy grabbed him as he tried to get at the jokester and dragged Duncan back into the seat beside him. "Take it easy, Web. He's just fooling around with you."

"Well, he needs to fool around with someone else. I'm not in the mood."

A half hour before they unloaded the bus, all conversation had ceased. When they reached their destination in Seattle, the bus driver, who was familiar with the routine, said, "Listen up. You guys are gonna be separated into different groups when you get in there. Everyone will probably get out at different times. The bus will be right here. If I'm not around, just stay in the bus. When you're all back, I'll get you home."

Two hours later, the boys began straggling back. One by one, they shared what took place and the results of their exams. All-League tackle Jimmy Locker was rejected—bad knee. Both the team's All-League running back and best wide receiver were rejected—diabetes and allergies, respectively. The team's center, "Yogi" Graystone, failed the physical as well—irregular heartbeat.

When the entire group had reboarded the bus, only two players from the football team had passed the physical and qualified for military service—Scooter Bennett, the team's five-foot-eight, 140-pound quarterback, and Duncan Webster, a rail-thin defensive halfback.

As a potential new soldier, Duncan was not necessarily opposed to serving his country. He hadn't enlisted and knew his draft status was precarious. He had dropped out of classes at the University of Washington when his father got sick, and he'd come home to help in the family's hardware store. As a result, his college deferral had disappeared, and he was prepared to go.

Two of his classmates had already been killed in the war, and another was reported missing in action. Most of the guys who wanted to avoid the draft had joined the navy or the national guard—anything that would keep them out of the army and the jungles of Vietnam.

Three months later, Duncan's next bus ride ended at Fort Lewis, the army's regional military base and basic training center in Tacoma, Washington. It was a hot day in August, and the bus ride with a group of apprehensive young men had been quiet. The air-conditioning on the bus was not working, which added to the draftees' misery. Things didn't get much better when they reached the base, and the nervous, rumpled group of kids filed slowly off the bus.

"Get a move on it, meatheads," bellowed their greeter, a crisp and cool-looking Black soldier wearing a Mountie-style hat. "We don't got all day. You boys look like you need a haircut and smell like you need a shower. Follow me and pay attention. From this minute on, you're going to be soldiers!"

Duncan looked at the beanpole eighteen-year-old who had been his silent seatmate on the trip and smiled reassuringly. The boy was as pale as an albino and gulping in air trying to steady himself. He said, "Hang in there, man; it's gonna be okay."

The boy bobbed his head up and down several times, but didn't answer.

They walked into the administration building, joining dozens of other confused new soldiers being sorted to various check-in stations. White kids, Black kids, Native Americans, and Latinos. Country boys and city slickers. All just kids. Every check-in station was clogged with draftees, all struggling to decipher shouted orders and follow instructions.

Boot camp at Fort Lewis was supposed to mold boys into men. It took Duncan about a half hour to realize that he was not going to be a good fit for the US Army. He hated being told what to do. Especially the army's obvious efforts to brainwash boys into soldiers. And soldiers into robots.

After basic training, the new recruits were transferred to Fort Polk, Louisiana, for jungle training and preparation for deployment to Vietnam. Fort Polk was the number one supplier of fresh soldiers, mostly all draftees, headed for service in 'Nam.

A month into the wartime training session, a pockmarked second lieutenant came to the barracks. Assembling the recruits, he said, "All right, men. Since you're almost ready for active duty, we need to get organized here. Before your trip, we need to handle some details. We're looking for a few volunteers for the military police. Same pay scale as all other soldiers. Different duties. MPs are supposed to keep things under control in the zoo. This here's a sign-up sheet for those who might want to help us out. It'll be posted up front. We'll review the volunteers and do some testing for acceptable grunts."

Everyone in the barracks had arrived with the same piece of advice from family and friends before they entered boot camp. That message was, "Whatever happens, *never* volunteer for anything in the army! Ever."

Duncan was planning to follow that advice. Especially when he heard a voice in the back of the group say softly, "Are you shitting me? MPs in 'Nam are probably the first fucking guys to get fragged."

Even the raw draftees knew *fragged* meant the deliberate killing of an unpopular member of a fighting unit by a pissed-off member of his own squad. Firefights are chaotic, and friendly fire was not always friendly. Victims were usually an unpopular officer or squad leader.

But Duncan had been thinking about ways to avoid the jungle. He was considering Officer Candidate School as a means of extending his stay in the States. He wasn't afraid of going to Vietnam. He was concerned about the incompetence of the people who would be telling him what to do.

Listening to the lieutenant, it occurred to him that military law enforcement might actually be a reasonable alternative. Until that moment, the thought of being an MP had never entered his mind. But now he was surprised that it had not.

From the first time he heard his uncle Harlan tell the story of the Lady of the Lake, he wanted to be a famous detective like Hollis B. Fultz. He knew being an MP wouldn't be detective work. On the other hand, maybe this crazy gig would provide an opportunity to test the idea of someday working in law enforcement when he had to get a job in the real world.

Besides, when he thought about it, he reasoned that MPs probably would not be on the front lines in Vietnam. There were plenty of soldiers over there who were not drawing the $65.99 per month battle-zone pay. On-base duty or even perimeter policing behind the front lines of the war zone—either seemed like safer placement options. Fighting units in the field would not have to be policed. On-base or local furloughs might.

When the group broke up, Private Duncan Magnus Webster worked his way through the GIs closest to the bulletin board so he could check the sign-up sheet. He heard a handful of soldiers break into hoots of laughter. When he was close enough to see the list, there was only a single name on the page. One of the unit's pundits had signed, "Private Jack Mehoff." Duncan skipped a space and signed his name.

Following a brief on-site training session in military-police operations, Duncan's Fort Polk company was ready for its war-zone deployment. Ninety-nine percent of the guys were going straight to Vietnam. When Duncan opened his dispatch envelope to check departure times and stationing details in Vietnam, he held his breath. Unfolding the paper, he stared at his posting in dumbstruck disbelief.

Military Policeman Duncan Magnus Webster would be stationed in Munich, Germany, as part of the American Army European Military Police serving troops on-site in Cold War Europe.

His daddy had always said, "I'd rather be lucky than good."

GERMANY

One day after arriving at the base in Munich, Duncan was ordered to report to Military Police Dispatch at one o'clock in the afternoon for an orientation meeting for new MPs. When he walked in for the meeting, there were five other young men standing around the room, all looking at their feet or fingernails, trying not to appear to be nervous.

A scruffy-looking master sergeant, wearing a name ribbon that said Donahue, sat at an equally scruffy desk, drinking coffee, smoking a cigarette, and thumbing through papers on a battered clipboard. His failure to acknowledge their presence was unsettling, and except for muffled coughs and throat clearing, the room was quiet. There was no greeting. No introduction. Not even any eye contact.

Sergeant Donahue had a steel-gray, one-inch-long crew cut and bushy eyebrows in desperate need of trimming…or mowing. Patches of whiskers were lost in the creases of his lined face. When he finally spoke, his voice was so gravelly it sounded as if someone had used a rasp on his vocal cords; coupled with a heavy Southern drawl, the new recruits strained to understand what the man was saying.

Donahue looked at the group. Shaking his head as if offended, he said, "Y'all might be the luckiest fuckers in the army. Most of y'all's buddies are dodging bullets in 'Nam by now. But if y'all do your job here the way I want you to, you're likely to not get killed.

"Here's all you need to know. Today, y'all'll be assigned a partner, and the two of you will probably be together for the next year or so. If you don't keep each other out of trouble, I'll make sure you end up being tunnel rats in 'Nam, and not military policemen in Germany. Do I make myself cle'a?"

After the group's "Yes, sir," all six soldiers glanced at the men standing beside them, wondering what they were getting into and whom they would be trusting to keep them out of the jungle as they counted down their tour time.

Master Sergeant Donahue had anticipated the nervous reaction. "Don't worry about who y'all will partnah up with. That's my job. And since that's always the first question grunts ask, we'll do that right now."

Studying the list of new policemen, he stopped short. "Well, looka here. We got us a rookie named Webster and another one named Bunny. I think you two sound like a perfect couple."

The only Black man in the room, an unsmiling and compact soldier, said in a hard voice, "Bunny is my first name, Sarge."

Donahue stared at the soldier, and the soldier stared back without flinching. The eye lock was easy for the newcomers to read—it was a hate-at-first-sight exchange.

The master sergeant answered, "What a surprise. It don't matter. It'll remind me that you country boys are special." He stared at Bunny. "At least one of you has a real name."

Duncan thought the man was trying to be funny. The Black man knew better. But the sergeant's earlier warning

"You got that right, man." Duncan held out his beer, and the two bumped their bulky steins. Duncan said, "We're supposed to meet for a briefing in the morning. Let's drink some beer and try to figure out a way to enjoy this gig."

The corners of Bunny's mouth twitched for the first time, and he said, "Oh, I'm gonna enjoy it. Don't worry about that. Just make sure you don't do anything that might fuck us up."

* * *

As the two military policemen settled into the routine of the job, they began to develop a relationship based on the hours they spent together. After a few weeks, they'd figured out each other's strong points and agreed each of them brought something to the job.

For Duncan, it took only a week or two to admit that he wasn't as tough as he thought he was, and at the same time, he realized that Bunny Archer, who was two years older, wasn't as diplomatic as he needed to be. Webster was forced to learn how to control his own fiery temper and become the levelheaded negotiator. Bunny thrived being the muscle.

After a while, Bunny began to realize that racism would not be an issue in the partnership. Duncan treated him like a friend and showed no signs of prejudice. The White boy was pretty sure Bunny considered his partner too naive to understand that the two of them might have differences.

Being a police officer in the army was a grind. Sergeant Donahue assigned all the schedules and duties for each of the teams. Somehow, the Bunny-Webs team seemed to draw the most undesirable shifts and locations. The worst GI hangouts, the most hookers, and the latest nights. When they tired of the routine, they sat in a *bierhaus* and reminded one another over multiple steins of beer that it beat the hell out of the jungle.

Bunny reveled in his enforcer role. He liked action and had a no-nonsense attitude. He didn't hesitate when a belligerent soldier needed a rap from his nightstick to get the message. He hadn't been kidding when he told Duncan not to worry about his enjoying the role of enforcer. When it came down to the nightstick, Bunny paid no attention to a man's size or color. He just liked to hit everybody.

Seven months into the partnership, they were sent to take care of a scuffle at a local GI hangout. They took a jeep and headed for the location. Arriving at the bar, they could smell stale beer from the sidewalk. Duncan looked at Bunny and shook his head.

Bunny winked at him and led the way into a dark bar where the beer smell was almost gagging, the music was blaring, and soldiers were shouting and laughing. The squabble must have been resolved. Bunny picked the rowdiest table and found himself nose to nose with a very large, very drunk soldier wearing an army tee shirt soaked in sweat and beer, with dog tags dangling outside, down the front. He was holding a huge beer stein supported by a thick forearm covered with a red-and-blue tattoo of a skull. The ink glistened from sweat or spilled beer. The big fella was a White man with buzz-cut dark hair, and he was not happy to see the MPs.

Bunny decided the man had had too much to drink. He jumped right in. "Time to go home, Soldier. You don't look like you'd enjoy KP for the rest of your ride."

"Home? You little pip-squeak," he said. "Without that stick and the candy-ass band on your sleeve, I'd bust you up like a scrambled egg. What's the MP on your arm stand for, major punk?"

Bunny answered, "You're comin' with us without any trouble. Or are we going to have a disagreement here?"

"Disagreement? Let's go outside, little man. I'm the heavyweight boxing champion of my battalion. It won't take me thirty seconds to settle any disagreement."

Bunny shrugged, then handed his nightstick to Duncan. "Watch my back," he said and walked toward the front door.

It took a moment for the soldier to recognize that Bunny had accepted the challenge. He looked around the table at his drinking partners and then rose unsteadily to his feet to follow Bunny outside. With noisy bravado, bar patrons stumbled to their feet, anxious to witness the slaughter. Duncan brought up the rear, keeping a close eye on the excited spectators.

When they reached the sidewalk, the challenger picked a spot between the building and a large truck parked at the curb. Flexing his shoulders to loosen his arms, and looking more like a drunk plumber than a boxer, he shadowboxed a half-speed flurry of punches.

Bunny laughed. "You sure you want to do this, mo'fuck?"

Before the man could answer, Bunny took one step and hit the champ twice in the mouth.

The punches caught the soldier by surprise, and the watchers could see that he was hurt…and beyond pissed. The boxer stance disappeared, and with blood smeared across his unshaven chin, he roared like a bear and bull-rushed Bunny, trying to smother him with his bulk.

Bunny moved aside and hit him once in the ear as he charged and once in the kidney as he steamed past. The blows were solid, and the GI began shaking his head in an effort to sober up enough to defend himself. After several more cautious advances by the big man, Bunny had still not been touched. The frustrated soldier was bleeding from his nose and lips. He circled warily just out of range, before trying again to grab his quicker foe.

Stepping aside from the man's next charge, Bunny delivered a vicious kick to the outside of the slower fighter's knee, dropping the bully to the ground, groveling in pain. The fight ended with the champion crawling underneath the chassis of the delivery truck parked on the street, trying to escape further punishment.

Looking at the man's friends standing on the sidewalk, Bunny said, "Anyone else?"

There were no takers.

When the two MPs dragged the soldier out from under the rig, the man watched as Duncan secured the handcuffs. Then Duncan and Bunny each gripped an arm, and the beaten man hobbled to the jeep without saying a word. Webster got into the driver's side, and Bunny took the shotgun seat.

"Holy shit, man. I thought that big bastard was gonna take you apart."

...y responded with a rare chuckle. "Those big mo'fucks are cake. It's the quick ones you gotta watch out for. Besides, did you see the H. A. initials below the skull tattoo?"

"No. What does that have to do with it?"

"H. A. stands for Hell's Angels. Those guys are always fat, slow, and high. I didn't even know they let those badasses into the army."

***

A week after Bunny's impressive display of martial skills, the two MPs were ordered to report to Master Sergeant Byron Donahue after their rare daytime-duty shift. The unkempt head of the unit was waiting for them, the ever-present cigarette stuck in the corner of his mouth. He took a drag, blew the smoke in their direction, and looked at them with a tight smile.

"Archer," he said to Bunny, "you got yourself in some deep shit here."

"Yeah? How so?"

Donahue smirked and said, "Seems like that soldier you ambushed last weekend has a real bad knee injury. He says you blindsided him when he was gettin' ready to leave the bar. The brass don't like that kind of dirty play, you know?"

Duncan butted in, "That's bullshit, Sarge. He did not ambush anyone. The son of a bitch was drunk, disorderly, and threatening. He got exactly what he asked for."

"Did I ask for your opinion, Webster? Shut the hell up. This ain't about you. One of our soldiers was attacked. Y'all fucked up. Someone's gotta pay. Ain't that right, Archer?"

"No, it's not right. But I should have known. Where you from, Sarge? Alabama? South Carolina? Mississippi?"

Donahue's face turned purple. "That's none of your business, boy. The soldier you attacked was one of ours. You crippled him. He told us everything."

"One of ours? You mean one of yours, don't you? And you ain't no different than all the rest of yours."

The sergeant said, "I told you fools when you got here, if you were dumb enough to screw up, you'd end up in the war."

Duncan jumped in again, "Sarge, you can't be serious. Bunny was just doing his job. Same as me. The guy was a Hell's Angel, for Christ's sake."

"You don't hear too good, do you, Webster? I said stay out of this. Unless you want to join your buddy in 'Nam, you better butt out. I've had just about enough."

Bunny looked at Duncan and did a quick shake of his head. "It's not worth it for you, Web. You can't change anything. It don't make no difference if I'm here, in the States, or with my brothers in 'Nam. Nothing's gonna change."

"Listen to your friend, Webster. That's the first thing he's said that makes any sense."

A week later, Bunny Archer received his orders for transfer to Vietnam. A day after that, he was gone.

And so was Duncan's faith in the military, the country, and the world. He could not wait to get home.

PORT ANGELES

Webster mustered out of the US Army in June and headed to the States, thankful for his stationing in Europe, but anxious to get back to civilian life. He was twenty-one years old and eager to look for a new job. Instead, he found a girl.

Stationed in Germany, there was little opportunity for female companionship, and most of the girls MPs met were not really drawn to military policemen. Hookers were never an option. Duncan was too Scottish to pay for sex.

He had been home for a week or two, thrilled to be back, anxious for his hair to grow out, and ready to rejoin the human race. In those days, there were still men's clothing stores in small towns throughout the Northwest, and by sheer chance, Duncan met a pretty girl in a Port Angeles men's shop when he was buying a necktie to wear to get ready for a job hunt. He saw the girl when she was looking through the sock rack beside the table of neckties.

Clearing his throat, he said, "Excuse me. Could I ask you a question? I just got out of the service, and my fashion skills aren't up to speed yet." Thinking fast, he lied, "I've got to look for a job pretty soon, and I need to make a good first impression."

Holding up two flashy ties, he said, "What do you think? Stripes or paisley?"

The girl laughed. Smiling, she said, "Well, welcome back, Soldier. Maybe I can help."

It was summertime, and the young lady was wearing a sleeveless white top and olive-colored walking shorts. She was unfazed by Duncan's question and appeared to be totally comfortable having been consulted. Which was good because this girl was beautiful. Honey-colored hair that reached below her shoulders and eyes that were the same shade of gold as her hair. Her skin was tanned and glowing. It was the kind of skin that needed no makeup and radiated natural, wholesome beauty.

Tilting her head to one side, she looked at the two ties he was holding and, with her hand on her chin, looked back at Duncan and said, "Are you applying for a job at a used-car lot or a circus?"

Duncan was speechless.

Then she laughed at her own joke. It was a great laugh.

He smiled back at her, surrendering to the teasing tone of the question.

Reaching across the table, the girl thumbed through the neckwear and picked a navy-blue tie with dark-red stripes. "Why don't you try this? Wear a blue blazer and a pair of gray or khaki pants, and you should be fine."

He stared at her, uncertain if she was messing with him again, then said, "Do you work here?"

She laughed the intoxicating laugh. "No, I'm just shopping for my brother."

Her name was Sasha, and the conversation soon went to other topics. After twenty minutes or so, Duncan worked up the courage to ask her for a date on the upcoming weekend. To his delight, she accepted…and that was how it all began.

Sasha was seventeen years old. Following her father's unfortunate passing, she had just moved with her family from a small town in Eastern Washington, to her mother's hometown in Port Angeles.

Duncan thought he was lucky when he was sent to Germany instead of Vietnam. He *knew* he was lucky when Sasha Frazier accepted his invitation for pizza and a movie. And after their second date, Duncan he also knew the newcomer was special. A girl who was as nice as she was beautiful was a rare treasure, and he considered himself to be smart enough to recognize a gift when he found one.

Ten months later, he married the girl from the menswear store. The young couple started their lives together in turbulent times. Anti-war protests, Civil Rights marches, and shocking assassinations dominated the news. The war in Vietnam raged on. There were moments of enlightenment. And times of tragedy.

Some of these iconic events were rebellious; there was no doubt times were exciting and stimulating as well. Social culture was changing with the times. Education, art, literature, and music were all evolving.

And if it was, as some historians have claimed, the decade of turmoil, there was no question that rock music was the new generation's choice of rebel poetry and the genre that fueled the revolution. Everything about the music suited the times. It was rhythmic, loud, edgy, and defiant. Parents, teachers, and the media hated it. Boomers loved it. It was the perfect voice for the new generation, a perfect way to protest social injustice and rebel against its causes. It was the war in Vietnam that anchored the unrest…and it was rock and roll that triggered the seminal event that would become the historical protest of the decade.

In August of 1969, just months after Duncan and his wife were married, the largest rock concert in history took place on a 660-acre farm in Bethel, New York, forty miles from the New Hampshire town of Woodstock. The event drew over 400,000 rock-music fans and was destined to be the apex of musical demonstrations of peace and love. Anti-war sentiment drove the passion for a better world, and Woodstock was a microcosm of the sixties generation's opposition to the war in Vietnam.

The anti-war rock group Country Joe and the Fish were the first group on stage following the famous thunderstorm intermission on the last day of the four-day festival. At Woodstock, the band warmed up the crowd with a rousing set, and with the listeners at fever pitch, front man Country Joe introduced the encore by starting with the group's usual concert-opening "F-I-S-H" cheer, shouting the individual letters of the word *fish*, which was the group's tradition at every concert they played at every venue during concert tours. The cheer urged attendees to repeat each letter by shouting the letter back at Country Joe.

Joe started by bellowing, "Gimme an *F*," to which the crowd shouted back, "*F*!" Then he surprised the audience by altering the spelling of the four-letter word *fish*, and for the next letter, yelled, "Gimme a *U*." They shouted it back with gusto. Then, "Gimme a *C*." The echo grew louder. He finished the chant with, "Gimme a *K*." Each letter was screamed back at the band, thundering with a deafening roar.

After the final *K*, Joe shouted, "What's that spell?"

The crowd shouted, *"Fuck!"*

Joe shouted again, "What's that spell?"

The crowd roared the expletive again. Louder.

He shouted one last time.

The crowd of a half-million crazed rockers—some drunk, some high, some sober—tried to blast the thundering echoes off the human decibel charts.

That awe-inspiring display of passion pretty much summed up the generation's feelings about the war in Vietnam.

* * *

Just after the Woodstock Festival, the newly married and still unemployed Duncan Webster decided it was time to get serious about finding a job. He and Sasha talked about a variety of options—law school, real estate, small-town stock broker—none of which interested Duncan at all. He was hesitant to choose a career in law enforcement.

After weeks of discussing pros and cons, Sasha convinced him to follow his heart. She knew that his experience in Germany had been a life-changing revelation for her husband.

Duncan struggled with subjecting his family to the challenges of choosing law enforcement as a profession. He was well aware of the stressful impact on body and soul.

Sasha sniffed her disagreement. "Duncan, we can make everything work. You were made for this job. You will be the best cop ever."

The next morning, she ironed his blue blazer and a white button-down dress shirt. After trimming his hair and stroking his ego, she kissed him on his cheek and pushed him gently out the front door.

With his military-police background papers in hand and wearing the outfit he had purchased on the day he and Sasha met, he visited the Clallam County Sheriff Department in the basement of the county courthouse his uncle had talked about during family gatherings when Duncan was growing up.

The military police connection, coupled with the reputation of a respected local family, fast-tracked the hiring process, and after a written test and a physical, he was a deputy sheriff. His military-police background was a huge asset for a new deputy. He was comfortable with the routine, aware of the confrontational nature of the position, and looking forward to having a job that would contribute to the well-being of his beloved hometown.

As the newest member of the Clallam County Sheriff Department, he was assigned the farthest-west region of the county. It was a traditional baptism for new deputies and, as the most isolated county territory, the perfect training ground for new recruits. Known to locals as the West End, it covered the county from the western outskirts of Port Angeles all the way to the Pacific Ocean, as far west as you can go in the continental United States. It was a hardworking population of loggers, fishermen, and free-spirited individualists who drank as hard as they worked. The department joke was, it was easy for one deputy to break up a bar fight in Forks, Washington, because it was always over before you could get there.

His first day on the job, he pulled into the Bear Creek Tavern, ten miles outside the town of Forks. It was 11:00 a.m. There were a few muddy, beat-up pickup trucks parked in front of the bar, and he wanted to meet the locals. The inside of the bar was small, but could not really be called cozy. There were three empty tables on the twelve-by-twelve dance floor and three customers seated at the bar. Duncan assumed they might be eating a late breakfast or an early lunch.

When he stepped up to the bar, he noticed none of the three seated there was eating or even drinking coffee. Seated at each end of a short row of barstools, one was drinking a Rainier beer, and the other two were working on a pitcher of draft.

Behind the bar was a woman of indeterminate age, with dyed-yellow hair sprouting from her scalp, similar to dark roots growing out of garden soil. There were wrinkles in her face, but a thick layer of makeup was more mask than touch-up, and bright-red lipstick drew the eyes from all other features. She was smoking a cigarette and staring at Duncan.

No one in the bar said a word, so he tipped his hat to the lady and said, "Mornin', ma'am. My name is Duncan Webster. I thought I'd stop in and let you know I'll be your law enforcement for a while."

The lady looked him over from head to toe, took a drag on her cigarette, then stubbed it out in an ashtray crowded with butts, and said, "No"—she paused—"you're too young."

Webster laughed. "I've had tons of responses nastier than that. Don't worry about me being able to take care of myself. I've been in the military police for almost two years. I'm pretty sure I can be useful if you need me."

"Well, no offense, Officer, but we don't need you." Reaching under the bar, she pulled out a beat-up double-barreled shotgun and said, "Lucy here don't need no help."

THE HERRICK ROAD

Four years later, Duncan was the point man for the Clallam County Sheriff Department's sector in the West End. He knew every tavern, bar, and disreputable house in the western part of the county. Every owner, bartender, waitress, and most of their customers. He had a pair of deputies sharing the territory and, as the senior officer, was working only on criminal cases, while the newer guys took care of domestic issues and most of the auto accidents and driving citations.

It was late October, and the sky was thick with fog so dark there were no clouds, just a screen of charcoal-colored rain shadows threatening to soak the surrounding countryside. Twenty miles past Forks was the Olympic Rain Forest, which averaged 130 to 150 inches of rain each year. Duncan knew every mile closer to the coastal forest increased the chance of rain…and knew the West End was going to get wet.

He had gotten a late start, having been tied up with department paperwork. Just outside the city limits of Port Angeles, he received a radio message from dispatch. The radio squawked, and Sharon Lopez said, "Hey, cowboy, if you're not too far out of town on your way to the zoo, I got a stop for you."

"Shoot."

"The boss man just took a call from a lady who lives on the Herrick Road, just past Lake Aldwell. She called the office to report a possible intruder. The boss wants you to stop on your way out if you're not past it already."

"No problem. I'm about ten minutes from the turnoff. Give me her address, and I'll check it out."

The woman lived just off the road above the Elwha River, on the privately owned side of the stream. As such, the house was part of county jurisdiction, not that of the park rangers who enforced the law inside the border of Olympic National Park. The caller had reported seeing a person lurking outside her home several times, then disappearing into the woods surrounding her unfenced, five-acre piece of property.

Duncan reached the Herrick Road ten minutes later and knocked on the front door. When it opened, he was stunned to be looking into a young woman's remarkable lavender-blue eyes. Eyes as rare as a cash-register silver dollar. He knew at once that it had to be Gitane Harper. They looked at each other without speaking, processing the shock of the unexpected face-to-face meeting after years of separation.

Gitane recovered first. "Duncan! What the hell are you doing here?" Then she engulfed him in a hug.

Wrapping his arms around his old girlfriend, he said, "I'm a deputy sheriff now, Gitane, and the department sends me to the West End for most of the week. I had no idea it was you living here. I didn't realize you were this far out of town." Holding her at arm's length, he said, "You look great."

Gitane blushed. She had gained some weight and, not expecting a morning visitor, wore no makeup. She looked tired, but was smiling and blinking tears back as they talked.

During the hug, Duncan thought he had detected the faint odor of marijuana. The fragrance…and that smile…made him happy. She was still a pretty girl. Tired maybe. But pretty.

"Yeah, right. Always the gentleman. Here's the real me, Duncan. Divorced. A mom. Almost broke and working a job as a bartender. That's my new life." She hesitated then said, "I hear you're married now. Congrats."

Before he could answer, she said, "I guess you don't get out to the other side of town much, or we'd have crossed paths in the restaurant."

"I knew you were working at the Rain Out Bar. The office keeps me up-to-date on what goes on in both sides of town." Smiling, he added, "Wherever they need me, you know? That said, I don't spend much time inside the city limits here, and with two kids, we're more likely to go to the Flying Saucer Drive-In. Anyway, what can I help you with? Dispatch said you might be having a little trouble."

"Not really. I think someone's been hanging around though. I caught quick glances of a person moving away from the woodpile, and I've seen some human-shaped dark shadows a time or two. Yesterday I found a cigarette butt by the edge of the woods…where I never smoke myself. It's just me and my daughter here, and now that I'm a mom, I'm a lot more careful. With April here, it's just creepy enough to make me a little nervous."

He raised an eyebrow. "Huh, if it makes you nervous, it must be serious. Can you show me around so I can check it out?"

"Sure, give me a minute." Gitane turned, walked into the kitchen, and returned carrying a toddler-sized little girl. "Duncan, this is my daughter, April."

A smiling little girl was holding tightly to her mother's shoulder. Gitane slid the little one down her side, settling the child on her hip, and said, "April, this is my friend Duncan. Can you say hi?"

The youngster buried her face in Gitane's neck.

Webster laughed and said, "Hello, April, I know you can't see me. Don't worry. I'm just here to visit with your mom."

The three of them made a tour of the backyard and the tree line surrounding the house. Gitane showed him the stack of firewood where she had seen the shadow of a person heading back toward the road and the spot where she had found the cigarette butt.

"How 'bout your neighbors? Any problems with any of those people?"

Gitane shrugged. "I don't think so. They're mostly loners, just getting away from town, same as me. There might be some druggies out here, but if there are, I haven't met them. Most of the people on the road are older."

"Yeah. Well, I think I'm going to visit them and see if anyone has noticed something unusual. I'll ask everyone to keep their eyes open. Listen, you be careful. If anything looks strange, call me. Don't take any chances, okay?"

"You know me, Duncan."

Rolling his eyes, he said, "Yeah...that's what scares me."

When he left Gitane's place, he found himself thinking about the surprise meeting with his school-days girlfriend. He hadn't thought about her in years, but smiled as he drove up the road, remembering the girl who changed his life.

Duncan considered himself blessed with a perfect marriage. With his wife, Sasha, and two young children, he never had serious romantic thoughts about other women. Even so, Gitane Harper would always have a special place in his heart. The surge of nostalgia was strong, and he realized some memories are impossible to erase. It was not about love. It was about recognizing a meaningful time of your life and how that time changed you as a person.

Gitane was, and always would be, free-spirited and exciting. Those traits, so opposite from his own, had helped bring him out of his personal shell. Try new things. Take an occasional risk. Develop a spirit of adventure. The bad news was, those same traits, taken to the level Gitane would take them, made her reckless and vulnerable. Duncan had not seen Gitane since before he got drafted. But he knew that nothing would redefine her spirit. And that made him nervous. Gitane was a single mom, living in the woods with a three-year-old child. There was no way in hell Duncan was going to let something bad happen to them. Even if this incident was just another sleazeball Peeping Tom.

When he got back to the Port Angeles office in the late afternoon, he asked some of the city deputies what they knew about Gitane Harper. She worked at a local restaurant called the Rain Out Bar and Grill, which was a favorite destination for thirtysomethings and good-time seekers. Live music on weekends and better-than-average food. People loved the bar's name, recognizing it had been chosen to provide an alternative destination when rain cancelled an outdoor activity.

An older deputy named Toby Wright was one of the in-town uniforms and a font of information concerning what was happening in the local bar scene. Duncan found him reading a newspaper in the break room, and asked, "Hey, Toby, do you know anything about a girl named Gitane Harper who works in the bar at the Rain Out?"

"Sure. Nice kid. Used to be a barmaid there and is one of the daytime bartenders now. Why?"

"Just wondering. Is she okay? Any problems?"

"Ha, did she tell you about her ex-husband? She used to run with a rough crowd. I'm sure she drank and maybe smoked a little weed. She got knocked up a couple years ago and married a real loser. A guy named Rodney Knight. When the baby was born, Gitane cleaned up her act, and her old man went apeshit. Things went from disaster to catastrophe. He knocked her around, threatened to kill her, and claimed the kid wasn't his. It got so bad she filed a restraining order…twice. When the first one was violated, she left the guy, and she moved outside of town. I think there's still bad blood about child-support issues."

Duncan was quiet for a moment, trying to process the disturbing information and wondering why Gitane hadn't mentioned any of it. "Thanks, Toby. I knew she had been married, but didn't know about the husband. Gitane and I went to school together, and she's out on the Herrick Road. She thinks she's being watched."

Toby grunted. "Yeah?" he said. "No surprise. Her ex is a real dick. If things get dicey, I know I'd start with him."

Duncan thought he might have heard the name Rodney Knight sometime in his high school years, but couldn't recall a face or a connection. He decided to take Toby's advice and check the records for Gitane's ex-husband. His track record wasn't pretty.

Rodney was two years older than Duncan and had an early start on his rap sheet, with a juvie record for vandalism and car break-ins. No auto thefts, but apparently looking for loose change or valuables which might have been left in the vehicle. As he grew older, Knight continued to add to his resume of county violations. There were a half-dozen traffic citations—speeding, running stop signs, defective auto-equipment violations. The usual harassment tickets for outlaws who drew pull-overs like magnets to steel.

Then it got worse. Disturbing the peace. Urinating in public. The two restraining orders.

Duncan was relieved to see, except for one marijuana-possession charge, there were only traffic tickets in the past few years. Still, he did not like the man's body of work, so Duncan made a mental note to ask Gitane as soon as possible about the current nature of their relationship.

Duncan visited Gitane again the next day. When he asked her about her nasty divorce, her face paled and, shaking her head, told him, "I try not to think about that monster, Duncan. He doesn't scare me. But he has made threats about April, and that scares the shit out of me."

"Has he hurt you, Gitane?"

"Many times. I can take it, Duncan. But when the post-divorce laws favored April and me, he went from bad to deranged. He has never paid a nickel…and I will not tell anyone because I'm afraid he might hurt April to get back at me. Please, please don't rock that boat, Duncan. Really, the two of us are doing fine."

Duncan reluctantly agreed, but he added a drive-by of Gitane's house to his daily West End route.

Throughout the summer and late fall, everything seemed to have settled down, and Gitane didn't call the department again. Gitane's history and fierce independence made him leery, and he still found himself drawn to the Herrick Road on a regular basis. She worked a day shift at the restaurant; every once in a while, the two shared a quick cup of coffee on her front porch in the morning on Duncan's way to the West End. If she needed a shoulder to cry on or a pat on the back, he tried to be there. Webster was busy out west, and the visits provided some smiles to start his day.

Eventually, Duncan's check-ins evolved from business to social. Gitane and April seemed to enjoy his visits, and it was fun talking about school days and their time together.

* * *

It was almost a year after Duncan's first visit to Gitane, and the deputy had spent a hard day at the Forks office. Two break-ins the night before, a fender-bender in downtown Forks, and a scuffle in the Chain Saw Tavern. It was almost 10:00 p.m., and Duncan had just finished the day's paperwork.

He was scheduled for a few days off starting the next day and changed into jeans and a flannel shirt so he could stop for a beer at the Bear Creek Tavern on the way home. It was good to interact with the locals and show them he could be one of the guys.

When he walked into the bar, the late-night drinkers recognized him immediately. A heavyset, logger named Pete shouted, "Hey! Look who's here without his gun!"

The group of bearded drinkers at the bar, all wearing dirty Hickory shirts and snagged-off work pants over heavy boots, turned in unison and raised their beer mugs in salute.

Pete hollered, "Rosey, get the man a beer, and let's see what he can do!"

An hour and a half and six beers later, Duncan was able to sneak away from his rowdy friends. It wasn't German beer, but he had downed them quickly.

Back in the squad car, he drove carefully. After crawling around the dangerous curves around Lake Crescent, he let his mind wander. It was after midnight, and the slow pace gave him time to think about the things people think about when they drink too much.

Without knowing why, when he reached the Herrick Road turnoff, he took a hard right and pulled the cruiser into Gitane's driveway. He flipped the roof lights on so if Gitane woke up, she would know who it was. He sat in the unit until a kitchen light went on and then watched someone pulling aside the curtain in the window.

Gitane met him at the door. "Duncan, what are you doing?"

When Webster didn't answer, she said, "Are you drunk?"

"Maybe." Looking at her, he added, "I shouldn't be here, Gitane."

"Then why are you?"

"I don't know."

She looked at him with tears in her eyes and said, "Well, I do."

She took his hand and walked him to the bedroom. They sat on the bed, and she cradled his face in her hands, her fingers massaging the skin on the sides of his neck, and kissed him, her lips slightly parted. Her eyes were closed, and when she tipped her head forward, he brushed each eyelid with his own lips.

The lovemaking was nothing like the urgent coupling in the back seat of Gitane's car the night they graduated. They came together as if they had been lovers for a long time, slow and gentle, a world away from the urgency and lust of their teenage years and their graduation night together. They let their bodies do the talking, savoring sensual touches and latent desires. They didn't talk much after it was over, both quiet and thoughtful. It had been unexpected. It was not planned. But it happened.

On his way home, the beer buzz was replaced by a headache, the pleasure pushed aside by guilt. Parking in front of his house, Duncan sat silently in the patrol car. He thought about his wife and their beautiful children. With a touch of sadness, he told himself that tonight would be the last time he would visit Gitane Harper when he had been drinking.

Webster kept his promise to himself and avoided nighttime visits. It was not difficult if he wasn't drinking. Nights when he had a few beers after work, it was harder. He still visited Gitane and April on his way to the West, but managed to resist nighttime stops.

* * *

Late autumn was the time of year the true nature of the Olympic Peninsula was on best display. It was *the time* locals reveled in their independence and toughness—cutting firewood, winterizing the house, hunting, and fishing for steelhead on the peninsula's famous rivers. Not to mention the glorious colors of the peninsula, the yellow and orange of maple trees and vine maples that flooded the valleys at the base of the Olympic Mountains. The natives were always happiest when the floods of tourists faded away like an ebbing coastal tide.

Deputy Webster's job stayed busy, and as the weather turned damper and colder, and with no additional sightings of Gitane's mysterious prowler, Duncan did fewer drive-bys to check on her and her daughter. The two friends agreed that it must have been some desperate drifter looking for a house to break into. With time, Duncan quit worrying, but he never failed to think about Gitane when he drove past the turn to the Herrick Road while going to and coming from the West End.

THE BABYSITTER

Jennifer LaBelle was running behind schedule for her babysitting at Gitane Harper's house west of town. She had worked late at the restaurant the night before and always miscalculated how long it took to drive from Port Angeles to the Herrick Road. She knew her friend had to be in the restaurant by 11:00 a.m.

The eighteen-year-old swung her VW Bug into Gitane's driveway, parked, and hurried to the door. When she got to the porch, she knocked on the door and, brushing hair out of her eyes, waited for Gitane to let her in.

No answer.

Knocking again, Jennifer called, "Gitane, it's me. I'm here."

When there was no response from her usually animated friend, she tested the door handle and was surprised when it opened with no resistance. Gitane had become more careful after her daughter was born; she always kept the doors and windows locked.

Walking in, Jennifer called again, "Gitane, I'm here. Where are you?"

She peeked in Gitane's bedroom. The bed was made. The bathroom door was open, and she could see it was unoccupied. She stuck her head into the little one's bedroom. The bed was unmade, but no one was there.

"That's weird," she whispered. "They must be running an errand or something."

Looking out the window at the parking area, she saw her friend's car parked in its usual spot near the edge of the clearing.

"Wow. That's strange."

Just to be sure, she checked the house again, pausing to listen when she thought she heard a noise from April's bedroom. She had taken care of April since Gitane had switched to the day shift at the Rain Out Bar and Grill.

Pushing the door to the room all the way open this time, she heard a soft, "Mama?" from behind the child's single bed.

"April!" Jennifer gasped. "What are you doing here?"

Sitting on the floor between the wall and the bed, the three-year-old stared at her babysitter with a blank face, looking almost catatonic.

"April," Jennifer said, "where's your mama?"

The little girl shook her head and managed a soft "Where's my mama?"

Jennifer was a bus girl at the Rain Out. She and Gitane were friends from work; Gitane tended bar. Both she and Gitane were free spirits, and despite the almost ten-year age difference, they had a good rapport. Jennifer was Gitane's regular babysitter, and April called her Auntie Jen.

Jennifer knew that Gitane would never leave her daughter alone, even if there was a grave emergency. Jen called the restaurant and Gitane's regular hairdresser to see if her friend was already in town. When no one had seen her, Jen had no idea what to do. With the little girl in her arms, she went outside and walked around the house and the edges of the woods surrounding it. She shouted toward the forest and then toward the road, "Gitane! Are you out there? Can you hear me?"

There was no answer. There was no noise, not even a bird or a chipmunk. Looking at her watch, Jennifer realized that she had been there almost a half hour, waiting, searching, and making calls looking for her friend. She went back inside and called 911.

Duncan Webster was doing his weekly paperwork in the Port Angeles office when he overheard the uniform at the front desk repeat the address of a distraught babysitter on the Herrick Road. He jumped out of his chair and told the officer at the desk that he would check out the call.

Duncan's mind was spinning as he headed to the Herrick Road. He knew Gitane's address and schedule. He thought this was probably just another example of Gitane's wild side. Or a hasty breakdown in communications. But he knew how she tended to April.

Webster and his wife had two kids, and he knew how fiercely Sasha protected their own children. He was sure that Gitane would never leave her three-year-old alone in the house. On the other hand, it was Gitane.

Lights flashing and siren wailing, he was there in less than fifteen minutes. Jennifer LaBelle was feeding the little one when he arrived, trying to calm and distract the confused child. Duncan could tell the babysitter was struggling to hold both April and herself together.

"This is not like Gitane. She watches April like a hawk. I don't know what's going on," Jennifer said.

"Try to relax, hon. We get missing-person calls all the time. Ninety-nine times out of a hundred, they're resolved in an hour or two. I'm going to check things out and see if everything looks all right."

He looked around the house for signs of disturbances or conflict. He checked Gitane's bedroom and the bathroom, looking to see if her toothbrush was wet or dry. Her makeup was lined up in a neat row. There was no sign of a hurried morning routine. No wet toothbrush, no makeup scattered across the counter. Everything was neat and clean.

"Have you called her family? I'm sure her parents live in town."

"I know. Her mom hasn't heard from her."

Listening to Jennifer's response, Webster began to feel a sense of urgency. Gitane had always been unpredictable, but he knew motherhood could change everything for a woman. Something didn't feel right.

"Jennifer, can you call Gitane's mother again and ask her to take the baby? When we get that taken care of, I'll get my crew on this thing. We will find her. I promise."

Hurrying back to town, he checked in at headquarters and requested permission to reschedule his usual office duties in order to handle the missing-person case.

The department protocol was to give the missing person twenty-four hours to return on their own. He had no intention of following that protocol. After alerting the staff of his concern about the missing mother and the circumstances of her disappearance, he placed a call to the city police department and asked for Sergeant Jonathan Kidd.

"Jon, I've got an issue with this one. Do you know Gitane Harper?"

"Sure. She works the bar at the Rain Out. Usually the day shift. There's just enough activity out in that area; we're on a first-name basis."

"Perfect. She's gone missing and left her four-year-old daughter unattended at her house on the other side of Lake Aldwell. I think we need to find her ASAP. She's kind of a rebel, and I don't trust the folks she used to run with. Can you get your guys to ask some questions? Maybe check some of the places where she hangs out when she's not at work? Or if anyone has an idea about where she might have gone?"

"You got it. I don't think she's a regular anymore, like she used to be, but if she's barhopping, we'll find her. I'll have my guys check around."

"Thanks, Jon. I owe you one."

He went to his desk and made some notes. If Gitane wasn't located immediately, he was going to start knocking on doors. He spent the rest of the morning making calls and the afternoon talking with Gitane's family and friends, waiting for a phone call or an embarrassed explanation from Gitane Harper. As the hours ticked away, the family grew more and more anxious.

Duncan stayed at the office until the swing-shift deputies started to arrive, waiting for an officer named Curtis Stagg. Curtis was a local Native America in his late-thirties and, like Duncan, had grown up in town; he knew most of the people in it. He had been hired as a county deputy after serving with the local reservation's tribal police force for five years; he had considerable experience with narcotics control and enforcement. Consequently, he knew about all the nightlife in the town and almost all the drug and alcohol players. His time working on the rez had given him a nothing-surprises-me outlook, and his contributions to the county were invaluable.

Curtis was short and powerful. He had prematurely gray hair and a sparse matching goatee. The occasional suspect made the mistake of misjudging his age, strength, and speed. Bad idea.

Duncan said, "Curt, what do you know about a guy named Rodney Knight? He's the ex-husband of our missing person, Gitane Harper, and I'm going to start with him if she doesn't show up soon."

"Rodney? Bad news, Web. He's had a rap sheet since he was fifteen years old, and he's basically switched from petty thief to possible drug dealer. In my opinion, the guy's a smoker and a joker and a small player in the local drug scene. He's been on the edge of some shady deals that we couldn't press charges on."

Curtis's face scrunched up like he had a bad taste in his mouth. "He's the front man for a local rock band called Rodney and the Roadsters. They're active in the local bars and clubs. Not too bad if you've had enough to drink. Knight thinks he's the second coming of Bob Seger. Long hair, tattoos, rides a Harley around town.

"All the band members are in their late thirties now. Still rockers and still driving muscle cars or riding choppers. They like to refer to themselves as the Rodsters, rather than the Roadsters. Probably Rodney's idea. They're all rock-group wannabes. Dopers, drinkers, and knotheads."

"Interesting. I knew, if Gitane married him, he'd probably be an outlaw."

"Outlaw?" Stagg said. "He's more like a nutcase. A legit pain in the ass. He's a druggie with an attitude."

"I'm not surprised to hear that. But it would be wise for him to skip his asshole routine when I talk to him. Gitane and I go back a long way."

RODNEY KNIGHT

Webster met with Gitane's ex-husband the next day, having tracked the man down at a dive bar in downtown called the Strait Shot. Except for a couple talking with the bartender, Knight was the only other customer, sitting alone at a corner table at the back of the room.

Rodney Knight was as thin as a razor blade, and his long brown hair and sorry beard looked unwashed and oily. He was wearing a black tee shirt, and his long arms—as white and thin as pieces of PVC pipe and covered with biker tattoos—would not strike fear into the heart of any potential foe. Still, the man had an aura of uneasy danger.

Duncan looked into Rodney's dilated eyes, and old photos of the deranged murderer Charles Manson flashed through his mind. It was 2:00 p.m., and there were a pitcher of beer and a half-empty glass on the table.

"Mr. Knight, I need to ask you a few questions. It won't take long. Just trying to solve a possible problem regarding your ex-wife."

Knight shrugged and said, "Which one?"

His question caught Webster off guard. "Umm...Gitane Harper."

"Oh, the second one. We're divorced and not on speaking terms. She's still trying to rob me for child support. What'd she do? She's always been a crazy little bitch."

Duncan felt the hairs on the back of his neck tingling and tried to stifle a flash of anger. "She didn't *do* anything. She just disappeared. Without her little girl. Does that answer your question? Does it surprise you?"

Knight shrugged. "Fuck yeah, it surprises me. The kid's the only thing she's semi-normal about."

Deputy Webster said, "I understand you had some unpleasant issues before and during your divorce. And that there's still some hard feelings between you. I need to know if you have seen her recently."

"No, I haven't seen her. We don't hang out; we don't talk; we don't like each other. I haven't even seen the kid since I got thrown out of the house."

Duncan snapped, "No? Too bad. That's your daughter, jackass. I thought you might be around Gitane once in a while because of your daughter. You sound like there might be bad blood between you and Gitane."

Knight took his time. He lit a cigarette and blew smoke over his shoulder. "Bad blood? Maybe. But not bad enough to make her disappear. And to be honest? I got no interest at all in that kid. I ain't even sure she's my kid."

The deputy's voice was cold and flat as he said, "Tell me where you were yesterday, Rodney…and the night before."

"Chill, man. I'm good. The band had a party that night. We drank our asses off at Wayne's place—he's the drummer— and crashed at his house. Everyone stayed there all night."

"Yeah? Anyone who might confirm that information?"

"Seriously? I got four band members and their old ladies. I said they were all there. I slept on the couch. Which is four feet from the door to the head. The bathroom gets used a lot at Wayne's. I'm pretty sure they all saw me during the night."

Duncan stared at the half-stoned rocker. He knew the man had a group of at least four liars to back up an alibi and verify his presence at the party. "Yeah," he said, "all model citizens, right?"

"They'll work, man. I guess that's all that matters."

* * *

The following day, Duncan drove out to the Herrick Road to interview Gitane's neighbors. It was late autumn, and the sullen gray sky reflected his own state of mind. He hoped that someone might have seen a strange car or anything unusual.

The Herrick Road did not get as much rain as the West End Olympic Rain Forest, but it got enough to have the same prehistoric feel. The tree trunks were carpeted in moss, and curtain-like sheets of the species shrouded the branches of spruce and hemlock trees. It had rained in the morning, and the woods were still dripping from the misty fog. The heavy air smothered the valley like a giant water-soaked blanket.

Duncan started at Gitane's home, which was the first house on Herrick Road, after turning off Highway 101, and drove from farm to farm, knocking on doors and visiting with neighbors who happened to be at home. He recognized several of the names on mailboxes and left his business card on the front doors of unoccupied homes. At the end of the road, in a stretch of old-growth timber bordering a rough pasture, he slowed to read the name on a roadside mailbox. He groaned when he read the faded black letters on the tin box. Too long to fit on a single line on the tin box, it read:

Adrian Adams Hawkins
Mechanic

He had forgotten, probably on purpose, that Adrian lived here, and had to force himself to pull into the driveway. He knew, as did every citizen in the town of Port Angeles, from frequent articles in the local newspaper and disruptions at civic gatherings, that Mr. Hawkins was one of the most vocal, stubborn, and annoying critics of local government in the entire county. Adrian Adams Hawkins, who insisted on being addressed at meetings and in newspaper articles by all three of his names, was the county's ultimate contrarian. If there was a contentious issue or conflict at any city council or county meeting open to the public, Adrian Adams Hawkins was there. Deputy Webster wasn't sure this was the day he wanted to deal with Mr. Hawkins, but so far, his stops had been futile, and he was determined to talk to any Herrick Road resident who might provide a scrap of information about Gitane.

He drove up to the farm, which was set just off the overgrown meadow. At the edge of the tree line was a haphazard collection of sheds and other storage buildings anchored by a rickety, unpainted barn. A small house of black-aged logs was nestled under a thick layer of moss. The little complex was adjacent to the meadow Duncan had seen from the road, which was a metal boneyard of rusting machinery—junkyard cars, trucks, and assorted farm machinery.

Duncan saw an early-era VW Bus, its two-color paint faded and spotted with rust, resting on axles without wheels. There was an old Ford pickup truck, minus a fender and its hood. What looked to be a circa-1960, boatlike DeSoto or Plymouth was poking out the front-door opening of the weather-beaten barn.

He parked in front of the house and watched a man with a long gray-white beard and wearing oil-stained coveralls walk toward his cruiser. He got out of the car and waited. Duncan could never tell if Adrian, with his long gray hair and beard, was old or just prematurely gray. He looked old, but he moved like a younger man and was always alert and energetic.

"Hello, Mr. Hawkins."

The man answered, "I know you. What do you want?"

"Not much. Just out asking for a little neighborly information if you can spare a minute or two."

"Information about what?"

"Gitane Harper has gone missing. Lives down the road a piece. We're trying to check to see if anyone has seen or heard anything that might help us find her."

"I know where she lives. I drive by there almost every day. Don't know the woman. Don't pay much attention. Folks up here pretty much want to be left alone."

"I understand. I'm looking for anything out of the ordinary. A strange car. An unusual visitor. Anything. I won't bother you if you haven't seen or heard anything that might have caught your attention."

"Why would I? I'm a busy man…and not a nosy one."

"Yeah, well, if you hear or see anything that might help, maybe you can let me know. Miss Harper has a little girl who's missing her mama. We would be obliged if you could help us out."

Handing Hawkins his card, Duncan said, "You restore these old cars?"

"Not no more. Used to." He almost smiled. "These things just took roots here. Part of the family."

"Yeah. Well, good talking to you. I'm sure I'll see you around. Have a nice day."

Adrian nodded. "When are you guys gonna do something about the traffic on 101? It's like a goddamn racetrack out there."

Driving back to the highway, Webster finished leaving messages for the last two places on the other side of the road. He hadn't learned a thing. There had to be something that would help explain Gitane's disappearance. He did know one thing—his concern was growing with every passing hour.

As it turned out, the hours would become months, and the months would become years. Gitane's vanishing act would remain a mystery for a long, long time.

A NEW SHERIFF

Six years after Gitane Harper disappeared, Duncan became the sheriff of Clallam County when longtime Sheriff Harvey Morgan died of a heart attack. At the time of Morgan's death, Duncan was chosen to replace his former boss. The following year, he was officially elected into office by the public.

His first day as the new sheriff, he hung a few award plaques on the wall and filled the bookcase across the room from his desk with criminology books and reference material. He was careful to clear out a space in the center shelf, at eye level from his chair behind the desk.

The following morning, he went to work carrying an unfamiliar briefcase. When he took a small stuffed animal out of the satchel, the gathered staff laughed and started teasing him about his choice of personal inspiration.

Rachel Evans, the white-haired, sometimes unfiltered, but always undisputed office manager for the last two decades, was dumbfounded. "Duncan, you're the sheriff here now. A macho guy, you know? I don't think the drug dealers and burglars will be too intimidated by your teddy-bear office decor."

He laughed. "That bear was a gift from an old friend who vanished off the face of the earth when I was a new deputy.

I'm putting it here to remind me every day that I promised myself, and her family, I would find out what happened to her. That bear will stay up there until I deliver on that promise." He studied the bear for a second before placing it in the center of the shelf. "This is for you, Gitane," he said. "He will not be leaving this office until I find out what happened to you. And neither will I."

The teddy bear was the same one he had received the day before Gitane ended their relationship during their last year of junior high school. After he married Sasha, he had shoved it into a box with his sports clippings, Polaroid instant photos, and old yearbooks...and forgotten them.

His promise to Gitane's family had popped into his head on the day he was sworn in. He did not want to let himself forget again.

For Duncan, being the sheriff was a whole new world. Moving from the field to the office, he had no idea the administrative duties would be so demanding. His passion was to remain a real sheriff, helping people, enforcing the law, and being a hands-on officer who could relate to his staff and his profession. Somehow, he came close. But it wasn't always easy.

His workload was intense, and he seldom had the opportunity to follow up on Gitane's case. The teddy bear stayed on the shelf, remembered only once each year on the first of January when he set goals for the department and himself. Every year, on that day, he grew more and more frustrated.

Gitane had left her young daughter and disappeared into oblivion. There was nothing. No clues. No motives. No witnesses. Only the emptiness of not knowing what happened. Had Gitane been kidnapped? Murdered? Suffered an accident? Or was she missing for some crazy reason that only she would understand?

As to solving the case as the years passed, the odds remained the same as they were at the time of her disappearance—it was a long shot.

Gitane's then three-year-old daughter, April, was the only person who might have seen what happened. Family and local law enforcement personnel had tried to jog her memory, to no avail. Early in the investigation, the Clallam County Sheriff Department called in a child psychologist from the University of Washington to question Gitane's daughter. The doctor was skeptical about the little girl's ultimate recovery, suggesting that if the youngster had seen the disappearance, and if it had been of a violent nature, the ensuing trauma probably induced a memory blockage of the incident. He explained that young children tended to block out bad memories. However, there were occasional cases where memories were regained. One day in the future, there might be hope of recovering a repressed memory. But that had never happened for April.

To Duncan's dismay, after seven long years of holding the office of county sheriff, the prosecutor's office classified the case as a "missing person with possible foul play." And deactivated the file.

For Duncan, there remained a hole in his heart. With every passing year, Sheriff Webster continued to monitor any violent-crime report that crossed his desk from any corner of the Northwest, trying to unveil some hint that would shed light on Gitane's disappearance. An item of clothing, a bloodstain, a repetitive pattern, or a sign of a similar pattern. There was nothing.

And then, almost two decades after Gitane disappeared, Duncan got a glimmer of hope. A nationwide serial killer named Sawyer Livingston, who had lived in the West End fishing village of Neah Bay, was arrested in Alaska. After hearing that Livingston had confessed to a dozen killings and claimed to have deposited at least one female body in Lake Crescent, Duncan waited impatiently for more details. The man toyed with investigators, divulging details of his murders sparingly and playing games to stall the process. Duncan was riveted to the media reports and even contacted the Alaska lawmen on the same day they released news that Livingston had hinted that he might have deposited several other victims in the national park's lake.

But two days after the news broke, Livingston hanged himself in the Anchorage jail cell where he was being held prisoner…before sharing the full history of his shocking trail of murders. Duncan was devastated.

Despite the years of frustration, though, Duncan never lost hope of coming across something to help with his promise to Gitane's family and friends. He made it a point to watch out for Gitane's daughter, April. The child had been adopted by Gitane's mother and father and was growing up in town with her grandparents.

April was nothing like her reckless mother. She was tall and thin, and had inherited her father's delicate bone structure. She sang in her church choir, was in church every Sunday and, except for singing with the high school chorus, had little interest in teenage social events.

As a high schooler, she met a young member of the church; he was as reserved as she. The relationship became serious, and the two were married a year after graduating from high school. Eventually, the couple's only child was born. They named their little girl Willow Harper Shepard, in honor of April's long-lost mother, Gitane Harper.

* * *

Gitane's personality seemed to have skipped a generation. Willow was like Gitane, not her mother. She dressed as she pleased, usually with clothing that represented different eras, from medieval robes to contemporary rock-star garb. She loved color and retro jewelry. Her hair was a painter's palette of bright red, blue, or orange. Willow did not hesitate to defy the norm.

She dropped out of Port Angeles High School in her sophomore year and attended the GED program for high school rebels because the alternative school was on the west side of town and within walking distance of her parents' house. She was often seen near the area, walking home from school, wearing a long black trench coat, her wrists loaded with stacks of bracelets, and a strange black hat that, except for a bent-over, pointed peak, looked very much like the headwear one might see on a Halloween witch.

When Willow was seventeen years old, her mother was diagnosed with stage IV breast cancer. The diagnosis was late; the chemotherapy and radiation, unsuccessful. The youngster quit the alternative school to take care of her mother. Willow spent as much time as possible with her mom and cherished the bonding and mutual love.

On a sunny and warm summer day before the girl's mother died, Duncan was driving an unmarked county car past a strangely dressed girl with dark hair streaked, on this day, with blue highlights. She was walking down the sidewalk carrying a large bag of groceries.

Duncan had already introduced himself to Willow when he'd stopped a time or two to talk with the young lady. So he pulled over, dropped open the passenger-side window, and said, "Hello, Willow, can I give you a ride home?"

"No thanks, Sheriff Webster. I'm just stretching my legs a bit."

They chatted about the nice weather, and he asked the girl about her mother's health.

Her eyes filled with tears, and she shook her head.

As he got ready to leave, Duncan said, "Has anyone ever told you you're a lot like your grandmother?"

Willow flashed a smile. "Yes, they have. With my mom being so sick, we talk a lot about her past life. I love that my gramma was a little unconventional. Being different is just a way of being yourself."

"Well, I knew your gramma, and I can tell you she was all about being herself. She would have been in hog heaven in today's free-spirit environment. Don't ever change, young lady. We should all be comfortable in our own skin. You tell your mom I said hello."

Pulling away from the curb after dropping off Willow, Duncan thought about Gitane. The fierce independence may have skipped a generation, and the two women's body types were not the same. But there was no doubt who the youngster took after—she was Gitane Harper's granddaughter.

For Duncan, Gitane's vanishing had remained his personal cross to bear. No one had stumbled across human remains in the back country. No skeleton was unearthed by a backhoe during a farmland building project. Still…nothing.

If Willow's presence was a gentle reminder of Gitane's unresolved fate, Rodney Knight's presence was a nightmare. The unsavory Mr. Rodney Knight burned in Duncan's gut with every sighting of the man.

Knight's group of Rodsters hung out in the bars, smoking and drinking while playing pool as a team in the local tavern league. The muscle cars had disappeared years ago, and although they all owned Harley Davidson motorcycles, they were now most likely to be seen in their Honda Civics or Ford pickup trucks. Rumor had it they had progressed from drug users to drug sellers, and the narcotics department knew them all on a first-name basis.

Even Adrian Adams Hawkins, one of the few remaining Herrick Road residents from that time, was an annoying constant reminder of Duncan's promise to resolve Gitane's disappearance. Adrian's high profile as a civic rebel brought the two men together often, and his mere presence made Duncan think of the Herrick Road. Mr. Hawkins had never changed. Like country singer Willie Nelson, both men looked old when they were twenty…and both looked exactly the same when they reached their sixties. Duncan preferred Willie.

* * *

The official Gitane Harper file was eventually moved from the department archives into the cold case database, where the lengthy time span since her disappearance recorded it as low priority. But with Willow's presence and the tired teddy bear on the shelve in his office, for Duncan the file was always open. Every detail, every interview involving the original case sat on the shelf beside the teddy bear, in a manila folder with creased and worn sheets of paper, held together by a stretched-out rubber band. The folder was woefully thin.

A RIVER REBORN

In 2009, Duncan had been the county sheriff for twenty-two years and had watched his home city evolve from a thriving logging and wood-product mill town to an economy driven by visiting tourists and senior retirees. The transition had been gradual, so news of an ecological project with the potential to impact not only the city of Port Angeles, but the entire world, came as a surprise to almost everyone.

Two separate hydroelectric dams on the Elwha River, by that time used only for supplementary energy support, were going to be removed in an attempt to rescue a river that had been choking to death for a century. It would be the largest dam-removal project in history, and it had the potential to create a global renaissance by returning the magnificent river to its original state and restoring the balance of nature.

The announcement of the removal of the two dams created a firestorm of civic controversy. Before the dams, the Elwha River was one of the most prolific salmon habitats in the continental United States. Old-timers claimed—only exaggerating a little—the annual salmon runs were so productive that you could walk across the river on the backs of spawning fish, and that early settlers used pitchforks, not fishing poles or nets, to harvest their dinners.

In 1913, a local entrepreneur completed the construction of a major dam on the Elwha River in order to provide cheap energy for local wood and paper mills. The dam was two miles from the mouth of the river, the gateway for six different types of salmon returning to their spawning grounds. That dam was responsible for the formation of Lake Aldwell, so named for Thomas Aldwell, the businessman responsible for its creation.

Thirteen years later, another dam was built above the Aldwell Dam, creating s second lake called Lake Mills. Both structures were constructed without bypass alternatives for spawning fish. Vital spawning grounds spread over eighty miles of prime fish-reproduction waters were destroyed.

When the Olympic National Park was created in 1938, the upper dam was located within the borders of the protected land. Seventy years later, the park's commitment to saving endangered ecosystems played a key role in the river's resurrection.

The dams weren't the only cause of the destruction of the fisheries. Polluted waters, global commercial fishing, Native Americans harvesting their rightful share of fish, and other challenges contributed to the alarming state of the resource. All of these connected entities agreed—any effort to restore the fishery was dependent on the removal of the dams. And others were just as passionate to fight for their retention.

* * *

Adrian Adams Hawkins raged from the podium with the deluded passion of Adolf Hitler, his long hair and beard adding a touch of surrealism to the scene, "We cannot allow the government to destroy our lives. This dam proposal is unacceptable. If it goes through, we will pay more for electricity, destroy two one-hundred-year-old recreational lake areas, and create a situation that has the potential to ruin private property and family homesites all the way from the Strait of Juan de Fuca to the border of the Olympic National Park.

"Furthermore, no one, especially the government, knows what is going to happen! There has never been a dam-removal project as large as this one. Turning that river loose after a century has the potential for disaster. We must put an end to this insane thievery immediately! We don't have to be lab rats for the goddamn government."

* * *

Duncan was in the office when the front desk buzzed him. It was a Saturday afternoon, which is usually too early for things to get interesting.

"Sheriff, Myles Reynolds here. Adrian Hawkins is raising a ruckus again. We're trying to hold a homeowner meeting at the grange on Black Diamond Road, and as usual, Adrian's fucking up the whole thing. You might want to check on him before I bust his neck."

Duncan sighed. "Myles, your direct approach never ceases to amaze me. Just hang on. We'll be right up."

The sheriff motioned to a deputy. "Okay, Leon, I'm bored. Let's take a ride and see what the hell Mr. Hawkins is up to now."

Arriving at the grange hall, they saw two burly loggers guarding the front door to the building. When they reached the porch, the bigger of the two nodded and said, "Sheriff."

"Myles. Is there a problem here?"

Myles Reynolds was clad in a Hickory shirt and red suspenders, standing with his arms folded and an impassive face. "Not anymore. We decided it might be better if Adrian waited for you outside."

"I trust he doesn't have a broken neck?"

Reynolds grinned. "Not yet." Jerking his head toward the porch, he said, "He's over there."

At the back wall of the porch, Duncan saw Adrian hunched down in a wooden chair. Myles's friend stood close by, guarding the door to the building.

Webster walked over to check on Adrian, Myles Reynolds following behind him. Duncan said, "Mister Hawkins. How's it going?"

Hawkins took a long drag on the cigarette he was smoking, dropped it on the dusty floor of the porch, and crushed it out with his foot. "I didn't do anything wrong. I was just speaking my piece. Protecting my property."

Myles said, "Yeah, he was speaking all right, just not letting anyone else speak. This is supposed to be a meeting where local landowners talk about the dam project. Not one fellow ranting the whole time. We'd be obliged if you could tell him to leave."

"Okay, Myles, I think we can handle this. Adrian, why don't you go home and settle down? It sounds like you had your turn."

"I'll leave, Sheriff. But I will not stay left. Taking those dams out just is not right. We can't let them do it."

"Adrian, you know you are always entitled to your own opinion. But ruining a meeting for folks is not all right either. It seems like you had your say. You go on home. Let your neighbors talk about alternatives. We will be happy to take you if you don't want to drive."

Hawkins grunted. "I bet you would. I know you fellows don't have anything else to do. But I'd prefer it if you'd find some other way to waste our tax dollars than driving me home."

"Just get in your car, Mr. Hawkins. And try to have a nice day."

As Duncan knew, Adrian Hawkins had a farm on the Herrick Road, just above the river and Lake Aldwell, which was created by the lower Elwha Dam. Adrian had declared war on the government's approval of the demolition project.

Opponents, like Adrian, argued that dam removal would be unpredictable and threatening to riverside homeowners, and that the dams reduced utility bills. In addition, the lakes provided fishing, boating, and nature watching, and had been a part of outdoor-recreation usage for over a century.

* * *

Once the dam-removal time line began to unfold, tension between supporters and objectors intensified. Highway 101 from Port Angeles to the West End was lined with home-made signs produced by rural landowners. Save the Lakes signs went head-to-head with Save the Salmon signs, both messages scrawled in paint on mini-billboards posted on roadside trees and fences.

The sheriff department received daily complaints reporting vandalism and stolen yard signs. Pro and con letters to the *Daily News* filled the editorial pages with rhetoric and raged in violent defense of each side's viewpoints.

Meanwhile, due diligence had addressed every possible bureaucratic roadblock. The Lower Elwha Tribe, the State of Washington, and the US Federal Government had assembled an airtight game plan for initiating the multimillion-dollar project.

Despite the inevitable outcome, anti-removal advocates continued to fight. When teardown crews arrived at the staging area, vandalism and minor sabotage efforts slowed the project. Workers arrived on some mornings to find slashed tires and broken windshields on some of their equipment and portable storage sheds graffitied with nasty anti-dam messages.

The demolition contractors, however, hired a nighttime security service, and the project went forward on schedule. A month later, in September of 2011, engineers began the largest dam-removal project in the history of the world. It was a complex procedure, which was undertaken with no previous comparisons to study and analyze. The Olympic National Park's involvement provided access to a deep pool of talented biologists, geologists, environment experts, and consultants eager to advise and document all aspects of the project. Meticulously researched and analyzed, the experts were confident about eliminating the dams, draining the lakes, and producing a safe rerouting of the river's natural path to the Strait of Juan de Fuca. The dismantling of the dams began in earnest.

DISCOVERY

Lake Aldwell was drawn down slowly, similar to snow melting in the high mountains during the spring thaw. Scientists monitored the water's drain pattern carefully, eager to see how having been one hundred years underwater would impact the valley and how a century of silt collected behind the dams would affect the release of the Elwha River.

The unveiling was unprecedented, and crews recorded every tree stump, discarded piece of logging equipment, and unusual rock as it was uncovered by the shrinking lake. On a daily basis, the exposed areas were revealing the landscape as it had appeared while being logged before the dam began to trap the river and fill the lake.

In addition to the jaw-dropping size of tree stumps, there were signs of early logging's disregard for the environment. Rusted saws, discarded tow chains, bottles, worn-out tools, and other discarded workplace castoffs were being discovered every day. Having been a popular fishing lake, workers also found a sunken rowboat and a variety of lost fishing lures, beverage cans, and one antique camping beer cooler.

* * *

Early one morning when the last dregs of Lake Aldwell were all that remained, Sheriff Webster received a phone call from Olympic National Park Headquarters.

"Webster."

"Hey, Web. Kent Merriweather with the park-service rangers here."

"Yeah. Hello, Kent, what's up?"

"I'm not sure, maybe nothing. We just got a call from the Lake Aldwell monitoring crew reporting an unusual piece of equipment beginning to show at the north end of the lake drawdown, about a half mile from the dam teardown. They think it might be a vehicle of some kind and say it is in a strange place for a mechanical piece to be. It's not totally uncovered yet, but whatever it is, they can tell it's been there for a long time, and it doesn't seem like a logging-show piece of equipment. Probably nothing at all, but I thought you might like a chance to check out the demo progress. Do you want us to keep an eye on it and give you a heads-up when its fully exposed?"

"Sure. Like most folks, I'm curious to see what's going on with the project out there anyway. Give me a shout when its uncovered, and you and I can take a look."

"Good idea. I'll keep you posted."

A day later the water level had dropped enough to confirm the object was an automobile, and the ranger thought it should be fully accessible sometime in the next twenty-four hours.

When Merriweather called again that same afternoon, he suggested they check out the rusted car the following morning. "Bring your waders, Duncan. It's not underwater now, but it is muddy as hell out there, and the lake bed is soft.

Nobody has wanted to get close to it yet. It'll be messy, if nothing else."

"What isn't? Why don't we meet you at the equipment-parking area in the morning, and you can take us to it from there?"

* * *

The next morning, Duncan rounded up Deputy Leon Berger, and the two of them met Merriweather in the demolition-team's staging area. They said hello and shook hands with Kent and another younger forest ranger.

The four men visited as they pulled on waders or hip boots. "This little discovery has the nerd crews all excited," said Kent. "It's in a very strange place, and the geeks are all fired up." Rolling his eyes, he added, "It's an old car, for Christ's sake...deposited, God knows how, in the middle of a lake with no road. Whoopee!"

Webster chuckled. "I'm sure you're right, Kent. But I got to admit, it's good to be out in the fresh air. I haven't had waders on since a fly-fishing trip to Alaska in 2003. Seems like a hundred years ago."

When they reached the lake, it was easy to see why the curious scientists were reluctant to check out the car. The lake bottom was soft and marshy with areas of standing water and exposed areas deep in mud. A hundred years of river silt had gathered behind the dam, spreading farther from the structure every year. The lake bottom looked more like a sullen swamp than the bottom of a pristine mountain lake. Two hundred yards away from either lakeside, they could see a dark boulder-like shape.

Deputy Berger said, "Bad choice for a parking lot, boss. This place looks like a freshwater version of low tide on one of the muddy clamming beaches on the Sound."

Duncan answered, "Yeah. Throw the car in, and I'd say more like a rusty pile of scrap iron stuck in a giant hog wallow."

Slogging through the knee-deep water and slime, they could see that the scrap iron was truly an automobile. The wheels had rotted away, and the body was settled into the soft mud, but there was no question it was a car. It was a smaller chassis size, the rear window was missing, and one front fender and the grille were gone. The group circled their way around the vehicle, the soft mud making sucking sounds with every step, trying to guess the make or year of the vehicle.

"Could be a midsize or a hard-roof sports car, I guess," Webster said. "It's not from the Model A era, though, which means it must have gotten here well after the lake was created…but it sure as hell isn't new. I'm thinking more in the sixties or early seventies. Let's check it out."

When Duncan muscled open the driver-side door, it came loose from the body, and he stepped aside as it fell into the mud. He leaned into the soggy interior and looked around. The visors, dashboard, and seat cushions were rotted away, the glove box open. No tools or luggage or personal items to be seen. Silt had snuck through the missing back window, and the floor and back seat were buried in muck.

"I don't see anything in here that might be unusual. Looks like an abandoned vehicle to me. Leon, see if you can open the trunk. Use that crowbar you packed in if you have to. We might as well do this right."

The trunk was jammed shut, and the other three men stood behind the deputy, watching him struggle with the crowbar while they visited about the project. Sweat was dripping off Leon's face when he finally loosened the lid. Shoving the stubborn trunk up with its rusty hinges squeaking in protest, he was able to force the lid open a foot or two from the rear bumper. Pulling a flashlight off his belt, Leon peeked into the dark space. Grunting like a gut-punched boxer, he dropped the flashlight in the mud and stumbled back from the car, almost falling into the sloppy lake bottom.

Leon looked at the three men, his eyes jumping from face to face, still struggling to process what he had seen. Sucking in gulps of air, he blurted, "Holy shit! There's a fuckin' skull in there!"

The men gathered around the back of the car while Leon and Duncan forced the jammed trunk all the way open. Then the others crowded closer. Everyone could see there was more than a skull. A jumble of human bones was strewn throughout the enclosure. A sparse rib cage with several bones missing and pieces of vertebrae were scattered like confetti about the floor of the trunk. Nobody said a word as they gawked at the scattered bones.

Finally, Sheriff Webster broke the silence. "Jesus Christ. This is incredible. These bones have been trapped in here for a long time. Nobody touches anything. We need to secure the car as a crime scene. This is unbelievable."

The others were beginning to recover from their various states of shock. "This doesn't make any sense," said Ranger Merriweather. "There is no record of even a skid road this close to the dam. There is no paved road to drive off. How could it get here?"

"I don't know, Kent. Look at all the tree stumps that trace where the riverside used to be. The loggers got here somehow. See if you can get a crew to look for old logging roads or skid trails. It is pretty obvious that they logged the side hills at some point in time.

"I know the lake's been here for a hundred years, but this car carcass isn't that old. The car had to come sometime after the dam was built and the lake created. I wonder if, through the years, the water motion or currents caused by the dam could have something to do with its location. Something must have." He grunted. "I don't think a helicopter dropped it in the middle of the lake."

Duncan thought for a second, considering options. "Leon, let's call the staters to check out both the car and the bones. Kent, can you make sure none of the workers…or the suits… get near this thing? No media or curiosity geeks either. I am pretty sure that a skeleton in a car trunk will be a crime scene, but you never know. We've got a lot of work to do."

Leon and Duncan postholed their way through the mud to the cruiser and returned with rolls of crime tape and stakes to cordon off the vehicle. They managed a somewhat-embarrassing perimeter. When they stepped back and checked their work, Duncan shrugged his shoulders and said to his deputy, "It ain't pretty. But it'll work."

The Elwha River dam-removal project was a subject of worldwide interest, and the television networks, social media, and cyber world were monitoring and recording the project's progress on a twenty-four seven basis. Webster knew the discovery of a skeleton in the trunk of a car had the potential to incite a frenzy of activity from the media, and he wanted no part of the circus he knew was about to take place.

"Kent, we need to have people here to keep the site secure until the state police can examine the scene. I do not trust *any* of the media people. I know you can handle it today, but we may need to hire some surveillance until the Washington State Patrol can do their thing. I have a hunch this is going to be something big. We've got to be extra thorough and extra careful."

When they got back to the department, the sheriff closed the door to his office and sat down to think. The minute he had seen the bones in the rusted auto's trunk, his mind went to two places—first, the legendary case of the Lady of the Lake from ten miles up the road; second, the location of Lake Aldwell, just one mile from the turnoff to the Herrick Road... where Gitane Harper was living when she vanished all those years ago.

* * *

Media sources went wild when they realized that the Lake Aldwell Dam drawdown had turned into a macabre crime scene. Although there was already a twenty-four seven camera monitoring the actual dismantling, it was not enough to satisfy the world's demands for in-depth coverage.

Northwestern television crews arrived with camera vans and helicopters. Newspapers sent reporters. The Internet news went viral, bombarded with hits. The flood of media exposure took the project, and the pressure, into the stratosphere. Who was the victim? How did the vehicle get into the lake? When? Why?

Duncan Webster did not know the answers. But his prediction was right about a media frenzy exploding at the news of the remains discovered in a newly famous lake. The news spiraled quickly out of control. When the first groups of television reporters and newspeople were so intense that deputies could hardly get to their patrol cars, Duncan knew the nightmare had begun. The demands of the media were constant, most of them aggressive and rude. The Internet quickly spewed questions and undocumented information. Within hours, wild theories were rampant online, most of them suggesting some type of conspiracy, aliens, drug runners, tree huggers…

Duncan was overwhelmed by the magnitude of the story. He knew a full-scale press conference would be unavoidable. But he was also aware of the nature of the forthcoming investigation. His department would need time to get organized and prepare a game plan for going forward. He decided to stall for time by issuing a written press release to be distributed to the media. Webster gathered available staff to keep them aware of the strategy and read the text of the press release to the team:

March 15, 2011

From the desk of Clallam County Sheriff Duncan Webster:

Human remains were discovered locked in the trunk of a sunken vehicle in the recently drained Lake Aldwell. The victim's identity is not known at this time. Make, model, and year of the auto is also unknown at this time. Nor have we confirmed that a crime has been committed. The Clallam County Sheriff Department is in the process of gathering this information and preparing an official case profile. We will make every effort to share information as it becomes available.

Thank you for your cooperation and patience.

When he finished, he said, "I think we all need to tactfully avoid the press as much as possible. At this point, we truly have nothing to report…and the intensive dam-removal coverage has put us in the spotlight. I'm afraid the media crews might be a bigger pain in the neck than solving the case. This is obviously a potentially criminal cold case. Everyone knows that a dated crime takes research and time. So it's not going to be easy."

Deputy Berger asked, "What are we gonna say, boss? We got no hope for current clues. DNA takes time. Bone analysis takes time, sometimes years of dead time—no pun intended—makes everything cold. They will finish the damn project—pun intended—before we can get a real case put together."

Duncan said, "I wish they would finish and get out of here tomorrow, but that is not going to happen; there is still another dam to go. They'll be here awhile. We're going to be on the hot seat for weeks, or maybe even months. We'll have to deal with it." He looked at the staff around the table, stopped at Leon, and said, "And you know what, Leon? I think this whole thing is going to get very interesting."

After the meeting, Duncan sat at his desk in the empty office, thinking about the day's strange turn of events. The discovery of a concealed body in Lake Aldwell was beyond belief. Since the first time he'd heard his Uncle Harlan tell the story of the Lady of the Lake fifty years ago, he'd dreamed about a mystery that might equal Harlan's once-in-a-lifetime experience. Now, nearing the end of a long career as a lawman, another stranger-than-fiction case eerily similar to the discovery of Hallie Illingworth's body in 1940 had turned up.

Even more mind-boggling to the sheriff was the fact that the discovery of these remains might be connected to his own past and the disappearance of a long-lost childhood sweetheart. He thought he was the only person—except for his good friend Detective Jon Kidd—who might think this scattered skeleton could be connected to Gitane Harper's disappearance years ago. The missing-person case was long forgotten, and all the other lawmen involved at that time were retired, dead, or never interested in the case when it was active. He decided not to disclose his thoughts regarding the Aldwell skeleton until crime-test results were completed. There was a good chance it might have nothing to do with Gitane Harper's missing-person case.

* * *

The Washington State Patrol were responsible for coordinating the extraction of the vehicle and safeguarding the remains until they were in the hands of the crime lab in Seattle. The vehicle would be evaluated by Washington State Patrol (WSP) people to ascertain the make, model, and year of the car; then it would be examined for possible clues. The skeletal bones would be rushed to forensic experts, who would perform a DNA test and a bone-analysis exam, hoping to determine how long the bones had been submerged and attempt to provide possible identity information. The Clallam County Sheriff Department would take care of the official investigation.

Webster phoned Dr. Monica Suzuki, head of forensics at the crime lab in Seattle. He had worked with her three years earlier and was well aware of her reputation for being talented but irascible. The doctor's feistiness was legendary throughout the state's law enforcement infrastructure, and for that very reason, Duncan was looking forward to the challenge.

DR. SUZUKI

M onica Suzuki was a pioneer in her chosen field. After graduating from Stanford University, she attended medical school at the University of Washington, after which, by virtue of hard work and a passion for science, she began her career in criminal forensics. She soon worked her way up from lab assistant to head of the forensic research department in Seattle.

Years later, she still had no idea that she was only five feet tall and that her once thick and black hair was now thick and gray. Having been in a cop-culture setting for her entire career, she could go head-to-head with any rude, pushy, and profane law officer in the state.

Duncan's phone call to the scientist was transferred quickly to her line. "Doctor Suzuki, Sheriff Webster from Port Angeles here. I expect you've already heard about the remains found in the Lake Aldwell Dam-Removal Project? We're going to be handling the case, and I just wanted to let you know how big this thing is going to be. We are all over the world on a daily basis now because of the project's publicity, and we're already feeling the heat. Evidently, the chance of a nasty little mystery is more important to the media than a historical, ecological breakthrough. We need some help here, and we need it ASAP."

The doctor said, "I remember you. What are you saying, Sheriff? That you want me to drop everything we are working on and put you at the front of the line? I don't think so. I am aware of your situation. You guys found a pile of old bones. Well, I've got dozens of piles of old bones…and bodies…here and all of your fellow cops are telling me they need information right now."

Webster smiled at the phone, thinking, *Some things never change.*

Dr. Suzuki and he had worked together on a cold case cadaver unearthed by a contractor's bulldozer several years before. Even then, she had thought Duncan was impatient.

"Okay," he said, "I just thought I would talk to you personally so we could figure something out. I can email you all the reports. But I can tell you, Doc, this one is not going away."

Webster hung up and made another phone call.

* * *

Two hours later, Dr. Suzuki received a message from the Washington State Attorney General.

Dr. Suzuki

Due to the global exposure of the dam removal project in Port Angeles, it is imperative that we handle the discovery of a potential murder in a timely manner. From a public relations perspective, this is a Code Red situation, which will be exposed to

*the world. For the State of Washington, a positive
image is imperative.*

Regards

Alice Cartwell, Washington State Attorney General

The Lake Aldwell body's remains arrived at the lab that afternoon. One hour later, Dr. Suzuki and an assistant were analyzing the bones.

* * *

Meanwhile, Duncan received the auto reports from the WSP and called his people together for a briefing.

"Here's what we've got so far. The staters say the vehicle was a 1965 Ford Mustang. Its original paint color was dark blue, and based on mechanical analysis, during its history it was most likely subjected to long, hard miles. There was front-end damage, and the grille had either been knocked off on impact with the surface of the water or removed prior to the car's submersion in the lake. The auto gearheads ballparked the actual time of submersion somewhere in the late 1970s."

Deputy Berger jumped in, "I think '65 was Mustang's first year. The baby boomers loved them."

"That is correct, Leon; 1965 is the year I graduated from high school. But there is a little more info in this report. There were no license plates or serial numbers. No clues as to who owned the car, and they noted that a vehicle stripped of all signs of ownership probably indicates a stolen car or, at the very least, a vehicle owned by a black-market mechanic who knew how to remove tracking information in order to separate themselves from an illegally obtained automobile. That's all the state guys have so far."

Sighing, he said, "At least we've got something to throw to the media. Those guys are relentless." The sheriff knew the car report was only one small step in the process. Mustangs were so popular in those early days that demand actually exceeded supply. And the WSP report of high mileage and excessive wear indicated that this car entered the lake years later than the year it was built.

* * *

Twenty-four hours later, Dr. Suzuki had processed the bones and prepared a preliminary DNA profile in record time. The remains were those of a woman. A young adult. The DNA from the bones would help, but Dr. Suzuki's email stated the contents of the car had not produced anything she could use for a positive DNA identification. She needed a smear of blood, a used toothbrush, or a strand of hair to cross-reference and confirm an exact DNA match. As an aside, she also called Duncan a "sneaky little bastard."

The contents of Dr. Suzuki's report encouraged Sheriff Webster. After a quarter century of frustration, he was afraid to even think there might be a connection of these bones to Gitane Harper. But the remains were female. A young adult. It was still a possibility. He had yet to share his thoughts and hopes with anyone. But if he could dial in the DNA, he could get an answer.

Duncan thought about how to go forward with the investigation. The science of forensic DNA evidence had advanced beyond all expectations, and every passing month produced technological improvements. He had hoped the vehicle's trunk would produce some sort of useful evidence that would connect the remains and establish an identity. Sex and time lines had been confirmed, but years beneath the water had erased any connective evidence, and forensics needed something to use for a final cross-reference.

Later that night, sitting alone in his office and thinking about tying the remains to Gitane Harper, he stared at the wall on the other side of the room, where his Gitane reminders sat on the center shelf. For almost three decades, the profile folder and scruffy teddy bear had been there, woefully useless and more a frustration than an inspiration. They had been there so long they had become invisible.

The skeleton in the lake had awakened interest and promises. Studying the bear now, something tweaked Duncan's subconscious. Struggling to grasp the thought, he pushed himself out of his chair and walked over to the shelf. The bear had been sitting there for so many years he knew it only as the fading memory of an unfulfilled promise.

He picked the bear up, trying to jump-start his memory. Around the teddy's neck, Gitane had added a makeshift collar of maroon-colored ribbon; touching it, Duncan's fingers felt a piece of jewelry. He held the bear closer to his body, trying to separate the brass-colored locket from the bear's fake fur. Over the years, the locket had darkened with age, and it now blended so well into the brown fur of the fuzzy toy that it was virtually unnoticeable.

As soon as he saw the bauble, he smiled, and everything came back to him. He knew exactly why his subconscious had drawn him to the gift and exactly why his memory would suppress its history. Duncan's hands started to shake as he fumbled with the catch on the locket, praying its contents might still be inside the piece.

Finally, he opened the cover. Inside was a snippet of honey-blonde hair. Duncan smiled again, dropped his chin to his chest, and blew out a long sigh of relief. He whispered, "Thank God for small favors…and crazy women."

* * *

The next morning, Duncan drove to Seattle to meet with Dr. Suzuki face-to-face. When he entered her office, the doctor was on the computer. She took her time acknowledging his presence, and he smiled at the frosty reception.

When Dr. Suzuki finally looked up, she greeted him with, "What do you want now, Webster? Thanks to you going over my head, we've already finished your little project."

Smiling sheepishly, he said, "You know, Doc, I've missed you too. We should have lunch someday to catch up on things."

Dr. Suzuki crinkled her face as if she thought he might be serious. "I don't think so. I don't have time to go out to lunch."

"I know. But you're going to love me today. I brought you a present."

"Quit fooling around, Sheriff. I'm not in the mood."

"No, really. I have a theory about the Aldwell remains you helped us with. If you can get me a positive ID, it might break this thing wide open. I think I know who the victim was. And I think you can nail it down for me."

As he talked, he watched Dr. Suzuki's face change from perturbed to curious. For all her tough talk, the woman was, above all, a skilled and dedicated forensic scientist.

"Go on."

"We have a cold case file from the eighties that I've been working on for a long time. A young mother who lived close to Lake Aldwell and suddenly disappeared. There were suspicions of foul play, but not a single clue, so our people ended up switching the file from missing person to a potentially criminal cold case disappearance."

"So?"

"Your WSP guys in Port Angeles tell me the car in the lake has been there at least twenty-five years. You told me the skeleton is female. So this is why I'm bothering you. I have a piece of the missing girl's hair, which I hope you can cross reference with those bones for a positive ID."

Suzuki raised her eyebrows and, switching to cop talk, said, "No shit? You *do* know most hair samples need the follicle attached for traditional DNA ID, right?"

"I did not know that—and this hair was cut—but I do know DNA technology gets better by the month."

She sniffed at his answer. "You're a lucky man, Webster. The science of DNA has come a long way. Technique advances and science...and a competent examiner...might be able to work with a strand of hair. With what we have already, and *if* we're lucky, I might be able to get enough DNA from hair that doesn't have a follicle. If your hair syncs up with those bones, we can get you a match." She paused. "Plus, in this case, you're twice as lucky—you have me to do it. And I like tough puzzles."

"That, I *did* know. And that is why I'm here."

He could tell she was excited about the opportunity to show off her skills. But he was not expecting what she said next.

"You know, Sheriff, that's not a bad piece of policing for a backwoods cop. But there is always a chance we won't get a match. What if your victim's bones aren't connected to the hair?"

He shrugged. "Strike one, I guess. We remove the girl who went missing from the list of possible victims." He cleared his throat. "Any chance you can put this at the first of the line, Doc? The media is going crazy. They won't go away until we figure this thing out."

Dr. Suzuki snorted. "Don't bother, Webster. I already got orders from the AG and the governor to drop everything and babysit your ass."

It was hard to hide his relief. "That's awesome, Doc. I knew you'd come through for us."

"Don't patronize me, Webster. You talk too much. Give me the hair, and I'll find out from my bones if it's your missing girl or not."

"Thanks, Doc. It's always a pleasure." He touched his forehead as if he were wearing a hat with a brim. "Have a nice day."

* * *

Back in the office the next morning, Duncan got a call form Dr. Suzuki.

"Well, Sheriff, it looks like you lucked out again. I was able to get a DNA sample from a strand of hair without a follicle, and guess what? Your hair is a match to my bones."

Duncan felt the hair on the back of his own neck rise. "Are you sure, Doc?"

He waited. There was no answer.

"Never mind. You're sure. Thanks, sweetie, I owe you one."

Dr. Suzuki hung up.

* * *

Dr. Suzuki had no idea how much luck had played into her discovery. It was true her science was critical. But so was fate. The sheriff knew forensic science had solved hundreds, if not thousands, of violent crimes. But if Lake Aldwell had not been unexpectedly drained, and a fifty-year-old gift of hair from a fifteen-year-old girl had not been saved all those years, they still wouldn't have a thing on Gitane's disappearance or the remains. Webster was the only one who knew that *if* the bones and hair were a match, it was a gift from Gitane Harper.

Duncan did not believe in black magic, but he was beginning to wonder if Gitane, the girl whose name translated to *gypsy* in French, might have had something to do with these discoveries.

And now, he had an opportunity to keep a promise on which he had almost given up the hopes of fulfilling. He knew where Gitane had gone, and he knew someone had taken her life. However, he did not know if that someone was dead or alive, and he really didn't care. If they were alive, they were going to be punished. If the murderer was dead, he or she was going to be exposed and reviled as the merciless killer they were.

He had sworn to find Gitane Harper. Now, he wasn't going to quit until he found out why her life had been taken and who had done it. He was on fire to have the lucky breaks and the new science put to the test. And to resolve what had started as a promise and evolved into an obsession.

COLD CASE

O nce the department had a positive ID, Duncan decided to take his personal file on the Gitane Harper disappearance to the Clallam County Sheriff Department Cold Case Squad.

The unit was created in 2001 and came about because of the number of talented ex-law enforcement people who had chosen the Olympic Peninsula as their dream retirement location. Members of the squad were strictly volunteer, but the quality of career experience and achievements was extraordinary. The squad was headed by a former California police chief from the San Francisco area named Julianna Judd.

Julianna was a legend within the women's rights movement in the police world and had set the bar for shattering the glass ceiling for women in a traditionally exclusive men's field. From beat cop, to sergeant, to captain, to chief, she had outperformed her male peers, rising through the ranks in one of California's most dangerous areas. She was revered as a role model by her law enforcement sisters and well respected by every male policeman with whom she shared a connection. Now retired and living in Port Angeles, she was a member of the cold case squad on the peninsula and the undisputed leader of the small group.

The rest of the crew consisted of a pair of retired detectives—one from Chicago, the other from Phoenix—and an ex-sergeant from a smaller town in the Midwest, all three of them men. The final members were a husband-and-wife team who had worked under sheriffs in separate police-force districts on the outskirts of San Diego.

All of the team members were police lifers, experienced, and dedicated...and bored. They all knew they had accepted the most difficult task in the field of law enforcement. It is common knowledge that, in homicide cases, time is critical in relationship to captures and convictions. Clues get colder by the hour, and the backlog of unresolved cases is overwhelming in virtually every metropolitan area in the country.

During the preceding fifteen years, the cold case team had resolved a handful of old missing-person cold files and tracked down a convict jailed in the Washington State Penitentiary in Monroe, Washington, who was serving time for a different crime, and traced the prisoner as the killer in a twenty-year-old unsolved local murder.

The cold case unit had their own file on Gitane Harper's disappearance in 1984 and were familiar with the case. Until now, it had been a low priority, waiting for any kind of clue to use as a starting point. The team gathered at a conference table in the group's rented office close to the courthouse, and the ex-cops were eager to hear why they had been summoned to a briefing.

Duncan started, "So...I know you guys have all heard about the remains found in Lake Aldwell. As of today, we have a break in the case. We now know who the victim was—and can connect her to one of your cold case files. So far, we are the only ones who are aware of this information. You have her file here and are aware of the missing-and-assumed-dead status."

Taking a long, slow breath, he said, "There's one other thing no one knows yet, and I hope never will. I wanted you guys to know in case it goes public...which it probably will." He stopped, took another deep breath, and said, "Gitane Harper, the Lake Aldwell victim, and I were childhood sweethearts, right here in Port Angeles."

The team of veteran police officers were seldom surprised, all of them having investigated brutal killings and unspeakable atrocities. Duncan could see puzzled expressions on every face, but no sign of incredulity; they remained silent, awaiting further information.

Webster said, "It all started when the two of us were in the ninth grade. And only lasted for one year. But I'm guessing, when that news gets out, the media will turn this thing into a soap opera. But despite the irony, and the potential bullshit, I also believe that with regard to the resolution of this murder, it's a huge plus for us.

"I'm the guy who delivered a lock of Gitane's hair to the crime lab. Which, when paired with the bones, has nailed down a match confirming Gitane's DNA identity. I want you guys to know everything. I've been looking for my friend since I was a deputy in the West End years ago. Now I've got a starting point, and I need you pros to help. We've got a body. We've got an ID. I need a motive. And a killer. I think it's possible the murderer is already dead. I'm hoping, with what we have now, we can put this thing together. Alive or dead, we're going to find the killer."

The group around the table looked at one another, trying to process the startling information. They seemed thoughtful. Not confused, but questioning.

Julianna broke the silence and asked quietly, "Are you still in love with her, Duncan?"

"What? No! I'm not sure I ever was. But I do know she was part of making me who I am today. And, maybe more important, part of giving me a clue for understanding what real love was all about. Which I recognized ten minutes after meeting my wife.

"Gitane and I were too young to know anything, Julianna. Just like Gitane was too young to die. I promised her family—and myself—I would find out what happened to her. And we are going to find the person who put her in the lake."

Judd didn't flinch. She said, "It's okay if you're in love with her, Duncan."

Webster snapped, "Goddamn it, Jules, I said NO!"

The room went silent. Julianna looked at the sheriff without blinking. He stared back.

She said, "I was wondering when I would see that famous quick temper of yours. Did I hit a nerve?"

Chagrined, Duncan lost the staring contest with Julianna.

Judd said with a straight face, "No offense, Duncan, but I've seen better temper tantrums from four-year-olds."

Webster looked around the quiet room. Someone started to laugh, and the rest of the room, Duncan included, joined in.

Julianna Judd smiled at the sheriff and said, "No need to apologize, Web. It's just another day in Cop Town."

TOMB WATER

T wo days after the public announcement of Gitane Harper's murder and the discovery of her remains, Duncan's cell phone rang at four thirty in the morning. He answered on the first ring, trying, without success, not to wake his wife.

"Sheriff Webster? This is Kerry Olson from the Port Angeles PD. Sorry to bother you so early in the morning, but we've just responded to a 911 report of a body on the truck route, underneath the Tumwater Bridge. Sergeant Kidd is still with the body, and we've got other first responders just arriving. Sarge asked me to call you for him. He says you should get down here as soon as possible."

"Why? What does this have to do with us?"

"He didn't say. I didn't ask. I'm just the messenger, sir. He said he'd like you here as soon as possible."

* * *

The western side of the city of Port Angeles spreads across the valleys of two creeks whose waters run from the Olympic Mountains into the Strait of Juan de Fuca. The valleys are spanned by a pair of bridges which connect the east and west sectors of the town—the business core of the city and its eastside residents, and the mostly residential westside of the city. The valleys are steep, and although they are only a short distance apart, both bridges span paved roads running beside the creeks below them. Coming from the east, the first stream is called Valley Creek. The second is Tumwater Creek.

Through the years, frustrated law enforcement had created their own name for the highest of the two bridges, which towered 140 feet above Tumwater Creek. Given its infamous reputation for hosting suicides, they called it Tomb Water Bridge.

Webster did not need to ask about the scene or the nature of the incident. He knew it had to be a jumper. Since their creation, both bridges had developed an ill-fated history of suicides. But the higher of the two earned its nickname by having averaged at least one suicide every other year. The Valley Creek Bridge was not as high, but was closest to town—impatient townies didn't want to go a 150 yards farther to end their lives.

An uncertain, but distressing, number of additional jump attempts had been aborted by quick-thinking passing motorists. Most of the preventions come in daylight hours, saving jumpers who did not really want to die. All of the suicide attempts by those who had actually jumped from either bridge had been successful. There were no records of any jumper surviving the free fall to the creek beds or pavement below.

As the years passed and the local drug culture exploded, the city had attempted a number of preventive measures. But the fencing and barricades had not stopped the broken people who could not cope with life any longer.

* * *

When Duncan joined the sheriff department, he'd realized being a lawman where he had grown up would not be easy. He knew almost everyone in town, and although that could be a good thing, there was a downside too. Through the years, he had jailed good friends and family, pulled neighborhood kids out of fatal car wrecks, and watched too many families lose children to alcohol and drugs.

But, for Duncan, the worst duty of his job was being a first responder to a suicide…of any kind. When some lost soul was so beaten down by living that their only escape was taking their own life, that death seemed more tragic than any other. Duncan dreaded the helplessness and sense of failure that working a suicide case would bring.

Driving to the bridge in a light rain, Webster could feel the muscles in his neck and back begin to tighten. There was an unfamiliar tremor in his hands, and he squeezed the steering wheel to control the shaking. The steady *thump-squeak, thump- squeak* of the windshield wipers was giving him a headache.

He had no idea who might have jumped or why his presence, in particular, at the scene was required; the Port Angeles PD's failure to tell him gnawed on his insides as if it were a dog working on a chew toy. Duncan's mind raced through a dozen worst-case possibilities. A family member? A friend? A coworker? But if it was personal, he thought Detective Jon Kidd would have made a point of calling Duncan himself, as a friend would usually do.

Driving through downtown on Water Street, he passed a group of marine-based industrial buildings and the log-loading docks. Just before reaching the boat haven, he turned onto the truck route that follows Tumwater Creek up to the bridge and beyond.

A half mile up the road, where the bridge spanned the creek, there were a cluster of vehicles, their red strobe lights rotating. A Port Angeles PD officer stood under the bridge with a flashlight, guarding the scene and directing any early morning traffic. When he saw Webster's county cruiser, he waved the sheriff into the group of first responders.

Just beyond the cluster of vehicles, two city cops were installing yards of yellow tape to secure the site during the body removal. The pallor of flashing light bars, crime-site lamps, and flashlights combined with the shadowy darkness and rainy drizzle.

After Duncan left the car, he drew in a long, slow breath and walked toward the group of first responders. He felt the familiar despair of a suicide site and could smell the sadness surrounding the tragedy

A slump-shouldered man in casual clothes saw him coming and hurried toward him. The man needed a shave, his whiskers gray, and his face was creased with fatigue. It was Duncan's old friend Jonathan Kidd, who was now a veteran sergeant and chief detective of the Port Angeles Police Department.

Kidd wasted little time. "Hey, Web, thanks for coming. I think you might have a connection to the jumper. The body's a mess, but my sector guys say they recognize her clothing as that of a regular westside walker. If it's who I think it is, I thought you might want to know. I wouldn't let them move anything until you got here. Can you take a look so we can use you for an ID?"

Duncan didn't answer. He simply nodded.

They started walking toward the group of EMTs under the bridge, both of them knowing the bodies of Tomb Water jumpers never looked good. When they reached the body, the Port Angeles PD people were setting things up. The corpse was covered by a tarp, and two EMTs were prepping a body bag, which would be needed when the crime team finished up.

Duncan tipped his chin to the firemen and said, "Detective Kidd sent me over. Any chance I can take a look at the body? Kidd thinks I might be able to help with an ID."

"We got some work to do, Sheriff. Can you take a quick look at the face and then check back in fifteen minutes?"

"Absolutely."

The man nodded his approval.

Webster knelt and gently pulled the tarp away from the top portion of the body, pulling the covering lower than necessary to get the best look possible. It was a young girl, tall and probably lithe. The body was at the side of the road, and the drop from the bridge had done a significant amount of damage. One side of the face was disfigured beyond recognition. Kneeling beside the body, he carefully lifted the chin and rolled it to get a better look. There were streaks of blue in her dark-blonde hair.

He had known who it was before he checked the undamaged side of her face. It was Gitane Harper's granddaughter, Willow Shepard.

Walking away from the body, Duncan found Detective Kidd, who looked at him and said, "It's her, isn't it? I thought so. I'm sorry, Web, I know how long you've been connected to this bad-luck family."

"I can't get my head around this, Jon. I know the kid marched to her own drummer, but from what I hear, she's been as solid as a rock. I've visited with her myself. She took care of her mom for months before she died. She dropped out of school to do it. She was smart. Happy in her own skin. It doesn't make sense to me. Would you mind if I look around a bit more? Maybe ask the techs some questions?"

"Of course, I don't mind." Hesitating, Jon added, "Make sure your heart's not looking for something that isn't there, my friend. But if there's even a small chance of foul play, I'm all in. We're too old for these fucking suicides. Let me know if I can help. You've got full access to the case."

The rain had stopped, and it was beginning to get light. Duncan went back to the scene. The EMTs were getting ready to load the body.

"Can I take a closer look now, guys? I'll make it quick."

"No problem," said the lead fireman. "We're just getting ready to take her home."

Pulling on a pair of latex gloves, Duncan unzipped the body bag. Avoiding looking at her face, he checked the pockets of her trousers in case the Port Angeles PD might have missed something.

Willow's left arm was obviously broken and jutted away from the body at a grotesque angle. He lifted both arms and checked the jumble of bracelets and bangles stacked four inches high on the wrist of the broken arm. He was surprised the baubles had survived the fall and decided the bone must have taken the brunt of impact and cushioned the jewelry. He fingered through the bracelets, curious about whether or not they had a particular meaning for the girl, but they were what you would expect on a ten-year-old, not a young woman. For the sheriff, the miracle of their survival added to the poignance of the tragedy.

He thanked the EMTs and left to check the site where the girl had been found. It wasn't hard to locate the point of impact. She had hit the asphalt close to the shoulder of the road, and investigators had marked the landing with parking cones—less permanent than a crime site's yellow outline, but no less heartbreaking.

In the early dawn's light, Duncan could see the faint curve of a crescent moon beginning to fade above wisps of valley fog. Looking up at the tall bridge, he tried to understand what a smart, attractive young lady would be thinking. Surely the discovery of the remains of a grandmother she never knew would not be a reason to commit suicide. He shook his head and spit the bad taste in his mouth off to the side of the road. He stared at the bridge above and whispered, "No fucking way."

The timing of the tragic death of Gitane's granddaughter this close to the discovery of Gitane Harper's remains was disturbing. In law enforcement investigations, there are very few acceptable coincidences. And this one just did not feel right to Sheriff Webster.

It was true the news of her grandmother's fate could have triggered an emotional meltdown. But it seemed unlikely the discovery of Gitane's bones would be traumatic enough to cause a suicide. It was a grandmother she never knew. Even during the months Willow had spent with her dying mother, every time he visited with her, she had a smile and a positive attitude.

During the dark days of Gitane's vanishing, he had never believed Gitane had taken her own life. Duncan had seen Gitane's same joy of living in her granddaughter. Willow was too confident, too free-spirited, and too comfortable in her own skin to have committed suicide.

Besides, he knew it was best to approach any violent death with caution because there is always a chance of foul play. It was just as possible someone threw Willow off the bridge. Until Kidd found a suicide note or medical red flags, Duncan was going to assume the worst-case scenario and work backward from there. And there was no doubt where he was going to start.

RODNEY KNIGHT

L ater that morning, Rodney Knight woke up at a quarter past ten and lit a cigarette. He was in his late sixties now and had long since been aware of his age. The years with a rock band had taken their toll, and contrary to famous groups who refuse to go away, Rodney and the Roadsters had packed it in long ago—just about the time the area's nightlifers started referring to Rodney and the Roadsters as Rodney and the Oldsters.

The music had gone away, but the rock 'n' roll mindset refused to die. Even after the band folded, the members hung on to their unsavory lifestyle. The dark side of the community had always controlled the local drug culture. The drugs of choice had evolved through the years, but from marijuana and cocaine, to meth and heroin, the band members continued to abuse themselves and others. They bought, sold, and used, avoiding jail time by means of experience and deception.

Knight was the brains behind the small-time operation. He was single for the fourth time and lived in a trailer park on the east side of town. A crafty businessman, he made a point of retaining contact with a younger group of users in order to sustain his presence in the local market. Like the other Rodsters, he stayed under the radar, one layer above the more vulnerable druggies and sellers, not big enough to be a threat to the serious suppliers. He used his age to disguise his drug-culture connection and worked hard to stay anonymous.

The local OPNET, an acronym for Olympic Peninsula Narcotics Enforcement Team, Clallam County's drug-control agency, suspected his connection, but focused their attention on more impactful suppliers. The little guys may have aided the problem, but they hadn't created it. It was the big guys that OPNET worried about and wanted.

Still, Rodney made a point of spending some time with prospective customers. He was careful never to be in the wrong place at the wrong time, or to associate publicly with any unfamiliar users—sellers or buyers. Though no longer the rock 'n' roll party animal he used to be, he was not opposed to an occasional evening of trying to keep up with a small group of customers and friends thirty years his junior.

The previous night was one of those times. He and two young friends had gone to the west side of town. It was a typical druggie function. They drank some whiskey, smoked some weed, and snorted some coke. The lost souls at the party chose meth, and the beyond-help shooters sought empty bedrooms or slid down to the basement for fixes of meth or heroin.

Knight had overindulged and was struggling to wake up. He sat up in his bed and tried to stretch stiff muscles and get his head to clear. He mumbled, "Christ, I must have gotten really fucked-up last night."

Rolling out of bed, he limped to the kitchen, fixed a bowl of cold cereal, and made a pot of coffee—Starbucks of course, his only concession to modern social behavior. He turned on the kitchen radio for the company the noise provided, sat down at the table, and lit a cigarette, groaning as he leaned back in his chair and blew a smoke ring out above his head. Local radio station KONP was running through the morning sports news.

He was watching the perfect circle of smoke when a "Breaking News" alert interrupted the program on the radio. He groaned again, pushed himself up, and turned up the volume.

"This just in. The Port Angeles PD has reported that, sometime early this morning or late last night, there was another suicide on one of the Eighth Street bridges. The body was discovered on Tumwater Drive by an early-rising motorist who called 911. The jumper was a female teenager, and although identified, the Port Angeles PD cannot release her name until family has been notified. KONP will keep you posted as we receive information."

The DJ finished the announcement and added his own comment, "Another tragic death for a troubled teenager. Will it ever end?"

Rodney listened carefully. The party last night was five blocks from the Tumwater Bridge. He finished the rest of the coffee and called one of last-night's drinking partners who had driven him to the party…and maybe back home too.

His buddy didn't answer the phone. So Rodney took two aspirins before lying down on his couch, paying no attention to the nicotine-soaked cushions and beat-up copies of smut magazines scattered on the floor around the piece of furniture. He needed a nap.

* * *

After Rodney woke up, the next radio announcement he heard came in the late afternoon. The DJ said, "KONP's Kim Crandell has just returned from the Port Angeles PD headquarters. What have you got for us, Kim?"

A young woman answered in a shaky voice a decibel or two too loud, "Well, Brian, according to Detective Jonathan Kidd, who is heading the investigation, the body has been identified as a young woman named Willow Shepard. The Port Angeles PD says the death of the eighteen-year-old girl was most likely a suicide. However, there was no suicide note, and her father and friends say there was never a sign of depression. Consequently, officials will conduct a routine investigation of the death. The body will be autopsied by the state's crime lab, and forensic techs will look for any signs of foul play."

She exhaled a breath and added, "There will be no further official press releases until cause of death is confirmed."

The DJ closed with, "Thank you, Kim. Better safe than sorry, right?"

Rodney Knight could not breathe. The suicide victim was his own granddaughter. His hands were shaking when he snapped off the radio and tried to light another cigarette

* * *

When Knight and Gitane were first married, they lived a rock-group's lifestyle—sex, drugs, and muscle cars. But when their daughter, April, was born shortly after the wedding, everything changed. Gitane switched from rocker to mother in less than three months after the baby's arrival; Rodney and Gitane's marriage ended. The baby canceled out any semblance of the bandleader's preferred lifestyle.

The couple's parting had been horrific and interminable. Rodney accepted no claim to the child, refused to pay child support, and focused on providing a living hell for his ex-wife.

When his daughter, April, grew up, married, and had her own daughter, Rodney Knight continued to reject any kind of familial connection. He had a granddaughter he had never seen...and he did not care.

FOUL PLAY?

When the media found out the suicide victim was the granddaughter of the recently identified remains discovered in the Lake Aldwell drawdown, the story went viral.

"These clowns have lost all interest in their purpose of being here," Sheriff Webster told his staff. "Something as unfortunate and sad as the deaths of these women—loosely connected to the dam removal—has turned the *New York Times* into the *National Enquirer*. It doesn't make any sense, and it sure as hell doesn't help us do our job."

Duncan held up the front page of a newspaper. The headline read:

Cold Sisters
Another LADY OF THE LAKE?

He said, "This is today's edition of the *Seattle Tribune*... trying to tie Willow's death to the Lake Crescent murder and referring to the Lake Aldwell death as a copycat Lady of the Lake. All sixty-four media sources are looking for the most sensational spin possible."

Deputy Berger said, "That's bullshit. We don't have any soap-statue body here. What we got is a closed murder case from the midseventies that no one has cared about for years, and now a girl who jumped off a bridge who *might* be connected to the skeleton found in the lake. All turned into a worldwide circus."

Sheriff Webster let the deputy ramble on and watched his team for their reaction. When Leon finished, Webster said, "First of all, somebody *did* care about the girl who was found in Lake Aldwell. *Me. I* cared about Gitane's disappearance. And I still do. Part of what you say is true, though. *Nobody else* cared. As to the suicide, with what we know now, I think it makes sense to look for possible ties to the two deaths.

"That said, for me, the suicide is what doesn't make sense here. The granddaughter is two generations removed from Gitane. What the hell's the point? Taking her own life after Gitane's remains were identified doesn't work for me. Why would she do that? No depression. No warning signs. No suicide note. Why?"

In response, there were several shrugged shoulders and lots of blank faces.

"I think I'll circle up with the cold case group. They're very good at connecting the dots. Even if this thing doesn't go back that far, they might give us some helpful information."

* * *

Webster met with Julianna Judd and her cold case team at 10:00 a.m. the next morning. He told them, "As the saying goes, boys and girls, 'the plot thickens.' I know you have all heard about the suicide, and I assume you know the jumper was Gitane Harper's granddaughter.

"Detective Kidd called me to the scene when they found the body yesterday. I was under Tomb Water Bridge, and I don't know if I'm buying the suicide. The body was so messed up that it's difficult to pinpoint any obvious foul play, but to me, it just doesn't feel right.

"Jon has asked me to be involved, and we need all the help we can get. We're sending the body to the crime lab in Seattle, and I asked Kidd to be the front man for the autopsy. Dr. Suzuki is not happy about the international press running her lab, and I think the Port Angeles PD can actually help separate the suicide from the dam project."

"Good luck with that," said Erik Landers, the ex-detective from Chicago. "The media guys working on the dam are so fired up about the skeleton in the lake, you can't take a leak in a San-A-Can out there without it going online."

"I know. That's why we need to resolve the suicide ASAP. Any ideas? Suggestions?"

"Yeah," said the detective, "get the cause of death nailed down. If she jumped, we need to find out why. If she didn't, we got ourselves two homicides—an old one and a new one."

"You're right, Erik. But if someone did throw her off the bridge, why would they do that? If Willow *was* killed, I think we have to look for a connection to the remains we found in Lake Aldwell."

* * *

Duncan was sitting in his office the next day when the telephone rang on his private line. He picked up and said, "Webster."

"Ah, Webster. This is Dr. Suzuki. I just talked with Detective Kidd and asked if he would mind if I shared this information with you. I guessed that you were the most interested person involved."

"What do you mean? The suicide is Jonathan's case. I'm just a sounding board for the Port Angeles PD."

"Don't bullshit me, Sheriff. I watch TV too. It doesn't take someone from the Paul Allen Brain Institute to know that when a body turns up and a relative of the victim's body dies two days later, there might be a connection. We ran the body this morning. It turns out you were right. The girl was dead before she went off the bridge."

Duncan tried to stay calm. "Really! What'd you find, Doc? It looked like a dozen things could have killed her."

"A dozen things could have. But only one did. Someone who knew what they were doing put a choke hold on her and left it there long enough to kill her. It's the submission tactic that most of your fellow police officers screw up and get in trouble for using. It is impossible to detect without an autopsy because you have to dissect the neck tissue. The diagnosis is asphyxia due to manual compression of the neck. This girl was strangled before she went off the bridge."

After a pause, she added, "And I must say, the method of the crime was quite ingenious. The murderer didn't use his fingers, so there were no external signs of trauma. The body was a mess, making the cause of death difficult to pick up, with all of the other body damage—broken bones, internal impact trauma, and massive skin abrasion. There is no way it would be detected without an autopsy. Unless it's requested, most of these types of suicides are not autopsied because of the obvious destruction."

Webster listened to the details, thrilled by the information...and sickened by the news.

"There's more, Sheriff. That girl was not dead very long before she hit the ground. I think she may have been killed on the bridge...or very close to it. If you're a killer and you want messy, you have to be quick. Rigor mortis can begin less than an hour after death. Rigor stops all bodily functions. Including blood flow. Your killing did not take place too far away."

Webster was riveted as he mentally calculated the blocks from Willow's house to the bridge.

"Thank you for the assist, Doctor. Suicide didn't feel right. She was different, but not mentally out of sync."

"Well, if she *was* out of sync, you and she had something in common."

"Yeah? What's that?"

"You forgot to tell me that the skeleton you brought me last week was an old girlfriend of yours, Webster. I don't like not knowing all the details."

Duncan was stunned anyone beyond the cold case unit and his staff would have knowledge of the childhood romance. "How did y—"

The doctor cut him off in mid-sentence, "Detective Kidd. If you want to keep things quiet, you should probably tell your friends to be careful what they say. Of course, after he slipped up, he made me promise not to tell you or share it with anyone else. I promised…but I lied. I don't feel too bad about telling *you* though." She paused and then said, "You know, Webster, I wouldn't have said anything if you had told me. And you can relax…because I won't tell anyone about it now either."

"I know. But you can see why I didn't. The bones we found in the trunk belonged to a schoolmate of mine. We were in junior high school when we dated. I couldn't care less who knows that…except for the newspapers, television stations, and Internet idiots who will turn it into something it wasn't. They'll make an ancient ninth-grade puppy love into Romeo and Juliet. I couldn't do that to Gitane…or my wife."

"I understand. That is why, next time, you should tell me. I'm a scientist. These types of things are irrelevant to me and always confidential." She added, "You might have noticed that I don't put up with much bullshit."

"No offense, but I think the hard-ass attitude is all for show, Doc. I get more indebted to you every time I work with you."

The scientist grunted. "Don't bother, Sheriff. I don't need any strokes from the peanut gallery. I can't believe you even had a girlfriend. Let alone one who would put up with you for more than a day or two."

Duncan laughed. "You don't fool me, Doc. I know you love me."

Dr. Suzuki hung up. Again.

As soon as Duncan got off the phone with the doctor, he called Jon Kidd. Not to embarrass him by mentioning his slip of the tongue—he was too excited by the doctor's news and more interested in talking about how the two law enforcement agencies were going to deal with the shocking results of the crime lab's autopsy.

"When the news of another killing breaks, the media people are going to be all over us. I'm almost positive these two cases are connected somehow, and I think the killer might have murdered the granddaughter because he's running scared. When the news goes public, it might spook him. What would you think if I met with the cold case team today to review the data from Gitane's original disappearance? If Willow's case *is* connected, the killing itself tells us the perp is getting desperate. I'll work with the cold case people to put everything together. Then we can meet to assemble a game plan."

The detective was quiet. When he spoke, he said, "I agree with you, Web...but we need to be careful here. This thing is getting dicey, and I think transparency is critical.

"I'm sorry about the girl. I know that's tough for you. But it just might give us something to work with that isn't twenty-whatever years old. Your logic makes sense to me. We know *someone* murdered Willow...and we don't want to spook the killer.

"But don't stall too long. Meet with the old-timers and let's get going."

* * *

For the second day in a row, the cold case squad and the sheriff gathered in the team's office to avoid media personnel who might be hanging around the courthouse. All the volunteers were there and excited that the crime lab had discovered the foul play. The possible connection of Willow's death to their own cold case involving the girl's grandmother gave them a unique opportunity to work on a case unburdened by the usual constraints of a cold case in which all information was ancient and most suspects long dead.

Duncan was just as excited about the news as the team of veteran police officers. Finding Gitane's remains was the first glimmer of hope in twenty-five years. Her granddaughter's murder might offer other clues. And he would have a talented group of elite ex-cops to help determine the relevance of the new information.

When he was investigating Gitane's original disappearance, he was focused on only one person of interest, her ex-husband, Rodney Knight. It was true her killer could have been a burglar or an unhappy lover, but Webster didn't think so. Duncan did not like Rodney Knight, and Knight was the only one who had a motive. But he had an alibi. Duncan didn't like the character of the man's witnesses—they were all band members and groupies—and he knew they would all lie for the man.

The sheriff knew that his own department needed to focus on the Willow Shepard murder. But the cold case team was a different story. He said, "I need you guys to concentrate on Gitane's cold case. If you find there *is* a connection, you will obviously be involved in both cases. We're all in this together, and I need your help to search for any hint of a connection.

"Julianna tells me each of you received a copy of Gitane's file yesterday. That's perfect. Does anyone have ideas or suggestions?"

Detective Erik Landers, the Chicagoan, cleared his throat and said, "I've been thinking about this since we got the file. This might be a long shot, but I seem to recall Gitane's husband's rock band had something to do with cars? Hot rods, maybe?"

"That's correct—Rodney and the Roadsters. All of them muscle-car geeks and motorcycle freaks."

"That's what I thought. So the WSP identified the car in Lake Aldwell as a 1965 Mustang, right? Does that seem like a car a hot-rodder might own?"

The question was like switching on a light in Duncan's head. Before Erik could continue, he said, "I see where you're going with this. It sure as hell does. The Mustang was at least ten years old when it went into the lake. Affordable. Desirable. Plus, it was confirmed that the Mustang in the lake was a 1965 model—which is the Mustang's first year of production. That makes it an iconic car...and a car guy's favorite."

Voice rising, Duncan continued, "Of course! How could I miss it? I'm an idiot." Looking around the table, he explained, "Gitane's ex-husband was a big-time car guy. His band was called the Roadsters, for God's sake. It is very possible that he might have owned a car like that. And, God knows, it could have been stolen and kept under wraps."

Julianna Judd spoke up, "Duncan, you are so obsessed with that man that you aren't thinking clearly. You missed it because you didn't have a car to put into the picture until three days ago. Relax—even if this guy owned the car, which will be hard to document, that does not mean he's the killer. He may be. But you have to keep an open mind. You want him so bad you're trying to mold him into being guilty. I think at some level you are not sure. Otherwise, you would have rung him up years ago.

"And, if you *can* get past avenging Gitane, don't forget Willow Shepard was Knight's granddaughter. If it's him, and the cases are connected, we've got to unwind the man's old alibi...and find a motive strong enough for a man to want to kill his own grandchild."

"Yeah, I know. But if anyone could go that low, it would be him."

WILLOW'S GRANDFATHER

Rodney Knight was not used to someone pounding on his door at nine o'clock in the morning. He rolled off his couch and teetered to his feet, shuffling stiffly to the door and barking, "What the hell?" as he jerked it open.

Sheriff Webster stood without speaking, looking at the old man standing in front of him. Knight's early-morning rising wasn't pretty. He was in his underwear, a stretched-out wifebeater, and scrawny legs were lost in a pair of baggy boxer shorts. His thin arms were covered with tattoos, now faded and distorted on loosening skin. On one shoulder, a black horse and armored knight looked more like a bruise than art, the ink more pathetic than intimidating. There was no beard, but he hadn't shaved for days, and the dark-gray whiskers made his face pale and sallow.

It took a few seconds for Rodney to realize that it was a sheriff. It took a few more seconds to recognize it was Duncan Webster.

"Mr. Knight?" Duncan asked as if he weren't certain who had answered the door. "Can I ask you a few questions?"

Rodney snorted. "We've done this dance before, Sheriff. Whatever you're going to ask me about, it isn't gonna do no good."

"Maybe not. But this time it's all about your own blood, not someone else's. I take it you know your granddaughter committed suicide two days ago, right?"

The pallid color in Rodney's face grew even lighter, a ghostlike shade of white behind the mottled patches of gray stubble. Rodney said, "Yeah, I heard. I don't know nothing about her. I don't think I ever talked to her after me and Gitane split up."

"That's a shame. She was a good kid. But, right now, I'm not interested in your feelings about your family, Rodney. I want to know where you were Saturday night."

"Saturday? Out with friends. At a party. Minding my own business."

"Can you prove that?"

"Yeah, I can. There was a shitload of people there."

"Where's 'there'?"

"I dunno. Over on the west side of town. I went over with a couple of friends. Didn't pay much attention to where we were headed."

"What time did you get home?"

"I dunno. I told you. I was with friends. Why?"

"What friends?"

Knight hesitated and then said, "Lonnie and Roach. A couple of the guys I hang out with."

"Lonnie and Roach? That sounds like a pair to draw to. Do they happen to have last names?"

"I dunno. But I got Lonnie's phone number. I don't know what you're looking for, but you can call him. He'll tell you that I was there."

"I will call him, Rodney. But like you said earlier, we've done this dance before. If you talk to them first, you tell your nameless friends, if they don't show up, I'll find out why they call one of them Roach, and everything else I need to know about both of them. Now, give me that phone number, and I'll give Mr. Lonnie a call."

Duncan waited a few hours to see if Knight would give his friends the warning. Then he called Lonnie and told him to round up Roach and come down to the sheriff department's courthouse office for a visit. Immediately.

The pair showed up less than an hour later.

Webster made it a point to be in the satellite jailer's office, located just past the holding cells, when they showed up. The sheriff liked perps to be aware of possible consequences. Most of them got the message.

"Well, well, Mr. Lonnie and Mr. Roach. Let's go back out front to check your IDs so we can confirm that you actually have last names. Easier to do background checks, you know?"

The two exchanged a glance and followed him to the front desk. They pulled wallets and driver's licenses out and handed them to the sheriff.

Duncan glanced at the IDs and passed them to the deputy behind the front counter. "We can go into my office and chat while the staff does a little research."

When the pair sat down, Lonnie said, "What's this about, Sheriff? We ain't done nuthin'."

"Maybe—I guess we'll find out about that while we talk. But this is not about you. Do you know Rodney Knight?"

Another exchanged look. "Yeah," said Lonnie, "he's an old guy who we babysit every once in a while. We took him to a party on Saturday. He's good for a few laughs early in the night. He's not a strong finisher. Usually passes out early, and we toss him in a bedroom until we split. Then we shove him into the back seat and take him home. That's what happened Saturday."

"Did he call you before I did?"

"No. Why would he? Did something happen to him? We just put him on the couch in his trailer and left."

"What time did the party get over?"

"Who knows? Me and Roach left a couple hours after midnight and took Rodney back to his trailer. Maybe two-ish?"

"You know, boys, we've had incidents with Knight before. It seems like every time he's a suspect, he's been at a party. And the partygoers cover his ass."

"Suspect? I don't know what you're talking about, but I can tell you this—we got no reason to cover his ass for nuthin'. Why would we? If he's done something to get him in trouble, we'll be out of the babysitting duties. We only hang out with him 'cuz he does a little business with us."

"What kind of business?"

"Oh, you know. Just business. Harley parts, some car stuff, shit like that. But we're not about to get involved with anything that has to do with the Rodster. We don't give a rat's ass about him."

Duncan snorted. "Harley parts? Yeah, right."

The sheriff had been a lawman for a long time. He could tell when a suspect was lying. Usually, guys like this pair were lying any time they opened their mouths. He didn't trust them and knew, odds were, they were not telling the truth.

But, today, his instincts weren't as solid as usual. It was possible these scumbags might actually be telling the truth. They didn't care about Rodney. And, unlike the members of the Roadsters, they wouldn't risk getting in trouble for lying just to give the man a break. Then again, maybe they were just covering for Knight to make sure that no damning information would rock their own dirty boat.

Lonnie Evers and Scott "Roach" Appleton had similar rap sheets—a variety of citations and court appearances ranging from traffic violations to possession of a controlled substance. The usual records of chronic offenders. Roach had a brief stay in neighboring Jefferson County's jail. Lonnie, despite a number of similar offenses, had managed to avoid jail time. Not dangerous criminals. But not exactly models of integrity.

After the pair left, Webster tried to organize his thoughts about how Rodney could be involved with both murders. Maybe the two designated drivers, or somebody like them, had done the dirty work. Regardless of the two men's information about Knight's presence, the odd couple's story was shaky at best. Duncan had no intention of writing Rodney Knight off as a person of interest.

To the sheriff, Gitane's scumbag ex-husband was the only person likely to have a strong reason to want Gitane to disappear. And even if Willow's murder was connected to Gitane's, as both the cold case team and the department suspected, why would a payback killing skip a generation?

* * *

The following morning, the desk phone buzzed, and Duncan answered with irritation, "Webster."

Julianna Judd said, "Duncan? Is this a bad time?"

"No, no, Jules. Sorry to be so brusque."

Julianna laughed. "It comes with the territory. The older we get, the crankier we are. So I'll get right to the point. I've been thinking about Detective Landers's car theory from yesterday. Erik's information got me wondering, and I reread your notes about your neighborhood research after Gitane Harper's disappearance. This might not be relevant, but there's a sentence or two in your notes regarding your visit to one of Gitane's neighbors."

Frowning, Duncan leaned forward, planting his elbows on the desktop. "On the Herrick Road, you mean?" he said. "Like what? I have memorized every word of that entire file. I don't recall anything suspicious from anyone on the road."

"I know. I wouldn't, either, without Erik's idea about the car. But there are two sentences there describing Adrian Adams Hawkins's house and farm. Apparently, there were several broken-down pieces of farm machinery and old vehicles scattered around the property. Is it possible he might have been working on a Mustang at that time? I know it's a shot in the dark, but is it something we might follow up on?"

Duncan didn't answer. He had read that file so many times; nothing seemed relevant. Thoughts ran through his mind as he tried to visualize what Adrian's messy farm looked like all those years ago.

Finally, he said, "Jesus H. Christ, Jules. I must be blind. Right in front of my face, and I missed both car clues!"

"For God's sake, Duncan, you keep forgetting we've only had the car to think about for well less than a week. There is no reason anyone would have picked up on it until Gitane's body was discovered when the lake was drained. It wasn't in the picture all those years ago. You've been studying that file for so long that getting out of the box will be impossible. Besides, this is just a thought. Just throwing stuff against the wall to see if anything sticks, you know?"

"I know. And I'm pretty certain Adrian isn't a killer."

Julianna said, "You would have seen it eventually. And besides, it might not help at all. I'm sure the WSP has checked the county's owner registrations, and we would know if they'd found anything there. But there are other resources dedicated to black-market auto marketers. Shall I get one of my people to dig deeper? Most stolen cars have a history... and that means a trail. It's another shot in the dark, but you never know."

"Absolutely. Tell those guys you're trying to help the dumbass local sheriff."

While he waited for the cold case team to do the research on Hawkins, he decided the possible car connection might be another excuse to shake Rodney Knight's cage.

* * *

The next morning, the same time as the previous day's visit, he rapped on the door to Knight's trailer, knowing that it would wake the man eventually and that Rodney would not be happy to see him.

It took even longer than he'd expected before he heard some movement and cursing inside the trailer. When the door finally opened, a very disheveled, very irate Rodney Knight stood glaring at him. "Goddamn you, Webster! What the hell do you want now?"

"Good morning, Mr. Knight. Did I wake you?"

Rodney had wrapped himself in a bathrobe with fifties-style, cord-trimmed lapels, and paper-thin elbows. Once burgundy in color, it had faded to dark pink—coral, maybe—and was mottled with coffee stains and other blotches of unknown origin.

"Very funny. Yeah, you woke me up. What do you want?"

"I just stopped by to see if you remembered anything about Saturday night. Lonnie and Roach tell me you took a long nap at the party."

Rodney's face flushed the color of his robe. "That's bullshit. I laid down for a few minutes maybe. I didn't take no nap."

"Really? Somehow, you guys are not on the same page."

"Fuck those guys. I know what I did."

"Maybe you should agree with what they said, Rodney. It would be helpful for you to be able to account for everything you did that night."

Rodney didn't answer, so Duncan changed the subject to what he really wanted to know. "Just a quick question. A blast-from-the-past type of thing. When you were with the band, what kind of car did you drive?"

"What? What in the hell are you talking about?"

"Just curious. It's not connected to anything. Humor me."

"Humor you! I don't have time for your stupid curiosity. I probably owned twenty different cars throughout those years. What does that have to do with this?"

"Like I said, nothing. Just curious. I know you were a car guy. Did you ever own a Mustang? One of the earlier models?"

Knight stared at him. "You're shittin' me, right? What are you talking about?"

"I'm talking about muscle cars. Any Mustangs in your past?"

"I have no idea where you're going with this, but the answer is no. Most Mustangs ain't real muscle cars. I'm mostly a Chevy guy. Had a couple of Camaros, a beefed-up Malibu, a cherry 409. A few other brands too, even a GTO for a while. Mostly, I rode a lot of bikes. Wrecked more Harleys than most people ever owned. Who cares what I drove, for Christ's sake?"

"How about your band members? The Roadsters? Any Mustang fans there?"

Rodney shrugged. "I don't have no idea. That was a long time ago. Those were fuzzy years. I don't remember every car those guys owned."

"Too bad. Just thought I'd ask." Looking Rodney in the eyes, Webster touched his hat. "Have a nice day. And, Rodney? Make sure you stay in town in case I need to visit with you again."

* * *

Rodney Knight's questionable alibi was frustrating. The sheriff had no doubt that Knight was capable of killing Gitane. But it was hard to imagine that in his obviously declining mental and physical state, he could plan and execute the crime that killed his granddaughter. He would have needed to leave the party undetected, hook up with a driver, perform the crime, throw the body off the bridge, come back to the party, and pass out again in the bedroom.

Even if Lonnie and Roach were lying, Duncan was beginning to wonder if Rodney was capable of formulating and performing such a demanding crime. The theory that Knight had killed Gitane was plausible, even probable, but killing Willow? Questionable. Had he used an accomplice? Were there two different killers?

Duncan's gut told him the deaths of two members of the same family had to be connected. His training told him he had to focus on the newest crime. Everything was fresh. He would keep the cold case team working Gitane's investigation. If there was even a hint of connection, Webster wanted to find it.

ADRIAN ADAMS HAWKINS

Julianna Judd's questions about Adrian Adams Hawkins were hard for Duncan to ignore. Hawkins had always been an enigma—a reclusive loner whose only public appearances were connected to civic debates of controversial issues. As strange as that was, it had been that way for as long as Duncan could remember, which was so long ago that the man's abnormal behavior seemed to be normal.

When Duncan became the sheriff, he had many opportunities to observe the annoying contrarian. Hawkins never missed a public hearing or a city council meeting. Despite the hair and whiskers, he never seemed to age. He'd looked old and grouchy when he got to town, and he'd looked and acted the same way for the past thirty years.

After Gitane's disappearance, the department had run background checks on all the Herrick Road residents. Details about Adrian were sparse. Nothing but age, birth date, and a single sentence about his military service dates. There were no criminal records at all. Not even a traffic ticket. Hawkins was in the military until the early sixties, and after several years in Maine and Montana, he'd bought his place near the Elwha River and the Olympic National Park. His presence at local civic events was so consistent that he was as invisible as the city-council chamber's furniture…until he got to the microphone, where he was always vocal, always ornery, and always a pain…but always harmless. And never violent.

Even so, the sheriff was not looking forward to visiting the county's most aggravating citizen. Duncan asked Deputy Berger to drive him to the Hawkins farm. He wanted someone normal to keep him company on the ride out and back.

Leon Berger was a local who had joined the department eleven years after Webster himself. Leon had grown up in town and gone into the navy shortly after graduating from high school. During his school years, he had always been one of the smaller boys in his class. As such, he was often picked on and the target of pranks and jokes.

When he enlisted, he was five foot nine and 135 pounds. When he came home four years later, he was six foot six and well past 240 pounds. The new Leon had black hair cut in the military style. Clean-shaven except for a dark mustache, he screamed "cop" to anyone who looked at him…in uniform or in off-duty clothes. Leon was an easygoing man who had a good sense of humor. He was fearless and impulsive. Sometimes too fearless and too impulsive.

Duncan and Leon drove past the still-muddy scar from releasing Lake Aldwell, watching the freed river as it carved out a new route through the valley. They talked about the future recovery of the land that had been underwater for over one hundred years. The unveiling had exposed rocks and tree stumps beside the river's natural course throughout the wooded valley. The bottom of the lake was still soft and silty—the visual impression, dark and foreboding—the expected recovery of river and valley years away from returning to their natural splendor. Both men knew the scientists were thrilled with the completion of the dam's removal and were predicting a swift and verdant finished product.

"Pretty amazing, huh, boss? I wonder how it will be when they blow the upper dam."

"I think it will be fine, Leon. Like my mother used to tell my father, 'You shouldn't mess with Mother Nature.' Whether you favored the dam removal or not, this is what Mother Nature had in mind thousands of years ago. What she didn't have in mind was man's failure to recognize the perfect balance of the natural world…and I hope it's not too late to fix it."

A mile past the lake site, they turned off Highway 101 and onto the Herrick Road. Webster looked out the window at the first house on the right and checked out Gitane's old home. It had been sold and resold several times throughout the years and appeared to be well taken care of by the current occupants. Two bikes and a small trampoline sat in the parking lot in front of the recently painted house. Only the roof, with its thick layer of rain-forest moss, hinted at its age.

Even in the early spring, the drive up the road was beginning to change. A weak sun softened the evergreens, and the alder trees were beginning to bud. The road was dry, and pastures cleared of the timber were green.

The private land next to Olympic National Park had become prime real estate over the years, and places were always hard to find since most of the land had been passed down from generation to generation by families who had tried to preserve the land as if it were inside the boundaries of the national park. One of the lucky non-pioneer family landowners was Adrian Hawkins, who owned the farm at the very end of the road, just across from where a trailhead led down to the river and into the national park.

The gated entrance to Adrian's home was ajar. Deputy Berger got out of the cruiser, opened it the rest of the way, and after he got back into the vehicle, they drove the cruiser up the graveled driveway.

Looking out the window, memories of his first visit to Hawkins's farm flooded Duncan's mind. The farm, like its irascible owner, appeared timeless; it was as if he were traveling back in time, going back almost three decades. The grounds were still a mess, with farm machinery and car bodies covered with moss and ferns, as if there were giant plant boxes growing out of rusted fenders and broken windows. Closer to the road, a pair of shedlike outbuildings housed tractors and cars in various states of disrepair.

"For crying out loud, Leon. This place hasn't changed a bit in more than thirty years. This junk must be different, but you could sure fool me."

"Kinda weird, boss. Big surprise, huh?"

They got out of the car and heard tools clanking and someone talking in one of the sheds. Apparently, the workers were focused on a project and hadn't heard them drive in.

Nearing the entrance to the barn-shed, Duncan called, "Hey, Adrian, is that you in there?"

The clanking stopped. "Huh? Is somebody there?"

"Yeah. It's me, Sheriff Webster. Sounds like you've got company. Can we interrupt for a minute?"

Wearing a dirty pair of coveralls and a Hickory shirt, the man came striding out of the front opening, wiping his hands on an even-dirtier rag. "What are you talking about, Sheriff. I don't have any company here."

Leon and Duncan snuck a quick glance at one another.

Hawkins said, "What the hell do you want? You got your ridiculous dam project forced through. I'm done with it. Just leave me alone, and let me watch it destroy things in peace."

"It's not *my* project, Adrian. I'm just the guy they call when someone makes trouble on any project."

"Yeah, right. Every time I see you outside of city hall, you accuse me of somethin'."

"That is because, every time you see me, you are probably causing trouble. But not today. This is just a friendly visit to get some information."

Hawkins cleared his throat and spit over his shoulder. "About what?"

"You heard about the girl who died on Saturday?"

"You mean the bridge jumper? I heard. I read the newspaper."

"Do you know who it is? Was?"

"How the hell would I know that? She doesn't live here, does she?"

"No, that's true. But her grandmother did. The girl that died is Gitane Harper's granddaughter."

Webster was watching the man closely to see how he would react. There was no facial change through the gray whiskers. Even the man's blue-gray eyes didn't change.

Adrian shrugged his shoulders. "So?" he said. "Am I supposed to know her?"

"No, but we think the girl's death might be connected to Gitane's. We're just looking for any information that might help."

"For God's sake, the Harper lady's disappearance took place years ago. How could I have any information?"

"Adrian, we are checking everything. In fact, I almost forgot. Have you ever worked on an old Mustang up here? I know you like playing with old cars. Ever had one of those, or worked on one for somebody else?"

"I've worked on machines for my whole life, Sheriff. As you can see from looking around here, most of them don't go too far away. And I got a good memory. No. I never have worked on a Mustang."

As they headed back to town, Duncan asked the deputy, "Leon, did you notice anything different about Adrian today?"

Leon thought about it. "Well, it's not too different, but I know he's a strange dude. You?"

"Not much. But he did seem to spare us a lot of f-bombs. And that is unusual in a private conversation with Adrian. It was almost like he was trying not to rock the boat for some reason."

"Maybe he's just being respectful, boss. I gotta admit, some of my friends might think it would be unusual if I didn't use the word."

Glancing at his driver, Duncan said, "Good point. But you're a cop—it's part of the culture. Maybe Adrian was just in his public-meeting mode. If he needs to be civil, he can be. But it seems odd in these circumstances. He's still pissed off about the dams, he's got us to complain to, and there's no audience."

Webster shrugged. "Or maybe that's just when he's around me. I seem to bring out the worst in the man."

COLD CASE WARMING

The cold case team was meeting every day now, and when Julianna Judd opened the session, she asked Duncan to share his thoughts about his visit with Adrian Adams Hawkins.

He started slowly, "I've been thinking about the guy all night and all day," he said. "I had to ask myself, *What do we really know about him?* He is a classic loner...until something controversial comes up...and then he's all over the negative side of any pro-or-con issue. He's been around for a long time, and no one knows much about him—where he's from or what he used to do. All we know is he can be a pain in the ass. Ask anyone about him, and they'll say the same thing— 'It's just Adrian.'"

Julianna asked, "You mean no one did a background check?"

"Of course, we did. But it was just a routine scan. Like I said, he's been part of the landscape forever...the cause of a thousand groans and ten thousand headshakes. Like the rest of the folks on that road, he wasn't really a suspect, just a distant neighbor."

The cold case leader said, "Yeah, a distant neighbor who obviously marched to the beat of a different drummer."

"Julianna, it's true Adrian's a piece of work; there's no doubt about it. But he's just a public nuisance, not a criminal. That is the way I handled it. I was, and still am, more focused on Knight. Who, as we know, has a rap sheet as long as my arm."

Judd said, "Duncan, you were young then. And too close to the victim. I'm sure at that time it was the right way to go. But from the outside looking in, this guy is a red flag." She paused and then added, "The good news is, from a background-research standpoint, he's right in our cold case wheelhouse. If this team can't do background checks, we shouldn't be here. I think you said at a prior meeting that Mr. Hawkins might have had a military background? If that's true, we should be able to access his records. Those bastards don't throw anything away."

She looked at Harold and Jean Carpenter, the husband-and-wife couple of undersheriffs from Southern California. "You guys worked the San Diego area for some time, right? You might have worked with the military-records people there once in a while?"

The couple exchanged a private smirk. "Every day, Jules, every day," Mrs. Carpenter said.

Judd was in her bureaucratic element. She knew there was more police work done on a computer than there was in the field. And she was interested in the original oversight. This was something that might provide another piece of the puzzle, and she knew her crew could excel at it.

Duncan sat with his arms crossed and his face impassive. He had visited every house on the Herrick Road, asking about Gitane the day she vanished years ago. None of them were suspects. None of them really required comprehensive background checks.

But one of them was different, and he knew it. He had spent all those years looking at the file without it registering. No matter what the team's intensive background check turned up, he knew he should have done a more thorough job on Gitane's case.

But he still believed the bad guy was Rodney Knight.

* * *

The next morning at 8:00 a.m., Julianna Judd walked into the lobby of the sheriff's office with a manila envelope under her arm. "Is Duncan here yet? I need to see him as soon as possible."

The uniform at the desk jerked his thumb toward the back and said, "He's been here for hours. I'll let him know you're here."

A few minutes later, the deputy came back to the front desk. "He'll see you now, Ms. Judd. He's on his way."

Duncan met the cold case director before she had time to step away from the front desk. He led her to his office and pulled a chair for her to the front of his desk, which was buried in stacks of messy crime reports and computer printouts.

"Hey, Jules, you're up early for a retiree. Can I get you a cup of coffee?"

"No thanks. I'm good."

He poured himself a third mug of black coffee, while Julianna fidgeted with her hair and examined her fingernails. Then he eased himself into his chair and turned to look at her, raising his eyebrows in question.

"I'm glad you sat down, Duncan. I've got some rather surprising news." She took some pages out of the envelope and did a quick scan of them.

Sheriff Webster watched her, trying to read her face for a clue about the nature of the news. *Surprising* could mean something good or bad. Leaning back in his chair, he said, "Shoot."

"The positive news is we found Adrian Adams Hawkins in some recently released classified military records. The bad news, and the surprising part, is the man is not, and never has been, what everyone thought he was." She took a breath and stopped.

"And?"

"According to the government, Mr. Hawkins was a decorated soldier before and during the war in Vietnam. But not just any soldier," she said. "For a short time, he was also an operative member of the United States Special Forces Division."

Duncan felt his eyes open wide. Staring at his friend, he tried to process what she had just said. Setting his coffee mug on his desk, he asked, "Special Forces? What are you saying? I was in the army myself. Spec Ops is elite stuff. What the hell are you talking about?"

"I'm talking about US Special Forces Operations and the Green Berets, Duncan. And Sergeant Adrian Adams Hawkins, who was injured in action in Vietnam during the war. The only Adrian Adams Hawkins in all four major branches of the armed forces. The one who was diagnosed with PTSD, post-traumatic syndrome disorder, and released from service with an honorable discharge. The one who would be the exact age as Port Angeles's own longtime nuisance of the same name. That is what I'm talking about."

The sheriff was beyond speechless, still wondering whether the cold case director was messing with him or was serious. Her stone-cold cop face did not make it look as if the news was a joke.

"So…you're saying…this guy…who's lived here for years… is actually a Green Beret veteran with an honorable discharge?"

She ignored the redundant question and went right to why she was there. "The man was discharged in the midsixties—diagnosed with PTSD. He drew Special Forces health benefits for years. Then, in 1979, the benefit checks he had been receiving, while living in Montana, ceased being cashed, and the army lost track of him. He disappeared. They tell me the suicide rate for Special Forces veterans is extremely high. So after several years of unclaimed benefit checks, he was classified as assumed dead, and his military benefits were cancelled.

"My team believes this guy is not the harmless pest that everyone thinks he is. We think his background screams you include him in your investigation as a serious person of interest. But, Duncan, you should know these things can be dicey when classified documents are involved. Covert-action records are often conveniently lost or misplaced. We were lucky to get what we did, and I think what we got is where we have to start. I don't believe there are too many Adrian Adams Hawkinses out there. If his name was Jim Smith, we might have been in trouble. But it is amazing how quickly computers can dial in on anomalies.

"With your approval, we will track down everything the government is willing to share. The political scars of the war have healed, and the changing times have made Vietnam top-secret records a little more accessible than they used to be."

The impact of this new information staggered Sheriff Webster. If it was true, it had the potential to turn this case upside down. He said, "I think you need to find out everything you can about Adrian's military history. A Green Beret? It doesn't seem possible, but if it is, Julianna, we most certainly have ourselves another person of interest.

"I'll visit Mr. Hawkins again this afternoon. If he confirms this information, and we can get him to talk, we may not have to deal with any of the army's possible covert roadblocks."

Still doubtful, the sheriff said, "It's hard to imagine the or-nery son of a bitch was an elite soldier. Those guys were, and still are, really something. And why would he kill Gitane? Where's the motive? There must be something else."

But Julianna Judd did not look as if she thought there was going to be something else. She knew military records were pretty much rock solid, and she knew the strange hermit who lived just ten miles outside of Port Angeles was, indeed, an ex-Green Beret.

VIETNAM

Adrian Adams Hawkins was born in Northern Maine in 1949 and raised on a small farm chopped out of the northeast woodlands in the corner of the state. His father, Rupert Hawkins, was a World War II veteran who had landed in Normandy on D-Day and fought in several key battles, including the Battle of the Bulge, the military campaign in which American forces suffered the greatest number of casualties of any battle in the war.

Rupert came home after the war with medals for bravery and a Purple Heart as a result of injuries suffered in action at the Bulge. He also came home with what his family and friends called shell shock or battle fatigue. Eventually, he would heal from the physical wounds, but would never escape the depression and anxiety of the war.

Mr. Hawkins never spoke of his wartime experiences. Adrian's mother told her son that his father came back a changed man and had never recovered his prewar, outgoing personality. Even so, he was proud of his service and did not begrudge his sacrifices.

Rupert had watched his only son grow up playing war with neighboring farm kids and dreaming of winning a Medal of Honor, like Audie Murphy or other military heroes. As Adrian approached his teens, his father's level of angst seemed to worsen. As much as Rupert loved his country, he loved his son more. The threat of another war, less than twenty years after his own, was unsettling for Adrian's father, who knew the true horrors of war.

Adrian had grown up a farm boy, tending livestock, mending fences, and fixing broken-down tractors and trucks. When he wasn't working or playing with friends, he spent every free hour in the Maine woods, hunting, fishing, and camping during all four seasons. He loved the outdoors with its survival challenges. He loved the solitude and the adventure of proving himself in the wild. And he longed to leave the farm and experience a more adventurous lifestyle.

Three days after graduating from high school, Adrian enlisted in the US Army. He had one goal—to become a member of a commando unit—fighter pilot, paratrooper, or, especially, Special Forces duty. That would fulfill his dreams.

In those days, Special Ops candidates—Green Berets—were required to serve at least three years in the regular army before being eligible to apply. Adrian had a gift for mechanics and spent his three years biding his time, stationed in stateside military posts as a motor-pool engine expert. Ever aware of his ultimate goal, he didn't smoke or drink, worked hard on a fitness program, and tried to be a perfect soldier. He re-upped, submitted his application for Special Forces a month before the end of his three years, and a week later was invited to apply for a position in the elite program.

The first day of the Special Ops training, Adrian met fellow trainee Morris Bullard. Where Adrian was of average height and slender, with sinewy muscles and small bones, Morris was six foot two inches tall and 215 pounds of chiseled muscle. He measured the lowest percentage of body fat of any man in the training unit. His skin had the leathery look that seems to be permanent for every year-round outdoorsman. Morris had done a tour in Vietnam without serious combat exposure and was eager to join a fighting unit. Adrian thought Morris Bullard could have been the model for Special Forces recruiting posters.

When Adrian shook hands with his fellow trainee, Bullard said, "Hey, brother, I guess we're gonna spend some time together." He grinned. "Let's have some fun, man!"

The taciturn Hawkins nodded; his conservative East Coast upbringing had left him unsure how to deal with the almost-giddy Idaho rancher.

"How great is this?" Bullard gushed. "It looks like we're finally gonna get to where the action is."

"Yeah, maybe. They say it's gonna be a long haul before we get the chance."

"Nah," said Bullard, "time flies. We'll be too busy to count the days. We're gonna see some action, bro. I can't wait."

For both soldiers, it was as if they had discovered a long-lost brother with whom their brains were hardwired.

As the training went forward, fellow candidates considered Adrian to be unusually intense. They thought Morris Bullard was deranged.

Throughout the twenty-two-month training program, the Maine introvert and the gung-ho Idaho cowboy developed a unique relationship. They shared unbounded passion for the cause and pride in their skills. Special Forces team members were a brotherhood of warriors dedicated to serving their country—and each other.

At the end of the program, and with both men having five years in the United States Army, Adrian Hawkins and his friend Morris Bullard were Green Berets.

Shortly thereafter, the two new sergeants were stationed in Vietnam, preparing for their first reconnaissance and training mission with their allies in the South Vietnamese Army. They were scheduled to depart that afternoon and had spent the morning organizing jungle-camouflage fatigues, checking and rechecking their small-arms weapons, and painting their faces and hands with glare-reduction "jungle grease." They talked quietly to calm their nerves and speed the time.

Bullard said, "Are you ready, brother? This is what we've been waiting for. I can't wait. Let's get this rodeo started."

Hawkins laughed. "Relax, Bull. We still got some time. What are you gonna do with your dog tags?"

"Good question. Why don't we do something cool to celebrate our first gig?"

On Special Forces missions, team members were not allowed to wear their identity tags. The covert nature of most missions discouraged *any* means of revealing the clandestine nature of the group.

Bullard said, "Let's hang these things together here at home base until we finish this gig, so's we always remember we're brothers, and we have each other's back."

Adrian nodded. "Good idea. We should make it a tradition when the missions start to get serious."

* * *

The helicopter rotors on the Bell H-13 chopper thudded in Hawkins's ears, and he strained to hear the squad-leader's voice over the beat of the metallic drum.

The lieutenant in charge, riding in the co-pilot's seat, looked over his shoulder and shouted to the soldiers, "We should be there any minute now. The good guys have hacked out a landing area in the jungle, and we'll debark there. Commando HQ says the friendlies will meet us and take us to their training area to set up the op."

Looking into the eyes of each team member, he continued, "Intel says there has been some Cong activity in the area, and they may have located the clearing. So be ready. We don't know what the fuck is going to happen."

The team members exchanged glances.

Sergeant Bullard winked at Sergeant Hawkins and flipped him a cool one-handed thumbs-up. "Bring it on, boss. We're ready." He looked at Adrian. "Aren't we, Hawk? It's time to rock 'n' roll!"

For the two new Green Berets, their first mission would be a training assignment, and each was disappointed it was not battle oriented or a recon patrol. Rather, it was a training session for South Vietnamese allies, and the team was trying not to get too amped-up.

Adrian said, "Relax, Bull. This is a teaching op. Just like boot camp, you know? Only we are the generals, and they're the dogs. I'm thinking we might have to save the rock 'n' roll for when we hit the combat zone."

Bullard shook his head. "I don't know, man. I've got a feeling about this one. Sometime on this assignment, we're gonna light those guys up."

The veteran pilot looked over his shoulder. "Get ready, girls; we're ninety seconds from the drop. I'm not seeing anything down there. Maybe our friends are late for the pickup. Be careful when you hit the ground. I do not trust anything out here. It feels a little too quiet for a friendly hookup."

He hovered the chopper above the center of the clearing, nice and easy, thirty yards from the edge of the jungle on all sides.

The lieutenant in charge of the op shouted over the pounding of the rotors and engine, "Sprint to the hut on the back edge of the clearing. Not too close together. We'll circle up there. The bird jockey is right. I don't like not seeing a welcoming party. They're supposed to be a big part of the mission."

The pilot shouted, "Be quick, Soldiers. I'm gonna touch 'n' go!"

The six Berets focused on the dangerous unloading, knowing they needed to land on their feet and on the run. The lieutenant jumped out of the bird, the others right behind him. When the last man hit the ground, the world exploded.

As if they were giant hailstones crashing onto a tin roof, a rain of bullets hammered the helicopter. Automatic-weapons fire streamed across the open field with no protection for the departing soldiers. The men scattered to spread the enemy fire.

Hawkins heard a man scream over the gunfire, not six strides from the chopper. He could hear the bullets ricocheting off, and thudding into, the helicopter.

The bird lifted off, rising twenty yards or so before the nose tilted down just seconds before it cartwheeled and crashed to the ground, bursting into flames and putrefying the air with the rancid smell of exploding fuel and boxes of ammo, which had been stored inside the helicopter.

Hawkins saw the looey and the second man sprawled out on the ground in front of him. The helicopter's crash drew cheers from the jungle shooters, diverting their attention from the troops who had landed.

Adrian ran, zigzagging behind Bullard, who was limping badly and trying to reach the jungle. He watched Bull dive into the dense underbrush and, five seconds later, threw himself into the heavy vegetation right behind his wounded friend. The surprise attack had been catastrophic. The two Berets low-crawled through the dense jungle floor, desperate to find a place to hide.

Bullard was gasping for breath, the resultant sound both hoarse and bubbling. The Idaho cowboy rolled into an overgrown, dry creek bed and buried his face in the leaves, lying on the damp ground.

Hawkins was right behind him and began pulling vines and jungle foliage over their bodies. Gasping for air, he wormed himself to his buddy's side. "Bull! Take it easy, man. They're gonna be looking for us. We've got to be quiet."

Bullard's head rolled to one side, and he croaked, "I can't move, Hawk. I'm shot up. Even my legs are fucked-up." Grabbing the ammo belts crossed over Adrian's chest, he said, "Don't let 'em get me, man. I don't want them to get me."

Hawkins whispered, "Just hang in there, big guy. The cavalry will be here soon. If we're quiet, we'll be okay." Hawkins rolled Bull onto his back and pulled his shaking body into his lap. He could feel the sweat and smell the blood, and hoped his friend could control his pain. "Just rest, bro. The boys will be here to get us soon. We've just got to stay quiet."

When Bullard's labored breathing finally ceased, Adrian knew he was holding a dead man.

Now he was alone. He had heard the Cong looking for them, but he didn't think they would search for long. The Charlies never stayed in the same place if they knew the US Army would show up. He knew the downed helicopter was more important than two dead or dying soldiers. And he thought Bull's silence ended the most dangerous threat of discovery. Without the sound of the dying man's fight for breath, Hawkins had a chance.

An hour later, he heard the chopper coming. He crawled out of the hole and, fanning his AK-47 back and forth from a crouching position, worked his way to the center of the clearing. He could smell the stench of the burnt helicopter, still smoldering in layers of smoke, and could see the charred body of the pilot.

The rescue bird circled over the wreckage before they spotted the waving soldier. The pilot was leery of a Viet Cong decoy trying to lure another victim to join the fate of the first copter. Only when his spotter recognized the Caucasian body and miliary garb did the pilot drop into the clearing. The two-man rescue crew urged Hawkins to hurry and pulled him into the helicopter.

Over the noise of the beating rotors, Hawkins shouted to the airmen, "We got bodies here, guys! We can't leave!"

The pilot shouted back, "They're sending a backup detail to get the bodies. Our job is just looking for survivors. If you're the only guy left, sit down and buckle the fuck up!"

"They won't find my friend. He's dead back in the jungle!"

"Just buckle in, Soldier. They'll find him. Did anyone else make it? Anyone else who might still be alive?"

"I don't think so. I'm the only one."

"Then let's go, brother. We'll get you home. They'll find your friend. It's what they do."

Hawkins hunched down in his seat, arms and legs pulled into his body. He was shaking, scared, and in shock. He understood only one thing—he was safe—saved because another man died. His best friend died. And he lived.

When the tremors began to slow, he checked his own body, which smelled of sweat, fear, and the jungle ground of rotted leaves and vines. He checked his hands, arms, torso, stomach, and legs. Not a scratch. Not a bruise. He was sore and dirty, and that was it. His eyes filled with tears. Just dirty.

Once the airmen found out he wasn't hurt, no one said a word to him on the flight back to the base. Hawkins held his face—a smear of camouflage paint, dirt, and tears—in his hands and tried to curb the terror of the failed mission. He began to whisper, trying to talk himself back to normal. He said the same thing over and over, "It's gonna be okay, Bull. We're gonna make it. We're gonna be okay." He had no idea those three sentences would haunt his dreams for the rest of his life.

WING IN PARADISE

A drian spent ten days in a Hanoi hospital before the army sent him home on an extended leave. Less than a month after the Viet Cong attack was over, Adrian's uncut dark hair and patchy new beard began to change. Six weeks later, both had turned to an ashen gray with a few streaks of black.

In the States, doctors at Walter Reed Hospital in Washington, DC, quickly determined the Green Beret was not suited for any further combat assignment. The United States Army mustered him out of service with an early honorable discharge.

Following his departure from the US Army, Adrian Hawkins struggled to cope with his emotional meltdown. He spent most of the next year living with his parents in Maine and trying to reconnect with old friends and classmates. The group had no clue about how to help their friend, and with a misguided attempt to take Adrian's mind off the war, encouraged him to drink until he blacked out every weekend and to get high whenever they were not drinking. Some of his more reckless buddies even coaxed him into experimenting with more dangerous drugs. The escape into alcohol and drugs didn't work. The nightmares and anxiety attacks grew worse, rather than better.

Finally, a three-day winter trek into a remote and trailless sector of the wild Maine woods served as a personal epiphany. The hike was dangerous, uncomfortable, and challenging.

And it was quiet. No alcohol. No dope. Before the end of the trip, Adrian knew that his only hope of controlling his depression would be isolation and solitude.

Two days after he got home from the woods, he stole his father's farm pickup and headed west. He wanted real mountains, wild animals, and rugged weather. A place where he could avoid people, stress…and reality.

When he first saw the beauty of the snow-covered Rocky Mountains, he felt alive for the first time in over a year. When he descended through Glacier National Park on the western slopes, he knew that somewhere in that wild mountain country was where he wanted to be. He spent the next three days searching the countryside in the United States and Canada, asking people questions, looking for the perfect fit.

In the northwest corner of the state of Montana, a few miles from the southern border of British Columbia, Adrian Hawkins found the treasure he was seeking. In a valley buffered by the Kootenai National Forest, and accessed by a road to nowhere, was a tiny town called Yaak. The miniscule anchor of the Yaak River Valley, the town consisted of four buildings—a small store, two dive bars, and a laundromat—to serve a population of less than a hundred full-time residents in the forty-mile-long secluded valley.

Adrian had stumbled on a valley of misfits living a lifestyle that could only be duplicated in the depths of the Alaskan wilderness. The valley was a time capsule for those looking for a simpler life in an isolated location.

Fifty miles from the nearest law enforcement, alcoholics could drive home without worrying about DUIs. Bail jumpers, child-support dodgers, and women not wanting to be found by abusive husbands lived in the valley. There were a few normal residents as well, but to live there full time required at least a touch of uniqueness—most of the folks who lived there were escaping from something.

The protected landscape was thick with uncut timber and home to a myriad of wild creatures. Deer, elk, and moose were plentiful, their populations kept in check by nature's predators; bears, mountain lions, wolves, and coyotes shared the woods. Prey or predator was the rule of the land, and the Yaak River its lifeline. Subsistence living was the norm… and a no-questions-asked code was the unwritten law. For Adrian Hawkins, the valley was paradise.

Adrian used some of the money he had saved from his Special Forces disability benefits to buy a piece of property on the river at the end of a rough, unpaved road. He used his farm skills to build a log cabin from timber cut from his own land with help of a ragtag group of locals. The helpers offered a variety of skill sets. The valley had one man with plumbing skills, one electrician, and a half dozen carpenters. Everyone who helped was paid with cash for their services. Like many of those living in the valley, all of the helpers were identified only by first names or nicknames—Mule, Pirate, Thunder, Bear, and even two different deep-woods Yaakers known only as Buck.

Adrian had always been called Hawk, but he thought that nickname was too close to his surname…and his military memories. He liked the idea of a subtle hint to his real last name and decided the name Wing would fit his new home. So from the beginning, the valley knew him only as Wing.

He picked up his monthly check from a post office box in the town of Troy, an hour's drive from the Yaak. That was the only piece of mail to ever occupy the box. It was addressed to A. A. Hawkins. Only the post office knew his last name. No one else asked, and no one cared.

As time passed, Wing created a reputation as the best hunter in the valley. Every season, he shot a trophy elk and the biggest whitetail deer. Those legal kills were the only ones anyone ever saw. Like most of the folks in the valley, he poached the occasional deer from the front porch of his cabin, and did so with a clear conscious—valley residents referred to the abundant whitetail deer population as hooved rodents.

Because of the circumstances of his war disability—and the clandestine nature of the elite Special Forces—his disability checks were generous. He did not work. He drove an older Ford pickup truck. He had the best firearms and camping equipment available, and he spent more time in the woods than in his cabin.

It was his love for the valley that drew him back to guarded social interactions. The Yaak was filled with free spirits determined to preserve their simple style of living…and intimate privacy. Passion for preserving their isolated retreat bonded a group of misfits working for a common cause. It was Yaakers against the world, and Wing slowly became a crusader for all Save the Yaak support groups. They fought against a state-paved road the length of the valley, they fought against telephones and television service; most of all, they fought against anything that would draw attention to their private paradise.

A year after he arrived, Wing met a neighbor named Clayton Cooper, who spent summers in a house two miles below his own, and the two men developed a close friendship. Several years later, Cooper moved to the Yaak himself, running from a nasty feud with an old enemy. When the neighbor's foe turned up seeking revenge, Cooper's friend asked Wing for help. In the following confrontation, Cooper, in self-defense, emptied a .38 caliber pistol into his adversary's chest. Wing was at the site of the killing. He was not the killer, but had fired his rifle and grazed the man before the fatal shooting.

For the scarred ex-soldier, the incident triggered a barrage of emotional confusion. The nightmares and anxiety attacks had never gone away, but the isolation had helped with controlling them. He thought the shooting incident and its aftermath of law enforcement legalities and media exposure would be unbearable.

The morning after the shooting, Wing packed his truck with gear, firearms, ammunition, and a few pieces of clothing. He took all of the benefit checks' money he had stashed around the cabin and shed. His friend had rightfully claimed self-defense, and Wing was certain the Montana legal system would uphold the plea. Even so, Wing wanted no part of the investigation or possible discovery. He was heading west.

The benefit checks continued to arrive after he left the valley. They were never picked up. He left no forwarding address. Eventually, the government determined he had indeed disappeared. This decision was not unusual, considering the high proportion of Vietnam War PTSD victims who'd ended their despair by committing suicide.

A year later, Wing bought five acres, which included a dilapidated log cabin and outbuildings, just off the eastern border of the Olympic National Park in the state of Washington. For the broken man, it was a new start. Wing was gone. He was Adrian Adams Hawkins again. He thought the government would have written him off as one of the alarming numbers of PTSD veterans who had taken their own lives. He wanted an escape in which he could fade into a normal life until he became invisible...and still be able to live where nature could calm his mind.

He soon felt comfortable with his new setting. His plan was to develop a small country-mechanic shop on the farm and gradually become a part of the normal world. After settling in, he went to a hardware store in Port Angeles and bought a farm-style mailbox and a packet of black stick-on letters. He knew he would not receive much mail during his stay, but he thought a mailbox could be used as a locator for those who wanted work done on cars or farm vehicles. He bolted the box to a four-by-four post and looked at the finished product.

Adrian Adams Hawkins
Mechanic

DOCTOR WILLIAM FONTAINE

After Julianna's discovery of Adrian Hawkins's military past, everything changed for Sheriff Webster and for her cold case team. Webster's stubborn refusal to consider different suspects began to break down. Adrian Adams Hawkins's background profile had "red flag" written all over it.

Julianna's own impression of Green Berets mirrored that of most Americans, military *or* civilian. Those men were the apex of the US Army fighting corps. Adrian's background was that of an elite soldier. It did not take a psychologist to connect Hawkins's unexpected background to his habitual civilian behavior. It explained everything about the man.

But Julianna knew Duncan would not let the background check make Adrian a murderer. Until the sheriff found a different connection to either Gitane Harper or her granddaughter, Willow Shepard, he would believe that Rodney Knight was the only man with a solid motive and that he had killed both women.

Julianna Judd had not become the chief of police in Oakland by accident. She was bright and tenacious...and tough. She recognized the possibility of Mr. Hawkins's being a victim of some type of war trauma that might greatly impact his profile and mindset. After her visit with Webster, she emailed the information to a San Francisco forensic psychologist with whom she had worked during her law enforcement tenure in Northern California.

Dr. William Fontaine had been a valuable resource in a handful of criminal court cases throughout Judd's California law enforcement career. As a noted psychologist and PTSD expert, he had a relationship with Walter Reed Military Hospital in Washington, DC, because of which he had often been used as an expert witness in California legal cases that centered around psychiatric issues.

Dr. Fontaine was an African American with the regal bearing of a tribal high chief. He was tall and graceful, with white hair and a matching beard. The facial hair was neatly trimmed and, along with eyes the soothing color of a pint of Guinness ale, created an elegantly strong face. He was a stylish dresser whose mere presence in the courtroom screamed "credible" to jury members—regardless of race or color.

When Julianna answered the phone, Fontaine's deep voice brought a smile to her face and a flush to her cheeks.

"Is this the elusive and attractive Julianna Judd who chose to retire in a godforsaken northwest wilderness?"

Julianna laughed. "Illusive? Yes. Attractive? I wish. Almost seventy years old? Yes."

"Ahh, Ms. Judd. You sell yourself short. We're only as old as we feel. What can I do for you?"

Julianna took a deep breath. "Well, it's complicated, William. I'm sure, like the rest of the world, you've seen what's been going on in our little town on the news or online?"

"I have. I thought about you right away. There was another murder two days after the body found in the lake, right?"

"Yes, there was. I'm heading-up a cold case team that's been working on a 1984 missing-person case of the woman found in the lake. As you may know, it turns out that the skeleton found in that case was the grandmother of the young girl whose murder has just been confirmed. Based on the family connection, we think the two killings have a good chance of being linked.

"In fact, we have just turned up a person of interest who is an ex-Vietnam Special Forces guy. I contacted you because we were able to find out the man has a medical history of PTSD and was given a medical discharge. He may not be connected at all—our local sheriff doesn't think he is. But I need to know about PTSD and its possible side effects. Characteristics. Consequences. Anything that might help me put together a decent profile sheet on the suspect."

"Well…that *is* complicated." He paused then said, "Where do I start? I can give you an overview, Julianna. But you should know it is impossible to pinpoint anything without working with the patient. Every PTSD victim's case is as different as everyone's fingerprints."

"I know. An overview would be great. Short and sweet, William. I'll cross him off the list if there's nothing that fits."

"Okay. Here goes. A war veteran who has problems with loud noises and has anxiety issues will react—and recover—differently than one who has lost half the men of his squad in a disastrous firefight. So symptoms are wildly diverse, ranging from alcoholism and drug use to anxiety, depression, or difficulty functioning in a normal work environment. If the sufferer is chronic, a variety of dark symptoms or side effects can ensue—anger issues, verbal abuse, violence. The worse the trauma, the less likely to achieve a full recovery. Suicide, usually by firearms, is always a high possibility.

"The most interesting thing is, PTSD has been around since the creation of mankind. However, it wasn't truly acknowledged as a wartime side effect until Vietnam. In the two world wars, it was called shell shock or battle fatigue, and never recognized as a significant mental illness. After Vietnam, it was so severe that today it has become a recognized disability in war *and* as a traumatic occurrence in everyday society."

Julianna interrupted, "William, this guy was a Green Beret. We don't know what happened, but apparently accepting dangerous missions is part of the gig."

"Ah yes, a Green Beret. Probably the most stressful branch of the US military in Vietnam. I would say there's a high risk he has some level of PTSD...depending on how and where he was deployed, and the extent of the trauma. There is no ceiling for possible dysfunction in a soldier at that level."

Julianna asked, "So what do you think?"

"I think you should get a psychological exam as soon as possible. Some PTSD patients have repressed their demons and function like semi-normal citizens. They cope, but they don't heal."

He hesitated and said, "You know, I have another reason I wanted to talk with you immediately. I've got an old friend in Seattle whom I owe a visit, and I don't have anything going on this weekend. If you can find your way out of that rain forest you live in, why don't I take you to dinner while I'm there? I'd love to see you again, and we can catch up on each other's lives. It will give me a little time to think, and maybe I can help."

Julianna was quiet for a second, then said, "Is this a date, Dr. Fontaine? Or a business meeting?"

"Both. I'll email you with my schedule."

* * *

On Friday, Julianna drove to Seattle and met William Fontaine for dinner at Canlis Restaurant overlooking the Seattle Locks.

"This is a fascinating case, William. We're trying to connect the dots before arresting the man who, to me, is a serious suspect. If he's our guy and did kill Gitana Harper years ago, we think he has to be a suspect for the girl's murder too."

"Hmm. Well, here's a thought. Both these deaths took place after your suspect's diagnosis of PTSD, correct?"

"Absolutely."

"I'm no Special Operations Group expert, but I do know that the common denominator for mind control, be it with religious groups, terrorists, cults, and even fanatic political groups, is all of them believe so deeply they can process everything to fit their own ideals. My guess is, *if* Hawkins is your guy, he sees himself, at some level, as vulnerable and is responding accordingly."

Julianna listened, trying to fit the information into the gray areas of the case. Before she could respond, Dr. Fontaine added, "Didn't you tell me, in your email, that Gitane's young child may have witnessed her own mother's fate? As a toddler?"

"I did."

"And the psychologist who examined the child at that time told the investigators that repressed trauma might be reversed at some point in time? Was that information made public through the media?"

"I believe so, but Willow wasn't even born yet!"

"I know… I think you also told me Willow was recently caretaking her dying mother."

"She was."

"It's not unusual for people who know they are dying to want to unburden long-suppressed traumatic memories. If Hawkins suspected that information even *might* have been passed on by Gitane's daughter, his PTSD could trigger a negative response. Maybe he panicked and decided to eliminate a possible threat. I mean, before Gitane's remains were recovered, he never had to worry about it because no one knew what actually happened to her. The identification of the remains in the lake might have pushed him over the edge."

Julianna had not touched her wine since the beginning of the conversation. Now she sat, bent over the table, her arms wrapped tightly around her body. "Holy crap, William. You might be right! Willow quit school to take care of her terminally ill mother. They spent months together. It could be. But how would Hawkins have known?"

"He wouldn't have. But neither do we. We're only putting possibilities together, and it seems like a possible theory. A paranoid PTSD sufferer might react unpredictably."

The waiter came by to see if they were ready to order.

Fontaine said, "Give us a few minutes, please. We've been talking so much we haven't been able to drink our wine."

When the waiter left, Dr. Fontaine raised his glass in a toast. "To Willow Shepard… As the Green Beret motto says, *De Oppresso Liber.*"

"What the hell does that mean?"

Fontaine smiled. "If I know you as well as I think I do, it won't take long to find out. Right now, let's just drink this wine."

* * *

When Julianna got home the following day, she went right to her computer and tried to learn as much about Adrian Adams Hawkins's military background as possible. She began by researching everything she could about the semi-secretive US Special Operations programs.

Dr. Fontaine's mysterious dinner toast was quickly solved. The vaunted warriors of the Green Berets were driven by an unexpected motto: De Oppresso Liber, which meant To Free the Oppressed, a noble commitment to defend those who are incapable of defending themselves. It is a concept so deeply ingrained that its believers commit their lives to its fulfillment.

Judd met Sheriff Webster at his office as soon as she finished her research. "Duncan, I don't know if this information impacts Hawkins's role in the case or not. What I do know is, it explains almost everything about the man's behavior."

"Meaning?"

"Meaning his obsessive compulsion to always take the underdog's side. In the time he has been here, with any issue involving controversy, he sided with the most likely to lose. I spoke to Dr. Fontaine again this morning. He called it positive brainwashing gone awry."

Listening to Julianna's theory, Duncan tried to envision Hawkins's behavior through the years he had dealt with the man. He failed to recall a single issue when Adrian had sided with the majority. He did not seem capable of doing so.

"But what does it prove, Jules? That the man isn't normal? We know that. It is not a motive."

"No, it's not a motive. Yet. But I think it's a damn good reason to dig deeper." She added, "I know you want it to be Knight, Duncan. And it might be. But you've not been able to nail him. Maybe it's time to look in another direction."

"Huh. Adrian is just an ornery old coot who's never had so much as a parking ticket. I agree we need to check him out. And, based on your news about his past, it makes sense. But it just doesn't feel right to me.

"Knight's our guy. He's been a scumbag his whole life. He abused Gitane both verbally and physically. He stalked her, spied on her, and threatened to kill her. That is what I'd call a convincing start for establishing a motive."

GRILLED

Despite Duncan's lack of enthusiasm, Julianna was convinced that Hawkins could no longer be ignored as a suspect in the 1975 murder of Gitane Harper. And she was running out of patience. She called the sheriff and asked Webster to meet with her staff in the cold case office at 4:00 p.m. When he agreed, she contacted her team members and asked them to come over as soon as possible to prepare for the sheriff's arrival.

Sheriff Webster was right on time, and Julianna got right to the point. "Duncan, we met earlier and did a reevaluation of Gitane's disappearance, factoring in the new information about Mr. Hawkins. We all agree Adrian is now a serious suspect. Connecting the dots, we put together a time line and possible cause. We think there is enough gray-area to bring Hawkins in for questioning. And maybe even enough to file charges."

The sheriff, arms folded across his chest, studied his friend and, after a deep breath, said, "Really? How so?"

Judd ignored the body language. "Think about it, Duncan. Hawkins lived less than three miles from Lake Aldwell. He was a backyard mechanic with an interest in old cars and, as we just learned, a trained soldier with a killer's skill set. Like you, we think Gitane's death and Willow's murder are connected. Hence, there's a good chance, if we can solve one murder, we can solve both murders. We don't know for sure if Hawkins killed Willow. But we all agree that this new information gives us a reason to, at the very least, check him out as a suspect in the Harper case…now."

"Julianna, you guys know that nothing would make me happier than to find Gitane's killer…and Willow's too. I'm not opposed to following up on any suspect other than Knight, but for me, it comes down to motive…and character. Knight's got a motive…and maybe the worst character in the sleaze-ball world."

Massaging her temples, Julianna rose from her chair and walked to a crowded grease board. Using a Magic Marker for a pointer, she went down the list of possible symptoms of PTSD sufferers, using those itemized by Dr. Fontaine. At the bottom of the list, three possibilities were underlined with double rows of black marker—anxiety, social dysfunction, and possible violent behavior.

Looking at Duncan, she said, "We're not saying these symptoms are all applicable to Mr. Hawkins. But we are saying there are red flags which need to be addressed. Your stubbornness is frustrating. It's time to forget your grudge and get on with it!"

Fighting to control his temper, Duncan didn't answer. He knew that Julianna was right, and he could not deny her charge…or reasoning.

Trying to control her own temper, Julianna said, "When this whole thing started, you asked the cold case unit to help with Gitane Harper's disappearance twenty-eight years ago. Based on the information we've been able to compile, we believe that if Hawkins had *any* concerns about the discovery of her remains, he would be a person of interest. Plus, one step further, he would have probable cause to be the most likely person to have killed Willow Shepard as well.

"For God's sake, we need to bring him in! With what we have right now, we think he might be your guy. We know Knight is dirty. But being Gitane's ex-husband is not enough motive for a double murder. A mental impairment like PTSD might be."

Duncan released a deep sigh and said, "I still think Knight killed them both. But you guys make a compelling argument. After all, I did ask for your help…and I do respect all of your work. I guess I'd be a fool to ignore it. I apologize for letting my personal hatred cloud my decision-making." He looked at Julianna. "I'm sorry I've been a little hardheaded."

He stood up and sighed again. "You win. We'll visit Mr. Hawkins right away." He paused. "And, Julianna, if it is Adrian, and he chooses to resist or fight, I can assure you that I will take his Green Beret ass down myself."

Finally, the concept of a killer besides Rodney Knight had taken root. Duncan's hatred for Knight had burned into his soul so deeply he had not been able to let it go. He *wanted* the man to be the killer…but after years of failure, Duncan knew it was time to admit someone other than Rodney Knight may have taken Gitane's life.

When he called Adrian Hawkins's home telephone number, the phone went unanswered. During the next few days, Duncan and his staff tried unsuccessfully to contact Mr. Hawkins. Based on the information presented at the meeting with the cold case team, Adrian's absence was concerning, and Duncan asked one of the West End deputies to stop by Adrian's place on the Herrick Road while en route to the West End and, if necessary, when he was coming back to Port Angeles at the end of his shift.

The deputy checked. On both stops, the entry gate was locked. On his second stop, when the deputy parked the cruiser in front of the locked gate and walked up to the house, no one was home. The deputy reported Adrian's usual vehicle—a battered Chevrolet Suburban, used in its better days as a logging company's crew bus—was parked beside the house. The man was nowhere to be found.

The news took Duncan from concern to alarm. The kindling of redirected vengeance was gaining momentum.

That afternoon, he and Deputy Berger drove out to Hawkins's farm. Webster's hope was the man had been on a project somewhere and would have returned from a weekend out of town. At the very least, he planned to poke around the place and see if anything looked suspicious enough to merit returning to town for a search warrant. Duncan would never break into a locked home. But he was not above looking into an open door or two, or looking through an uncurtained window.

Adrian Adams Hawkins was now a suspect he could no longer ignore. If he was home, they were planning to question the former Green Beret and, depending on the results of the conversation, bring him back to headquarters for a more official interview.

It was 10:05 a.m. when they pulled up to the farm. The gate to Adrian's driveway was still chained shut.

"Park here, Leon," Duncan said. "Let's walk up to the house and see if our friend just forgot to open the gate this morning."

Berger grunted. "Yeah, right. He's always been quick to welcome visitors."

The two men squeezed through a space between the tubular farm gate and the barbed-wire fencing, and walked the fifty yards to the house. It was quiet and appeared to be empty.

Knocking loudly on the door, Duncan shouted, "Adrian! Are you in there? It's Sheriff Webster. We need to talk."

There was no answer, so he twisted the door handle. It was locked. The two lawmen walked around the house, looking through curtainless windows and checking open floor space for a fall or accident victim. Everything looked neat, clean, and waiting for the owner's return.

Duncan looked at his deputy and shrugged. "Well, we didn't see a body in there, so I guess he isn't dead. Maybe he's working on a project in the woods someplace and took a truck. Let's take a look around the outbuildings and check to make sure he hasn't busted a hip or something."

* * *

The farm's owner watched the two lawmen walk up his driveway from the loft of the old barn he used as one of his work sheds. He had ignored Webster's phone calls and, when he saw the cop car pulling up at the gate, had hurried up the ladder to the loft. He had used the same tactic to avoid a different deputy who had been nosing around his place a few days before. After that one left, he had gone back to the house and brought his .30-06 hunting rifle up to the attic and leaned it in a nearby corner…just in case.

Adrian did not like noncustomer visitors. He did not like cops. Seeing Duncan Webster this soon after the other cruiser's drive-bys was unsettling. He decided on recon instead.

When the two men began to walk toward the farm's outbuildings, Adrian slid down the loft ladder and hurried to a storage closet beside his workspace. The door to the room was almost invisible; sealed by weathered barn boards, it blended into the gray interior walls. It also had a dead bolt on the inside and was safer than the open loft. And it was close enough to eavesdrop without detection.

Waiting in the dark closet, he hoped the sheriffs would poke their heads into the work shed and then move to the other outbuildings.

The two sheriffs walked straight to the barn.

Deputy Berger said, "This here is the main workshop, I think. It's the same building he was in the last time we visited, remember? He was having a nice conversation with himself out here."

Webster chuckled. "Yeah, I remember. Welcome to your future, Leon."

"Not me, boss. I ain't going there."

"If you live long enough, you are. Everyone goes there if they last that long."

The deputy wasn't paying attention. He was already looking around, peeking in corners, kicking at piles of rusted parts and tools. In contrast to the neat appearance of Adrian's living quarters, the workspace was a disaster.

"What are we looking for, boss?"

"We're not looking, Leon. That's not legal. We're just checking to see if Mr. Hawkins is here and okay. But if we accidently stumble across anything unusual, we'll figure out a way to come back with some paperwork. Anything that might be unusual."

"Great. Everything is unusual here, and everything's a mess. This guy's a world-class hoarder."

Duncan ignored the deputy and tried to focus. He knew Hawkins was a mechanic. He remembered the man's adamant rejection of ever working on a Ford Mustang. Sheriff Webster thought there was a chance he had forgotten parts of the past. Now, he knew Adrian was a PTSD victim, and he may have been lying.

Either way, or neither, it was obvious Adrian didn't throw much away. They saw groups of car parts and scraps scattered around the barn, and Duncan used a booted foot to untangle several of the stacks of junk metal and wires.

In the farthest corner of the building was a pile of larger auto parts—a fender, some corroded bumpers, and discarded batteries. It looked as if they had been there as long as the building had. Dump parts. He poked at the top of the pile in a half-hearted effort to check the contents. There was nothing interesting.

Turning away, something gnawed at Duncan's gut and stopped him from leaving. He swiveled back to see what might have tweaked his internal alarm system.

There was a John Deere tractor poster hanging on the wall just above the stack of debris. It was framed in a black-plastic material and looked oddly out of place where it was positioned. Something wasn't quite right. The poster wasn't new, but it was definitely fresher and less dust-coated than everything else in the barn. It was blocked by the junk pile and looked to be inaccessible. Curious, Webster started moving some of the mess so he could take a closer look.

Leon stopped poking around and said, "What are you doing, boss? I thought we weren't going to look too close."

"I know. I guess I forgot."

Climbing over a jumble of auto rejects was awkward, greasy...and illegal. Duncan was no longer an agile man, and he could see by the look on Leon's face that indicated Duncan's balancing skills weren't too impressive.

When the sheriff reached the lower corner of the poster's frame, he managed to knock it askew enough to see what was behind it. It looked as if someone had tacked a piece of faded plywood to the wall. Looking closer, he could tell the heads of nails holding the board in place appeared to be fairly new, and there were nails in each corner of the three-foot-square sheet.

"Leon, find me something I can use as a crowbar. I want to check this out."

"Okay, but I don't think you'll find anything more than a hole in the outside wall...or maybe an empty rat's nest."

"Maybe. Just get me the pry bar."

While Leon did as he was told and then returned to watch, Webster cleared out more of the wires, hoses, and scrap metal. When Leon stretched himself across the pile with a gigantic screwdriver, the deputy said, "You want me to do this, boss? I might be a little more limber."

"Just give me the damn tool, Leon. This job needs finesse not muscle."

Webster levered the first nail out, then carefully loosened the others so he could remove them without damage. When the plywood was freed, he balanced the sheet on top of the pile and looked inside the hole. He could see what looked like a piece of chromed automobile tubing, rectangular in shape, which appeared to be about two feet long. As soon as he pulled the piece from its hiding place, he knew what it was. And he felt a surge of rage tighten every muscle in his body.

Duncan was holding the front grille of a small car; it was made of rusty chromed tubing. In the center of the piece, inside the tubing and far smaller in size, was a metal identity emblem—the image of a galloping horse.

"What is it?" Leon said. "It looks like just another piece of junk to me."

Through gritted teeth, Webster said, "Really? It looks more like a car grille to me."

"So? It's a grubby old car grille."

"It is indeed, Leon. And what kind of car did they pull out of Lake Aldwell last week?"

The big deputy's eyes opened wide as the light came on. "A 1965 Mustang!"

"You got it. A Mustang with a missing front grille. Maybe just like this one. Very well hidden for a man who claimed, the last time we were here, that he'd never in his life worked on a Mustang. I'm guessing this hidey-hole was created right after we talked to him that day.

"We've got ourselves a very sick, very dangerous suspect here. What the hell was he thinking? Most people would have just tossed it in some deep water somewhere or buried it in the woods. But he's obviously a hoarder. It's a sickness." He shook his head. "I think Adrian might be losing it."

"No kidding. What now?"

"Now we put it back, tidy up a bit, and go home to see if we have grounds for a search warrant. And even if the judge denies one, we are going to find the bastard who tormented my life for the past thirty years."

* * *

When the sheriffs left, Adrian sank to a seating position. He clapped his hands to the sides of his head and rocked back and forth on the dusty floor. With a superhuman effort, he choked back the usual panic attack and managed to keep control. He had heard every word. The lawmen had been excited and eager to get back to town to process a search warrant.

He wrapped his arms around himself, still sitting on the floor, rocking, and moaning, "Nooo."

When he heard the car pulling away from the gate, he left the closet and stumbled to the grille's hiding place. He would get rid of the grille as soon as possible. But he knew the damage had already been done...most of it a long time ago.

UNLUCKY

Adrian first noticed Gitane Harper on a warm spring day in the late seventies. On his way home from a meeting at the Port Angeles City Hall, he turned off Highway 101 and onto the Herrick Road. Nearing the entrance to the first house on the right, he saw a young woman with a little girl on her hip, checking the contents of her weather-beaten mailbox.

Slowing down to take a look at the girl, he pulled over to the shoulder of the road, got out of his truck, and leaned across the driver's-side front fender to say, "Hey, neighbor. You doing okay? Can I help with anything?"

The girl looked at Adrian, with his long hair and shaggy gray beard, without a shred of prejudgment. She smiled and said, "No thanks. We're just picking up the mail."

"Okay. Just checking. I go by here most every day if you ever need a hand."

"Oh, thank you. That's nice to know, but I think we can handle most everything. We pretty much take care of ourselves."

Hawkins nodded and got back into his truck.

She watched the truck head up the road, turned around, and walked away. She had probably forgotten all about him before she reached the house.

Adrian, on the other hand, had a rare smile on his face as he drove up the hill. Over the next few days, he paid attention when driving past the house, watching for his pretty neighbor.

Later that same month, while tramping through the woods, looking for deer or elk antlers that had been shed, he found himself searching the wooded parcel of dense timber bordering Gitane Harper's house. He was careful to stay out of sight and, from force of habit, surveyed the terrain.

The house was positioned at the back of the lot and appeared to be a small prefab home. There were toddler's toys in the front yard—a Big Wheels trike and colorful, oversized plastic building blocks. At the front of the parking space, a supply of firewood was stacked close to the tree line, undetectable from the road.

As the weeks and months passed, he began making occasional recon trips, staying hidden in the woods while tracking the girl's daily routine. He noted she lived alone, but on occasion there were two different cars parked at the house during the day. A Chevy Vega was there every day; it was replaced by an orange VW Bug from midmorning until 5:00 p.m. most weekdays.

One misty morning while watching from the woods, he saw a young woman get out of a VW and jog to the house. Ten minutes later, Gitane Harper hurried to her own car, beeped a happy goodbye on the horn, and drove down the driveway. He assumed that the woman worked days, that she'd hired a babysitter to watch the little girl until the early evening, and that when the sitter left, the woman was alone for the night.

As Adrian watched, his admiration began to evolve into obsession, and his original intelligence gathering grew from curiosity to stalking.

* * *

It was two years before Adrian found the courage to address his obsession. He knocked on the girl's door just as the day was fading into night.

It was autumn, and darkness came quickly in the forested valley. Before leaving his house, Adrian took a bath and brushed out the beard that reached well below his chin. He got in his truck, drove down the road, and parked his rig on an abandoned farm side road a half mile from Gitane's house; he wanted to walk the rest of the way. *That way,* he thought, *the woman won't be aware of my visit until I'm at her door.*

His knock was quick and friendly, and the door opened almost at once with no "Who's there?" or cautious peek through a one-inch crack.

They stared at each other for a moment before she said, "Yes?"

Hawkins cleared his throat and asked, "Any chance I can come in?"

"Why? Is something wrong?"

"Nothing's wrong. Just a neighborly visit."

She raised her eyebrows. "Now? It's almost my daughter's bedtime."

"I know. I've been thinking about you though. Worried. A pretty girl like you living up here all alone. I thought you might need some company."

"I'm not alone, Mr....?"

"Hawkins. Adrian Adams Hawkins. You can call me Adrian Adams," he answered. "What's yours?"

Gitane ignored the question. "Well, Mr. Hawkins, I do know you live up the road, and I would be happy to visit with you sometime. But not now. It's getting late, and I'm not exactly comfortable with the timing."

Hawkins pushed the door open, brushing her aside and stepping into the room. "It's okay," he said, "I just want to talk."

Glancing at her daughter's bedroom door—which was ajar—and lowering her voice so as not to alarm the child, she said, "You're beginning to make me uncomfortable, sir. You need to leave. Now." She then lied, "I'm expecting company any minute." Glancing toward April's bedroom door again, she began to inch her way toward the toddler.

Hawkins said, "I'm not trying to be a bother here. I just thought we might get to know each other a little bit. We can check on the kid and make sure she's all right." He took two steps toward April's bedroom.

Gitane grabbed his arm. "Don't you dare! My daughter is none of your business."

Adrian pulled his arm free. "I said we can check." He started for the door.

Gitane screamed, "No!" Jumping on his back, she reached around his head and tried to claw at his eyes. "Get out!" she shouted. "Get out! Get out!"

Hawkins grabbed both her arms, dislodging her with ease.

The girl was frantic—screaming, kicking, and trying to bite him.

With hands like vises, he twisted her arms to turn her body to face away from him and threw his left arm around her neck. The girl was desperate and difficult to control, but Adrian applied pressure with a choke hold learned while in training with Special Forces. It was a tactic taught to control violent opponents or enemies.

Nine seconds, they'd said. Nine seconds to unconsciousness.

At twenty seconds, the girl was still trying to kick and elbow him. Adrian applied more pressure. Her body continued to jerk and tremble, but muscle control began to disappear.

At thirty seconds, she began to lose consciousness.

At forty seconds, all movement ceased.

Hawkins laid her gently on the floor and waited for her to come around. He patted her cheeks. He rocked her shoulders.

Nothing.

"Wake up," he whispered. "Wake up! Wake up!"

Nothing.

Looking at her pale face, he pressed two fingertips on the side of her throat, hoping to feel the pulse of a beating heart. When he felt nothing, he groped around the soft neck in panic. Grabbing the girl's wrist, he used his thumb, searching for any sign of life.

When there was no response, he cradled his face in his hands. Then stretched his arms in front of him and stared in horror, not believing those arms were his own.

The girl was alive and uninjured minutes ago. She wasn't supposed to die...only settle down. His whole body began to shake, and he moaned and moaned.

He stayed on his knees beside the body, trying to calm the quaking inside his chest and head. He looked around the room to make sure that he had touched nothing and that the house showed no signs of the struggle between the two of them. Everything looked the same. It had been a mismatch from the second she jumped on his back.

Lifting the dead girl in his arms, he twisted the doorknob and pushed the door open with his foot. He took a quick look over his shoulder, checking to be sure he had left no sign of his presence. Carrying the body, he made his way through the woods and back to the road where he had parked his rig.

* * *

From the window in her bedroom, the confused little girl watched the man carry her mother outside and disappear in the dark shadows of the woods. After they went away, she tiptoed into the living room. The front door was still open, and she walked over to it, looking into the night. Shoulders drooping, she closed the door and went back to her bedroom.

She found her blanket and Rose, her sleeping-bunny. Then she lay down on the floor rug between the wall and her bed and fell asleep.

* * *

After Adrian walked up the dark country road, carrying Gitane to where he was parked, he set her gently into the bed of his pickup and drove back to his own place up the road. While he was driving, his hands were choking the steering wheel, and the tears in his eyes made it difficult to see.

But as he drove, his military training, so intense and so deeply rooted, began to take over. There had been no helicopters, no bullets, no blood. No dead brothers. He let his survival instincts guide his body and prepare his mind, knowing that the aftermath of this night, like Morris Bullard's death, would haunt him forever.

LAKE ALDWELL, 1975

When he returned to his farm, Adrian went directly to the barn where he was finishing some work on a Ford Mustang that he had rescued for a song from a local scrap dealer. He had been working on the car for weeks, and now it was drivable, but it still had some grille and body damage, and had yet to be tested on the road.

He went to the vehicle, climbed behind the wheel, and turned the ignition key to start the car. The 289 Ford engine coughed a time or two and then rumbled to life. Adrian sucked in a chest-full of air, puffed out his cheeks, and exhaled a noisy sigh.

Leaving the car idling, he got out to move the scattered tools and equipment blocking the doorway; then he slid behind the wheel, eyes closed, and listened to the motor.

The girl was lying on the ground beside the barn's open front door. He backed out and stopped next to the body. Opening the car's trunk, he lifted the woman into the empty space, arranging the still-flexible corpse into a fetal position, then closed and locked the lid. He went back inside the barn and found an ax, a bow saw, and a pair of shears, and put them all in the back seat of the car.

Adrian forced himself to think. He knew he had to get rid of the body. Looking at the Mustang, something triggered a thought. There was a string of three lakes bordering Highway 101. Lake Aldwell, Lake Sutherland, and Lake Crescent. Sutherland and Crescent were almost ten miles away. Lake Aldwell was only one mile from the beginning of the Herrick Road. Lake Sutherland was ringed with cabins and summer homes. Crescent had year-round homes, resorts, and Olympic National Park campgrounds and rest sites.

Lake Aldwell was inside the national forest, and there was only one boat launch on the lake. And not a single cabin or house on its densely timbered shoreline. Adrian had fished it often, and its rainbow trout had supplied many a meal. He knew where the deepest water and the biggest fish were located…and he wanted everything to go away as soon as possible.

Driving toward the lake, Hawkins's mind churned. Thoughts of Vietnam and his friend Bull fought with thoughts of the night's gut-wrenching disaster…and the famous Lady of the Lake legend that had trigged his desperate plan to hide the girl's body.

Halfway up the long hill beside the lake, he crossed the centerline of the road and pulled into a wide section of shoulder just above Lake Aldwell, which was snuggled in the forested valley below. The wide shoulder was bordered by knee-high salal bushes and ferns. The overgrown brush shielded the presence of an old logging road used before the lake was dammed over a hundred years ago.

Adrian had discovered the hidden road by accident while walking up the hill on a day hike, looking for a private place to relieve himself. A decades-old, bulldozed skid road for older and smaller log trucks, it had quickly morphed into a convenient game trail. Hidden from the road by dense salal bushes, the deer and elk had prevented new timber growth and created nature's version of a safe descent to the lake below.

Hawkins took the bow saw out of the car and studied the jumble of salal brush and ferns that hid the entrance to the long-forgotten road. Second-growth hemlock and spruce had narrowed the road, but animals always choose the path of least resistance, and their constant use had maintained a pathway to the lake.

The Mustang was a narrow car, and if Adrian could get past the heavy brush, he knew he didn't need to reach the lake. There was a better way. And if it worked, it might be years before someone would find the car.

Using the saw, he cut three small alders as close to the ground level as possible. The heavy brush hid any trace of the trees or sawdust; Adrian took extra care not to create any obvious opening in the tree line.

When he had cleared enough brush to get the road somewhat navigable, he was able to drive the car forward, bending the resilient salal under the car as it pushed past the opening. Using his tools, he was able to clear a workable passage. He inched past the hidden entrance and, using only a flashlight to see, was able to widen a path roughly equivalent to the two-track wheel span of the narrow Mustang. Bit by bit, the car crept forward; Adrian was careful to avoid high centering, cutting the occasional rogue sapling when necessary. Ten feet before he reached the rock face of the bluff, he stopped to survey the terrain. The cliff he was planning to use was a sheer drop of sixty or seventy feet.

Setting his tools on the ground, he double-checked the interior of the car, on the chance it might, by some miracle, be discovered. He had filed all identification shortly after he acquired the car, but he wanted to be sure. He took the keys out of the ignition and threw them over the cliff, and then went to the back of the car, leaned against the trunk, and said, "I'm sorry, pretty lady. I didn't mean to hurt you."

Hawkins was a strong man, and the front wheels of the small car were close to the edge of the cliff. Pushing the car over the edge, he heard the splash and some distant gurgles.

After a while, all that remained was silence, dark shadows of the trees, and the deep water in the lake below.

UNHINGED

T wenty-eight years later, Lake Aldwell unveiled the near-perfect crime. After authorities confirmed that the remains of the skeleton discovered in the drained lake were those of Gitane Harper, media sources spread the news around the world.

The crush of television, newspapers, and social media exposure was staggering, and Adrian Hawkins began to lose his fragile grip on reality. The news, and the fear that the worldwide interest would demand a resolution, pushed his anxiety level to the breaking-point.

* * *

Gitane's daughter, April, was in the house the night Gitane vanished. April had since passed away, and the threat she'd recover her repressed memories had died with her. But April's own daughter, Willow, had quit school to take care of her mother for the months prior to April's death. If April's childhood memories had surfaced, who knew what secrets a dying mother might share with her daughter?

Adrian had monitored April and her daughter for years, relaxing his vigil only after April's death. He knew Gitane's granddaughter lived in the same house with her elderly father. It was Friday night, and the girl was a teenager. Adrian thought there was a good chance she would be out with friends.

Two days after the news of the Lake Aldwell victim's identity went public, Hawkins had dressed in a brown-and-green camouflage suit, which he had picked up earlier in the summer at a garage sale, and a black balaclava with the eyes cut out and a long throat cover for his beard.

When dusk turned to darkness, he backed the Suburban out of sight beside a vacant lot across the street from the Shepard house. He sat in his rig, watching the neighborhood for late dog walkers or night owls. The sky was overcast, and there were no stars or moon to light the dark shadows.

He had reconned the house earlier in the day. It was in a quiet neighborhood and sat on a corner lot, a dense laurel hedge separating it from its only neighbor. The building was a faded and peeling Craftsman-style house surrounded by a profusion of overgrown bushes as old and neglected as the house itself. Scruffy rhododendron bushes lined the brick walkway leading from the street sidewalk to the front porch.

When it was totally dark, Adrian got out of the Suburban. Moving quickly into the shadows, he worked his way to the corner at the end of the street and slipped into the unlit alley behind the house. He watched the backyard for almost an hour, saw a kitchen light go on for a minute or two then go dark. He waited another half hour, before low-crawling under the windows of the building and worming his way to the safety of the overgrown front-yard shrubs.

Out of breath from the crawl and unfamiliar adrenaline rush, Adrian found an opening behind the branches of an old rhododendron bush three-quarters of the way up the brick walkway. He squeezed into the center of the bush and broke off some small branches to clear a sight line, then scraped the ground below the branches, clearing a carpet of dead leaves, and hunkered down to wait.

There was no guarantee the girl was away. But the front-porch light was still on, and it was Friday night...and the kid was a teenager. He checked his watch; it was 10:40 p.m.

As the hours dragged by, Adrian struggled to stay awake and made a point of stretching and flexing muscles to keep his body as loose as possible. Shortly after 1:00 a.m., Adrian saw a small pickup truck pull up to the curb beside the house. He heard doors open and the laughter and hubbub only three teenage girls could create after a night on the town. He watched as all three girls hugged one another, giggling and chattering. The driver and a shorter friend, wearing an over-sized black hoodie, got back in the truck. Pulling away from the curb, arms waving out the windows of both sides of the cab, they beeped a cheerful goodbye.

Willow was alone. The girl was in no hurry, watching the truck disappear until it turned the corner. She stood on the sidewalk as if she was savoring the silence of being alone in the still night. Adrian watched as the tall, slender girl loosened the scarf she was wearing. She took several deep breaths and pushed a streak of bright-blue hair off her forehead. Seconds later, she started walking toward the house. She was humming a song as she drew near, lost in her own world.

Adrian's body trembled like a cat ready to ambush an un-suspecting songbird. Crashing onto the girl from behind, he slapped his left hand over her mouth. With the strong hands of a lifetime mechanic, he pulled her tight to his body, wrapping his right arm around her throat and locking the neck into the inside of his elbow.

The death grip did not take long…and was much quicker than her grandmother's demise almost three decades earlier. The girl was too surprised to struggle and the crushing grip too deadly to allow any sound. She gagged and her body stiffened into a rigid seizure, then relaxed like a damp dish towel. Adrian rolled her body face down in the grass, turned away, and bent over with his eyes closed and his hands on his knees, sucking air into his lungs as he tried to regain control of his senses.

When he looked back at the body, he could see that the tee shirt Willow was wearing had somehow been pushed up from the waist to the center of her shoulders. Her bared back was white and childlike. He looked away, and his own body began to shake. When the tremors stopped, he stood, forcing himself back into mission mode.

Pulling the corpse into the bushes, he rechecked the body and the ground around the walkway. Nothing had been disturbed, and no blood shed. He threw the body over his shoulder in a fireman's carry and hurried across the street to his rig.

Driving the five blocks to Tumwater Bridge, he didn't see another car. He stopped in the middle of the bridge, where the highway below the tall structure was centered. He lifted the body from the back of the rig and, looking up and down the street once again, carried the body to the four-foot-high green-wire fencing at the side of the walkway of the bridge.

Gathering his strength and wits, he looked down at the drop, and noticed a slash of black letters graffitied on the concrete that supported a four-foot-high wire fence. The message, centered directly on the road beneath the bridge, read, "Spatter, don't shatter." Adrian grunted, quickly looked away, lifted Willow's body to the top of the barrier, and pushed it over the fencing.

The revulsion, horror, and panic were the same as those when Gitane died at her home on the Herrick Road, but the girl's death was even more disturbing. Still, he was a Green Beret, and he had been taught that sometimes the end justifies the means. He had been trained to kill. And, like it or not, he had done the same thing to her grandmother years before.

This time, though, it was not an accident.

TOMMY LEE RHYSACKER

Hawkins's disappearance after the Mustang-grille discovery left little doubt about Adrian's probable connection to the murders. The cold case team and the Clallam County Sheriff Department met to assemble a strategy for locating and arresting the new suspect. Despite their best efforts so far, phone calls had gone unanswered, and drive-bys up the Herrick Road by westbound deputies had produced only a locked gate at the farm's entry.

Duncan, whose hatred for Rodney Knight would never disappear, found a new villain in ex-Green Beret Adrian Adams Hawkins. Driven by his own failure to recognize Gitane's murderer, now he wanted to avenge Gitane's murder and his own years of frustration.

The sheriff wasted no time in calling the meeting to order. "I'm not certain what's going on with Mr. Hawkins, but it appears he is either hiding somewhere or gone. Either way, something must have put him on high alert. We need to find him before he disappears completely."

"You're right, Duncan," said Julianna. "Somehow, someway, it seems like he got nervous, and according to Dr. Fontaine, some of these PTSD guys are smart, even if they aren't normal. We need to find him quick."

"I agree. We'll get ahold of the Port Angeles PD, the staters, and border patrol, and set up a search strategy. My staff will do an APB and network it out from here. If he's just spooked, he might be laying low. If he thinks we *are* on to him, this thing is going to turn into a monster manhunt."

Deputy Berger asked, "Do we even know what he's driving now? Our guys say that piece of trash Suburban, which was there two days ago, hasn't been there since. Maybe he ditched it. Or maybe he got one of his beater wrecks running and is driving that."

"Or," Webster said, "maybe he stole, or plans to steal, something else. There are lots of options."

Judd offered, "Right. But it comes back to whether or not he thinks we're on to him. Even if he's driving something different, unless he's changed his appearance, he's not too hard to recognize. If he got a haircut and shaved, who knows what he looks like."

"Not Brad Pitt," Berger mumbled.

Joan Carpenter from the cold case team said, "It's possible he's just getting ready to run. All those drive-bys would make anyone suspicious. If we get an APB out, and he's still on the peninsula, we've got a good chance to nail him."

Berger said, "You're right, Sheriff. An old guy with PTSD might not be quite as smart as he used to be." He looked around the room at the veteran police officers. "Umm, no offense…not all old guys, of course."

* * *

Hawkins was closer than the local crime team could hope for. He had a good friend, maybe his only friend, who lived in an abandoned hunting cabin in the Sol Duc River drainage between Lake Crescent and the West End.

Tommy Lee Rhysacker had served in the US Marine Corps in Vietnam and, as a fellow PTSD war vet, had met Hawkins at the only regional support-group conference that Adrian had ever attended in Tacoma, Washington. Both men were living on the Olympic Peninsula, and they became good friends.

Tommy Lee was big and burly. Like Adrian, he had a gray beard. Unlike Adrian, his beard was neatly trimmed, and his head was as bald as a light bulb. His personal grooming made him appear much more conventional and far less notable than the mad-zealot persona of his fellow vet.

However, his normal exterior disguised a severely compromised mental dysfunction. The damage Tommy Lee had suffered during the war was far more evident and disconcerting than Adrian's postwar disorder. Rhysacker was plagued by bouts of anxiety much like those of Tourette's-syndrome sufferers—talking became screaming, and screaming became profanity. These attacks had upset the business district of downtown Port Angeles, and a sympathetic fellow Vietnam vet had offered Tommy Lee an escape to the solitude of a rustic hunting cabin he owned but never used. Located on a remote piece of barely accessible land on a bend of the Sol Duc River, it was deep in the woods, twenty yards from the river, and purposely hidden from the eyes of national forest rangers. The cabin was old and rustic, but a dream base-camp during hunting season.

Rhysacker was happy there; the isolation allowed him to poach an occasional deer and fish the river whenever the spirit moved him. With his small military pension and medical-benefits checks, he shopped in the grocery store in the three-building burg of Beaver and got on as well as he could.

Hawkins had been his only visitor throughout the years, so when he showed up at the cabin and asked his friend if he could stay a few days, Tommy rolled out a dirty sleeping bag and said, "Be my guest."

* * *

Thirty-six hours after arriving at Rhysacker's cabin, Hawkins was ready.

Tommy Lee said, "Where you headed, Hawk? I thought you was laying low for a while."

"I am. I just need to go back to the farm and pick up a few things."

"Shit, man, why? You can bivouac here for months if you want. Even the church guys don't show up around here. I ain't seen two people here in the past three years."

"I know. But I've got something I have to do. There's a firefight coming, Tommy Lee, and I need to get ready."

"I hear you, dog. Those firefight fuckers never did nothing for us. Even if you won, you lost. Am I right?"

"You're right. Nobody knows what it's like until you've been there. When you've come back from hell, only another soldier can understand how bad it is." He threw Tommy Lee a sloppy salute and climbed into the Suburban.

Adrian Hawkins was going back to his beloved Herrick Road farm. He had tracked the times of the sheriff-department drive-bys, and he was gambling that those visits were based on their coming or going to the West End as part of their regular patrols. If he was right, the county's westbound lawman would probably be well past the Herrick Road on his usual patrol route.

Adrian knew his plan was risky. Driving the speed limit around Lake Crescent to avoid park-ranger cruisers, he made the trip in less than forty-five minutes. Driving up the Herrick Road, his eyes jumped from house to house and from driveways to front porches, looking for nosy neighbors as he drove up the hill toward his farm.

When he got to the end of the road, the farm gate was still chained shut, and there were no signs posted to indicate the place was locked down or secured. He unlocked the gate's padlock. Unwrapping the chain connecting the gate to the fence post, he drove up to the house, hunched over the steering wheel, and scanned the grounds.

At the house, he got out of his rig and took a minute to study his longtime retreat. The old farmhouse had been his safe house for thirty years. He looked at the blanket of rain-forest moss covering the roof, the aged-black log walls, and the small windows providing the safety of darkness and privacy.

Opening the front door, the familiar smell of a thousand woodstove fires permeated the kitchen and living spaces. He stood still for a moment, eyes closed, breathing in the familiar smell of home.

In the center of the space was a smoke-stained vertical support post that anchored the open ceiling. Hanging on the post were a pair of beaded neck chains. Attached to each was a set of military dog tags. Adrian had panicked after Webster found the Mustang's grille, and in his rush to get away, Hawkins had forgotten his most cherished belongings.

He took the chains off the hook and separated Morris Bullard's tag from his own. Rubbing the lettering of his friend's tag between his thumb and fingers, he read the worn name and talked to the tag in a low voice, "One more mission, brother. Just one more." He slipped both chains onto his neck and headed for the door.

That was it—the sole reason for returning to the farm.

He hurried to his rig, drove down the driveway, got out of the Suburban, and resecured the padlock. Leaning against the tubing of the farm gate, he stared up at the place that had been his retreat since he left Montana. A small farm nestled in the valley of green-black virgin timber. The sanctuary that had saved his life. It was beautiful.

* * *

Roland Cross looked through the blinds of his kitchen window and watched his neighbor across the road from his house. Adrian Adams Hawkins's place was blocked by the heavy woods, but the gate to his farm was visible from where Roland and his wife, Belinda, lived. In fact, from the gate, Hawkins could see the Cross's place as well, but Roland was careful to peek through the narrowest crack of slat blinds.

Cross had been cleaning some vegetables at the kitchen sink when he first noticed the gate to his neighbor's place was open. He'd moved to the window with the better view and waited to see who might be visiting.

When he saw the Suburban, Roland whispered, "God-damn, it's Adrian." He watched Hawkins lock the gate, take a step back, and take a long look at his place. The man finally got back into his rig and pulled away from the gate, throwing gravel behind the spinning back tires as he headed down the road.

* * *

Duncan took the call transferred from dispatch. "Webster here."

"Sheriff, this is Roland Cross. Your deputy stopped by a day or so ago and asked me to call if I saw any sign of my neighbor Adrian Hawkins around his place."

"Yeah. Thanks, Roland. What's up?"

"Adrian just drove out of his driveway a minute ago. Headed down the road. In kind of a hurry, I think."

"Really? What's he driving?"

"Same old, same old. That beater Suburban of his."

"Roland, I can't tell you how much we appreciate your help and your prompt response. Thank you so much."

"What's going on, Sheriff? Is Adrian in trouble?"

"Thanks again, Roland. I gotta run."

THE HUNT

"Leon, we just got a break. Roland Cross spotted Adrian coming out of his farm. Believe it or not, he's still driving the Suburban! We need to set up a perimeter net ASAP. From the Herrick Road, he's only got three options for getting off the peninsula.

"We need to keep Deputy Johansen in the Forks area to handle things there. Get someone up front to call the staters and see if they have a unit close to Forks. If they don't, let them know what we're looking for and that we need one of their guys on the highway headed this way. That'll take out 101 West.

"See if you can get Oliver Welch and his border patrol guys to cover the two exits to Highway 112. You and I will start from here, and if he's planning on going east, he'll have to drive past us to get there. Just in case he slips past, let's see if the WSP can keep a unit at the floating bridge.

"If he stays in his rig and tries to get off the peninsula, that's all there is. If we don't get him, he'll have to be hiding somewhere, and we'll make sure those three options are blocked until we've got him. The only other option is by water, and I don't even want to think about that."

"I got it, boss. If he heads west, he's got a ten-mile head start on us. We'll have to go like hell to catch him. And I wanna be there when we nail his ass."

They hit the siren and lights before getting out of the courthouse parking lot. Leon was driving, and the man could make Duncan nervous even when they weren't chasing somebody.

The sheriff tightened his seat belt and said, "If you kill me before we get him, Leon, I'm going to find a way to kill you too."

"Relax, boss. I got more speeding tickets in my early days than I've written," he joked. "I know how to drive fast."

"That's not comforting, Deputy. Remember, we should have a unit coming toward us if he gets around the lake before we catch him. Let's don't get too excited here."

Westbound traffic pulled off the road to let the rocketing cop car pass. Both men eyed every vehicle headed their way, hoping each one would be the easily recognizable Chevy Suburban.

They kept in touch with the other units via radio and cell phones. No one had seen anything yet, and Duncan began to worry. If Adrian had reached one of the Highway 112 exits before their net units could get in place, they would be in trouble. He also knew how dangerous the older road was—fraught with tight, blind corners and logging truck traffic. He did not think a fleeing driver would choose a road that would slow him down.

Leon had to reduce speed to cross the Elwha River Bridge at the bottom of the hill, but they were going eighty-five miles an hour as they whistled past the turnoff to the Herrick Road. Speeding past Lake Sutherland, they crossed the boundary into the Olympic National Park at the east end of Lake Crescent.

The road around the big lake—a narrow track of twisty curves, scenery-gawker pull-offs, and very low speed limits—was even more dangerous than Highway 112. Webster thought Adrian would slow down to not risk getting pulled over by park rangers. So he contacted the state patrolman in the town of Forks and told him to watch carefully as he drove toward the lake on the highway.

Lake Crescent is twelve miles long and about a half hour from Forks. If Hawkins was still driving, he had to pass a law enforcement vehicle either way he went. If he stayed in the Suburban, he was trapped.

Duncan reached to his hip and touched the grip of the holstered Smith and Wesson .357 Magnum. It was a reflexive gesture, and he smiled at the thought. In his forty-five-year career, he had never shot a gun at anyone.

They drove slowly around the lake, being careful to check the many viewpoints and pull-offs created to provide visitors with photo ops or picnics, or just for nature lovers stopping to savor the beauty of the setting.

Webster said, "I don't think he'll stop here, but you never know. I'd hate to miss him if he had to make a pit stop or something."

Leon answered, "Well, even if he does, he's not going too far. The staters are coming the other way. We got him, boss."

"Maybe. The guy's no dummy, and I don't think this is his first rodeo. We know he's a mental case, but a deranged perp is a whole different world. The shrink was adamant about unstable and unpredictable behavior."

They drove on in silence, paying attention to the lakeside road and monitoring the eastbound traffic. Webster squirmed with frustration at every empty space. When they reached Fair Holm Grocery at the west end of the lake, they still hadn't seen any sign of Hawkins. Highway 101 ascended the long hill behind the little store and lake. At the top of the hill, the highway straightened, and the speed limit picked up accordingly. They could see approaching vehicles from a long distance.

"Here comes the WSP," Deputy Berger said as he spotted the rotating lights on top of the familiar white cruiser. "Want me to pull over for a chat? We got us some wide shoulders here for a ways."

"Yeah. Let's have a visit."

The state patrolman saw them pulling over and crossed the centerline to their side of the road. He stopped beside them, side by side, and both drivers lowered their windows.

Duncan leaned forward from the passenger seat and said, "Any luck?" He knew the answer, but hoped for something helpful.

"Nope, I left Forks as soon as I got the call. There's a bunch of side roads, but he definitely didn't pass me on this highway."

"Dammit, something isn't right here. The lake should have slowed him down enough to keep him away from any of these side roads. We don't have enough bodies to roadblock every highway side road, and it doesn't make sense for him to risk being pinned down on one of those backcountry dead ends."

Leon said, "Nope, so what's next, boss?"

The sheriff was quiet, thinking through alternatives. Looking at the state patrolman, he said, "Can you get border patrol and the others to work some of these side roads? Maybe the prison can spare a man or two who knows the country. If you can, work with both sides of the highway turnoffs. Pick the obvious ones first, and go from there.

"If we can keep him on the peninsula, we can round up teams to do a house-to-house search if we have to. This whole thing just doesn't feel right. He shouldn't have had enough time to clear the lake. We'll backtrack and see if he tried to give us the slip somewhere on his way out."

The officer nodded. "I'll try. Let me know what's goin' on, and call if you need me."

"We will. Thanks for the help. And good luck."

The trooper touched the brim of his Mountie-style hat and said with the same lack of sincerity given to the unhappy recipient of a no-seat-belt ticket, "Have a nice day."

Webster tried to wrap his mind around what it was that did not feel right. It was an intangible, a gut feeling that came from all the years of trying to think like the bad guys.

This was Adrian Adams Hawkins. An eccentric. A war casualty who appeared to be coming apart at the seams. Dangerous...but smart. The sheriff thought about what those things might mean, and the dark corners of his subconscious began to clear.

THE DEVIL'S PUNCH BOWL

"We need to go back, Leon. I think I might know what's going on here."

They turned around and drove down the hill, backtracking the lake route. They drove slowly, braking beside each pull-off and surveying cars parked there or in any hidey-holes screened off from the road by trees or brush, looking for Adrian's Suburban, or for anything unusual that might give them a trail to follow. Duncan was on high alert, sensing they were on the right track, trusting his gut, and expecting a sighting at every new site. With each failed stop, Webster's confidence in his instincts grew stronger.

They were drawing closer to Lake Crescent Lodge, which sat at the base of the legendary Mount Storm King. When they reached the entrance to the complex, Webster said through clenched teeth, "Here we go, Leon; this is it. I can feel it in my bones."

"I hope so, boss. My bones are tired of being in this car. I hope we find the crazy bastard soon."

"Be careful what you wish for, Deputy. We don't know what's going to happen if we find him."

What they found next would kick both officers' cop instincts into the red zone and erase any thoughts of aches or discomfort. Easing past the lodge's parking lot, they checked parked cars that might be suspicious.

Duncan, who knew the complex well, said, "Let's check out the back parking lot, where Barnes Creek empties into the lake. It's a lot more private."

They drove past a row of rustic cabins between the lake and Barnes Creek Cove. Parked in the far corner, shaded by parklike old-growth hemlock and spruce trees, was a dirty orange-and-cream-colored Chevy Suburban. Both men knew there was only one vehicle in Clallam County it could be. Adrian Adams Hawkins had been—and might still be—here.

"Well, Deputy. It looks like your aching body better heal up real soon."

Smiling with tight lips, Leon said, "Bring it on, boss. I'm ready."

"You better be. Take a look—a careful look—around the area. If you find any sign of him, call me. I'm going to get us some backup and check out the lodge. And, Leon, don't do anything careless. Joke time is over. We got us a dangerously disturbed Green Beret to deal with. You hear what I'm saying?"

"I got it, boss. Nothin' stupid."

Duncan watched Leon get out of the car; then he slid across the bench seat to the steering wheel, threw the unit into a tight U-turn, and headed back to the lodge. He parked in front of the entry porch, ignoring the visitors sitting in the iconic swinging benches and Adirondack chairs facing the lake.

The main entrance had a massive stone fireplace, with a fire burning day and night, and a cozy seating area. There was a huge taxidermy head and antlers of a world-class trophy elk with a bronze plaque dating back to before the lake was designated as part of the Olympic National Park.

Duncan did not see any of these treasures or the relaxed charm of the rustic building...but he could not help recognizing the surreal coincidence of the familiar setting.

There was a college-aged girl at the desk by the bar, and he said, "Young lady, I need some information, and I need it fast. We've got what may be a dangerous situation here, and I want it handled in the safest way possible."

The clerk nodded, her face paling. She licked her lips, clearly upset by the uniform and tense demeanor of the white-haired lawman.

"Relax," Duncan said, "it's going to be okay. Have you seen an old man, about my age, with long hair and a longer beard? Checked him in, maybe? Shown him the way to the restaurant? Maybe just walking through the room?"

"You mean an old man who looks kind of like a wizard?"

"A wizard? Yeah...yeah, I guess I do."

"He was in here maybe thirty minutes ago." She looked at her boat-rental sheet. "His name is A. A. Smith. He rented a rowboat. Said he was interested in seeing the Devil's Punch Bowl from the water and only needed it for the afternoon. Paid in cash."

"Smith, huh? Get me a manager, young lady. Right now. Then call the park service and get me some park rangers out here, quicklike. Tell them Sheriff Webster is here and that we're tracking a dangerous suspect...and that we need back-up...ASAP. Then get me whoever is in charge here...and tell them they better get here. It's an emergency."

The manager was on the far side of the complex, and it took him almost ten minutes to get back to the lodge. While Webster was waiting, his mind worked to put the pieces together.

The Devil's Punch Bowl. He knew it well. It was the same place he had taken Gitane Harper almost fifty years ago. The same place the Lady of the Lake's body rose from Storm King's Graveyard in 1940, the most famous display of the mountain's power to punish humans who dared desecrate the waters of his lake.

The Devil's Punch Bowl was still nestled in a small cove by walls of rocky bluffs, and the water in front of the cove was still some of the deepest of the lake. For Duncan, it had always seemed foreboding—dark, deep, and dangerous. As much as he now hated the man, he was not looking forward to dealing with Adrian Adams Hawkins in the devil's territory. And he knew if Adrian chose the water for his exit, it would be difficult to find a body.

* * *

Deputy Berger was with him now, and the two lawmen watched as a young man wearing a day pack and a Seattle Mariners baseball cap hustled across the parking lot to where they were standing. Out of breath, he said, "Steven Muller, Sheriff. How can I help you?"

"We've got a big problem here, Mr. Muller. Unfortunately, time is of the essence, and we can't wait for backup to get here. We're tracking a potentially dangerous suspect who's heading for the Devil's Punch Bowl. We need a boat and a driver to get us across the lake. It's an emergency, and it might be dangerous. I'm going to bend the rules here and ask you for your assistance. Can you help us out?"

"Of course, I can take you myself. The boat's right behind the dock."

* * *

With Mount Storm King looming behind them, the lodge's outboard-powered boat sped across the lake toward the Devil's Punch Bowl. Duncan swore at himself for forgetting to throw a bullhorn in their unit to communicate with Adrian if he was holed up somewhere. He was leery of getting too close to the ex-soldier.

The once-treacherous train tracks around the Punch Bowl had been replaced by a paved path known as the Spruce Railroad Trail. The surrounding country was as beautiful as ever, but that beauty and its long reputation for danger still harbored a palpable taste of foreboding. Webster kept that in mind as the shoreline grew closer.

Leon shouted over the noise of the outboard motor, "There's a boat out in the cove! I think it might be fishermen, but I can't quite tell."

Duncan had Mr. Muller throttle down so they could figure out how to approach the boat, which all of them could now see. It was several hundred feet in front of the Punch Bowl.

Leon said, "It ain't movin' much. We might get a break here."

"Is it a rowboat?"

"Yeah, looks like it."

As they drew closer, still out of shooting range, Webster had Steven Muller make a wide circle around the smaller boat. If Hawkins had a weapon, there was no doubt in Duncan's mind that he was capable of using it. None of them could see a rower in the aluminum boat, and the early afternoon sun produced a distorted shimmering image from what they hoped was a safe distance.

"Looks pretty quiet, men, don't you think?" the sheriff asked the other two.

Muller nodded, and Berger said, "What the hell? I can see the oars. Can't you guys? I don't see anyone rowing though."

"No, Leon, neither do I. But it might be a decoy of some kind, an ambush, or…who knows…it could be anything."

"Well, if it's a decoy, boss, it sure as shit ain't working on us. Decoys are supposed to draw you in."

Duncan scowled at the deputy. "Let's get a little closer, Mr. Muller. And take it slow and easy."

The manager was hunched down beside the outboard motor, trying to make himself as small as possible.

Leon was half-standing, trying to get a better look. "Pretty quiet," he said. "I think it's empty."

"Hold your horses, Leon. Let's just watch for a minute."

They floated closer, nobody speaking, watching the boat bob and rock. The two oars dangling at its sides were disconcerting, wobbling in their locks as if an invisible rower was treading water, waiting for them to arrive. Minutes passed.

Leon fidgeted. Finally, he said, "If it's an ambush, it's a really skinny guy laying on the bottom of the boat."

"Okay, Leon, that's enough. There might be explosives or some other kind of booby trap." Duncan looked at the boat driver and drew in a deep breath. "Pull up beside it. Let's take a look."

Ten feet from the boat, they could tell it was empty. Steven Muller blew out a sigh of relief and started to breathe again.

As the two vessels touched, Leon grabbed the rowboat. Scanning the empty boat, he said, "I'll keep everything steady if you want to check it out, boss. I don't see no bombs or anything."

There were no bombs. But from the center of the resort's boat, Duncan leaned across the port side of the rowboat and studied its contents. Wrapped around the black-rubber handle guard of an oar was a silver chain. Dangling at the end of the chain were two sets of military dog tags. He leaned into the boat, unwrapped the chain, and slipped it into his pocket to be submitted as evidence.

THE SEARCH

Park-ranger backups arrived twenty minutes after Webster's group found the empty boat. They questioned the two sheriffs and hurried into action, knowing that the only hope for the successful recovery of a Lake Crescent drowning victim—unless the location was immediately reported or had taken place in one of the rare shallow beaches—was a quick start...and luck.

The rangers started by calling the coast guard in Port Angeles and requesting a helicopter and trained divers to help with the search. Park headquarters mobilized their own dive team and began contacting local rescue teams with water-search skills.

The coast guard helicopter was the first to arrive and dropped two divers close enough to the bridge to meet with ranger rescue advisors to organize search strategy for the large expanse of water leading to the Punch Bowl.

Despite the urgency, it took over an hour before volunteer responders began to arrive...and another half hour to organize logistics and assignments as teams hurried to the Punch Bowl. The rowboat was found almost a half mile from the shoreline, in some of the deepest water in the lake. Everyone knew finding the body quickly was essential to the search's success.

Through the years, even science had failed to solve the mystery. From sonar devices to one-man research submarines manned by trained oceanographers, every delayed start had failed. If the body wasn't located quickly, even science had been thwarted. The frustrated experts could only surmise that a complex system of underwater currents, lake-bottom crevasses, and possibly carnivore species of fish contributed to the mystery.

* * *

Leon and Sheriff Webster were standing on the Spruce Railroad Bridge at the middle of the Punch Bowl, watching the growing flurry of activity and trying to orchestrate the search effort.

When Port Angeles PD Detective Jon Kidd arrived at the scene at the national park's boat launch, the two sheriffs welcomed their good friend. Kidd was an ex-navy frogman himself and, in his younger days, had moonlighted as a technical underwater expert throughout the waters of Puget Sound.

Sheriff Webster was standing beside a group of law enforcement big shots arguing about the logistics of the search. Washington State Patrol, park rangers, and county officials all had an opinion. Webster was tired of the talk and stood away from the group. He had bummed a cigarette from his deputy and was smoking it with unconcealed frustration when he met Kidd.

"Hello, Sheriff. Looks like you need another man or two," Kidd said with poorly disguised sarcasm.

Webster whispered over his shoulder, "Jesus H. Christ, Jon, it's like being in the army here. Too much brass, not enough soldiers. My guys would call it a real shit show." Duncan, a longtime nonsmoker, took a deep drag on the cigarette, dropped the butt on the plank bridge, and ground it out. He looked at his friend and said, "Thanks for coming."

"I'm just here as an advisor for you, Web. I've probably spent more time in the water than all those kids out there put together. This won't be easy, man. It is almost as impossible as finding a body in the ocean. Harder maybe, because the bodies in the lake never float up to the surface. I have no idea how many bodies have been found during a search, but I *do* know no group I worked with ever found one."

Webster snorted. "Well, these guys seem to think they can. We'll search until dark. Then, if we need to, start again in the morning."

"Good idea. I don't want to rain on your parade here, but you should know that your world is about to get worse—any minute now, this place is going to be crawling with media. The news is out in town, and they're all going to want to interview the sheriff."

Duncan frowned at his friend. "Great. Just what I needed. But, even worse, is that we're in the national park. God knows, if we don't find this murder-suspect's body, the FBI might decide to join the party. Some of the bosses are already worried about Adrian faking his disappearance as part of an escape plan. They want to make sure it is really a drowning and not just a clever ruse. They're talking statewide alerts and setting up traffic checkpoints around the peninsula."

Kidd nodded. "I don't know, Web. I'm not so sure the Feds will move in. Neither murder took place in the park, and this ain't a national threat—no highjacked airplane, no ransom, no skydiving. But I agree; finding a body would make things a hell of a lot easier." Looking up at the darkening sky, he added, "Let's hope they find one soon."

The light continued to fade, slowly squeezing darkness closer to the now-dark-blue surface of the lake. The search chaos began to ebb; tired crews straggled back to the bridge walkway over the Devil's Punch Bowl. Small groups of two to five rangers, rescue teams, and skin divers were questioned and asked—or ordered—to reassemble at daybreak the following morning. All the responders were frustrated, knowing that every hour was critical for a successful Lake Crescent recovery.

* * *

Just before the weak sunlight smothered the final light of the day, an old man stepped out of dense woods near the top of the mountain behind the Spruce Railroad Trail. Pyramid Peak was directly across the water from the higher Mount Storm King, but, like the big mountain, its lower flanks were rugged and thick with spruce and cedar trees. When silhouetted in the western sky at dusk, it was a near-perfect outline of its Egyptian architectural namesakes.

That afternoon, the man had abandoned his rowboat in the deep water outside the Devil's Punch Bowl and had swum with commando stealth to the shoreline just past the abandoned railroad tunnel on the popular Spruce Railroad Trail. He scrambled across the pathway and disappeared into the uncharted backcountry on the western side of the mountain, bushwhacking his way up the slope and clambering over downed trees and through thorny devil's club bushes and slippery moss and lichens. Like the Punch Bowl, Pyramid

Peak was on the more remote side of the lake, which limited its popularity for hikers, so it was far less visited than the highway lakeside and its more accessible country and trails.

Near the top of the peak, Hawkins heard the first helicopter thunder over the lake, and he knew the boat had been discovered. He slipped back into the woods and waited patiently for the cover of night.

From his lookout, hidden in alpine scrub, he could see most of the lake and had watched the chaos of boats and choppers. In the thinner air at 3,000 feet, he could hear muffled shouts and orders and feel the urgency and frustration of the searchers. He thought the confusion would keep searchers busy for days and allowed himself a rare smile. Then he crawled into his lair and closed his eyes, power napping and saving energy.

Minutes before the light disappeared, Hawkins looked across the lake toward Barnes Cove and the foot of Mount Storm King. His eyes stopped at the top of the peak, where the sky was slate gray and matte-black clouds gathered like troops assembling an assault. Adrian knew it would be raining soon.

The first drops came, and when he felt their cold touch on his face, he knew it was time to go. Turning on his headlamp, he shouldered his knapsack and focused on the coming mission.

* * *

Reaching Tommy Lee Rhysacker's hidden cabin would be a challenging cross-country hike in the darkness, rain, and tangle of dense national forest. Adrian had a small survival kit, prepared before Willow's killing, which contained another headlamp and a handheld compass. There was an older .45 caliber semiautomatic military handgun and a wad of fifty-dollar bills cached through the years for an emergency. Every piece in his pack had been wrapped in field-tested, waterproof containers and packed in an underwater-diver's bag.

Adrian sat on a log just outside his lair, closed his eyes, and took several deep breaths. He tried to focus on his military training and think only about the coming mission. He planned to stay in the backcountry until he reached the dirt road leading to the western end of the lake. Once he was on the road, he would only have to cross Highway 101 before sunrise...without being seen.

As the crow flies, Tommy Lee's cabin was twenty-miles away, but in total darkness and rugged country, the trek was much more difficult than a daylight walk on a maintained park trail. But once he found the road, he knew it could be done.

When he got to the cabin—if he made it alive—he planned to sleep most of the day and then lose himself in the least accessible areas of the national park, resting during the day and bushwhacking through the night. He thought the head start provided by the water-search focus would slow down a land search and give him enough time to disappear.

If he was able to work his way out of the park undetected, his plan was to flee again to the wildest country—Canada or Alaska. He did not know if he would be caught or live long enough to start over one more time. But what he did know was, one way or the other, he would not die by another man's hand.

STORM KING'S GRAVEYARD

The next morning, the search continued in earnest, with the Olympic National Park coordinating the operation. The Clallam County Sheriff Department, Washington State Patrol, and border-patrol-reinforced teams of search volunteers all focused on combing the waters of the lake.

Lake Crescent drowning searches were always intense, and the surrounding media exposure added to the urgency of locating this victim's body. As days passed with no results, the park even asked residents living around the lake for help using ski boats and fishing boats. Normally banned jet skis were authorized for search-and-rescue efforts as well.

The park requested the use of University of Washington's marine minisub—a strategy that had been tried—and failed—in previous drownings. Unfortunately, the sub was out of the country and not available as a last resort.

The lake hunt for Adrian's body went on for nine days. The failure to find a body, even with the lake's long history, sparked public speculation of a daring escape attempt. Adrian Hawkins was a Green Beret. Could the man, despite his age, use his military background to pull off such a bold ruse? Traditional news resources and social media junkies around the world reveled in the possibility of a new-era conspiracy similar to that of the infamous D. B. Cooper heist and disappearance in the early 1970s.

Sheriff Webster refused to accept any chance of a conspiracy theory. He believed Adrian Hawkins's disappearance was a suicide. Duncan had carefully studied the two sets of dog tags wrapped around the oar handle of the rowboat. One tag belonged to Adrian. The other, to a soldier named Morris Bullard. Bullard's tag was almost unreadable, the stamped letters smoothed almost flat by years of thumb rubbing. Due to the discovery of Hawkins's PTSD background, the sheriff thought Bullard was a Green Beret brother killed in Vietnam, and the dog tags were Adrian's way of dealing with the loss of a close comrade—they were the broken man's suicide note. Adrian had joined the long list of PTSD victims who had taken their own lives.

For Duncan himself, the end was not without cost. Forty-seven-years in law enforcement had been long enough. He'd seen his share of sorrow, and Willow Shepard's tragic death had crushed his spirit. The lack of documented closure was a soul-deep pain, and he felt the despair of all the families who had lost unrecovered loved ones in the lake. Despite fulfilling his promise to Gitane, the modern-day demonstration of the Storm King's history of horror scarred his soul.

* * *

It has now been over a decade since Adrian Adams Hawkins disappeared, and his fate is still unknown. Since his disappearance, Storm King's curse has never gone away—swimmers and boaters have disappeared; a local attorney was lost after launching her kayak and purposely leaving her life jacket in the car; a twenty-year-old girl on a road trip stopped at a view pull-off on a warm summer day and floated off on her air mattress. The air mattress was found six miles away.

Each drowning was followed by an extensive search. None of their bodies was ever recovered. Uncertainty is the crux of the mountain's revenge, and nothing is more heartbreaking than denying the living their right of closure.

The ceremonial rites of passage remain forbidden...and for the dead and the living, the verses of their death songs will never be sung.

EPILOGUE

On June 9, 2023—four years AFTER the first draft of *Storm King's Graveyard* and two more unsuccessful body-recovery searches in Lake Crescent—the mountain struck again.

A man and his fiancée were kayaking on the lake in separate boats when high winds swamped their kayaks. Cast into the water, neither wearing life jackets, and trying to keep both boats afloat, the man was overcome by hypothermia and drowned. Frantic to get help, the woman managed to swim to shore and alert a passing walker, who used a cell phone to reach authorities.

A search for the man's body began that afternoon and continued for almost two weeks before officials canceled the hopeless effort.

Days later, the boaters' families located a unique Midwestern search-and-rescue organization specializing in the recovery of deepwater drowning victims. The company immediately sent a crew cross-country to conduct a search.

Sixteen days after the drowning, the new searchers recovered the body…at a depth of 394 feet…in less than twenty-four hours! State-of-the-art technology, computers, sonar, and underwater cameras pulled off the deepest recovery in Lake Crescent's history. It was viewed by many as a technological breakthrough with the potential of ending a 10,000-year reign of terror and revenge.

There were—and still are—questions. Was this the beginning of a new era? Or was it an outlier of luck and coincidence? In some places, the lake is two hundred feet deeper than the depth of the recovered body. The lake is seventeen miles long, and the bottom is rocky, uneven, and unexplored.

The recent recovery is encouraging, and it appears that Storm King's mystery is on the brink of being resolved. Even without the graveyard, there will be drownings, and where there are drownings, there will be tears and gut-wrenching grief. But for the families, there will be closure.

May all the souls in the mountain's graveyard rest in peace.

The End

Storm King's Graveyard is Rob Sorensen's second novel. A longtime bibliophile, book collector, and part-time writer, he is addicted to books that tell good stories. Born and raised in Port Angeles, Washington, he and his wife, Alexis, share a passion for the natural beauty, charm, and history of the Pacific Northwest…which they consider to be the country's "last best place."

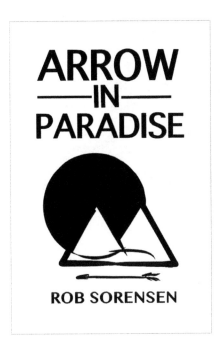

Writing Arrow in Paradise has been a labor of love. Composed while living on the banks of the Yaak River in a once-notorious bar called the Hell Roaring Saloon (which was converted to a home in 1998), the novel captures the essence of this remote valley as well as its unique collection of inhabitants—both humans and animals. Although the book is pure fiction, the wild country is real. . . and crafting the story within that context makes all the difference.

ISBN Hardcover: 978-1-61244-706-3

ISBN Paperback: 978-1-61244-707-0

Printed in the USA
CPSIA information can be obtained
at www.ICGtesting.com
BVHW051951010823
668084BV00002B/3

9 781637 653975